The Tomboy

Mary Lou Rich

J

JOVE BOOKS, NEW YORK

THE TOMBOY

A Jove Book / published by arrangement with
the author

PRINTING HISTORY
Jove edition / February 1996

The Putnam Berkley World Wide Web site address is
http://www.berkley.com

ISBN: 0-515-11810-9

A JOVE BOOK®
Jove Books are published by The Berkley Publishing Group,
200 Madison Avenue, New York, New York 10016.
JOVE and the "J" design are trademarks
belonging to Jove Publications, Inc.

PRINTED IN THE UNITED STATES OF AMERICA

10 9 8 7 6 5 4 3 2 1

To my editors:
Melinda Metz, who introduced me to the Daltry clan, and Jennifer Lata, who helped me tell them good-bye.

To all the other *Sons and Daughters* authors, especially Lorraine Heath for sharing her research material.

To my dear friends and colleagues:
Vella Munn, Tallie Thompson, Pat White, and Sue Rich,
who kept me on the right road along the way.

One

JEHOSHAPHAT! PESKY VARMINT! ONE EYE FIXED ON THE WILD horses, Atalanta Daltry stealthily eased her hand to her cheek and sent the blood-sucking insect to his just rewards. No sooner had she lowered her palm than another mosquito, just as tenacious, landed on her chin.

She'd heard it said that May in Texas was akin to spring in hell, and had no cause to doubt it was the honest truth. The sun overhead seemed intent on broiling her alive, and everything that could either crawl or fly had taken a chunk out of her this past week—except for snakes. She stayed clear of them.

Dotted with insect bites, her skin looked like she had a bad case of measles, and she itched from head to foot. It took every bit of willpower she possessed not to indulge in a frenzied fit of scratching, but she knew any movement on her part would send the wild mustangs to running.

She squinted toward the opposite side of the ravine where Hal Anderson, her partner in the roundup, slumped lazily in the saddle. Both he and his buckskin appeared to be sound asleep. She couldn't fault him any for that. She'd probably be asleep, too, if she'd been smart enough to pick the side of the canyon with a tree.

Sweat tickled a trail between Allie's shoulder blades and sent a shiver up her spine. Enviously eyeing the sycamore's shade, she pressed her cracked lips together and wondered just how much more she would have to endure.

Whatever it took, she decided. At least it was better than being home, listening to all the hullabaloo about tomorrow.

Tomorrow. Allie shuddered.

Her twentieth birthday. Just the thought of it knotted her stomach. Envisioning the coming ordeal, Allie was certain she'd rather be caught in the middle of a stampede.

That was one reason she had spent the week helping Hal catch the wild mustangs. Even if it hadn't been for her birthday, she would have been out here anyway.

She stealthily vanquished another mosquito.

Truth was, she'd walk barefoot through a cactus patch for Hal and was sure he'd do the same for her. Her grandma Minerva had wondered if in another life she and Hal might have been twins. Of course everyone thought Minerva to be a little strange and notional anyhow, but to Allie, the idea had more merit than fantasy. She couldn't remember a time they hadn't been together. She'd been able to read Hal's mood, his thoughts, as if they were her own—at least until four years ago.

Allie's older sister, Venus, before she'd married and left for India, had insinuated that Hal had new interests now that he was grown up. She'd whispered it was common knowledge that Hal had been seen keeping company with that redheaded hussy who sang at Lucky's saloon.

Even though her sister's words hurt more than she cared to admit, Allie refused to accept that as the reason. It was about that same time that Hal's mother died of pneumonia and his pa, Jack Anderson, started drinking. Then Mr. Anderson lost their hard-earned mortgage money in a game of cards and the bank foreclosed on the ranch. Hal and his father had been left destitute, except for the parcel of land Hal had inherited from his grandpa. They might have moved there, but Hal feared the place held too many memories for his father.

Allie had been afraid Hal might give up, too, but her grandma loaned Hal enough money to get him and his pa settled in town. Minerva would have paid the bank, too—heaven knows she had enough money—but she said that with Jack drinking the way he was, he would have ended up losing the ranch to somebody else.

Sometimes Allie wanted to shake Jack Anderson, tell him the dead were dead and no amount of grieving would bring them back, but that wasn't her place. Besides, as much as she missed Hal's ma, she wouldn't have had the heart to do it anyhow.

In a way she knew how Jack felt, losing his wife. She'd only lost a small part of Hal and it hurt something fierce.

She gazed wistfully across the canyon at the long-legged cowboy, her pard, her best friend. Even though she loved her family and they loved her, she'd always felt like she'd never quite measured up to their expectations. Hal accepted her as she was. With him she'd always been able to say anything, do anything she pleased. He didn't look down on her because she wore her brothers' cast-off baggy britches and her pa's old shirts. Hal didn't even care if her face was dirty, or if she smelled like horses, which she did ninety percent of the time. She could tell him anything without fear of ridicule or censure. He knew her thoughts, her hopes, her dreams, things she'd never shared with her own siblings.

But lately she felt as though she didn't know her pard at all. The two of them had spent a week alone on the range rounding up the horses, and even though they were still close, there was a part of Hal that remained hidden, shuttered, even to her. It made her sad that he'd lost the old eagerness, the joy of life. It hurt that he no longer told her his secrets, his aspirations for the future. It was as though he were drifting, going through the motions but not really living. The special something between them had gone, and no matter how hard she tried she hadn't been able to get it back. That's why this herd of mustangs was so important—and not just because Hal needed the money to pay Minerva. Allie hoped capturing the horses would make him remember his dream.

A blue fly buzzed around her mare's haunches, and Circe stomped restlessly and swished her tail.

"Easy, girl," Allie hissed low, tightening her grip on the reins to keep the animal quiet.

Since they were children, Hal had talked of breeding a special kind of horse. One that could live on the barest desert and get by. Texas tough, yet with strength and speed. She wasn't sure breeding such an animal was possible, but as long as Hal thought it was, that was good enough for her.

Allie slackened her hold and allowed Circe to drop her head and graze.

Although she tried not to look too often, for fear one of the mustangs would catch her eye, she noticed the horses had steadily inched nearer to the trap, where a fence made of brush and poles would block the tree-shaded box canyon once the animals were inside. *Go on, you ornery cayuses.*

The mustangs edged a few yards closer. Then, just when Allie was certain they had them, a sudden gust of wind tripped among the tumbleweeds, picking up momentum as it swirled toward the herd.

The leader, a gunmetal-gray stallion, shifted uneasily.

Nostrils flared, he stared into the wind. Allie prayed the wild stud wouldn't catch their scent. If the herd bolted now, she knew they would be gone for good.

Dang it, Hal. Allie peered anxiously toward her companion, who still appeared to be asleep. *What's he waiting on—Christmas?*

As if sensing her agitation, Hal straightened in the saddle; then, taking his hat from his long, sandy-blond hair, he looked her way and nodded.

Allie tensed, alerting Circe for action.

Hal swept the hat down, giving the signal. His buckskin lunged toward the herd, effectively closing his end of the circle.

"Kii–yii!" Allie yelled, sending her silver mare racing forward.

The heads of the mustangs shot up. The stallion let out a shrill neigh, then he reared, pawing the air.

Fearing he might break past them, Allie yelled and waved her arms again.

Finding his escape blocked, the stud spun and fled into the canyon. The rest of the herd surged after him.

Whooping and swinging their hats, she and Hal followed. At a spot where the chasm was narrowest, Hal slid his gelding to a halt. "Don't let them turn back, Al," he shouted, dismounting to pull the first length of the heavy brush fence into place.

"I won't." Allie raced past him and cut off the mustangs that had wheeled in an effort to escape. Unable to evade the little Arabian, the strays rejoined the herd. Allie didn't pursue them any further, but pulled Circe to a halt and waited.

The wild bunch gradually slowed its frantic pace; then, reaching the shadowy end of the canyon, they stopped and milled about uneasily. After a while, when they saw Allie had no intention of following, one or two dropped their heads and began to graze on the sweet green grass that edged a musky-smelling spring.

Circe nickered and tossed her head. Knowing her horse had caught the water's scent, Allie ran her gloved hand down the mare's sweat-drenched neck. "Sorry, old girl. We'll both have to wait until we get home." Wistfully eyeing the pool, Allie licked her own parched lips, then turned the Arabian back toward the mouth of the canyon.

Hal waited beside the makeshift gate. His green eyes dancing, he grinned when she approached. "You took so long I thought you might have decided to spend the night."

"Not on your life." She edged the mare through the crack in the fence, then dismounted to help Hal tie it shut. "After a week of sleeping on rocks, I'm looking forward to stretching out in my own feather bed."

"Getting soft in your *old* age, Atalanta?" Hal teased, reminding her that tomorrow would be her twentieth birthday.

He would have to bring that up, she thought resentfully. "I'm not in my dotage yet. Even tired as I am, I bet you a dollar that I can still run the legs off you."

"After chasing those broomtails all week, I'm of no disposition to enter any footrace," he said with a groan. "So you can keep your money."

"I intended to keep *my* money," she said. "It was *your* dollar I was after."

Hal laughed, then turned toward the canyon.

She followed his gaze to where the seventy or so wild horses happily munched on the grass. "We did it, Hal," she said with wonder.

He slapped her on the back. "Course we did, pard. I never had any doubt we would. Did you?"

"None a'tall," she lied.

They spent the rest of the ride back discussing how to

spend the money that would remain after Minerva had been paid.

"Think I'll order that roping saddle I've had my eye on," Hal said after much debate.

Allie took her foot out of the stirrup and eyed her bedraggled footgear. "After climbing around in those rocks all week, I guess I could use a new pair of boots."

A lock of hair drifted into Allie's eyes; she shoved it aside only to have it fall forward again. In exasperation, she removed her hat and looped the rawhide thong over her pommel, then she reached for the scabbard on her side and took out her knife.

Hal chuckled and shook his head. "The way you're always whacking your hair off with that Arkansas toothpick, it's a wonder you aren't bald."

"If yours gets any longer, people will think you're a girl," Allie said, noting the length of the straw-colored hair poking out beneath his hat.

"That's one thing *you* don't have to worry about. With your hair sticking out every which way and dressed in your pa's shirt, they'd more likely take you for a scarecrow."

"Caw. Caw." Allie flapped her arms.

Hal gave a hoot and doubled over.

"You know I don't give a dang what anybody thinks," she said. "And if *you* don't like the way I look, then point your nose somewheres else."

"I wasn't talking about me. It don't make no never mind to me what you look like," he teased. "Long as the horses don't seem to care."

"Any objections, Circe?" Allie asked, bending over her mare's mane.

When the mare shook her head, they both laughed.

The Texas sky seemed ablaze, with shades of crimson, purple, and gold coating the brown, grass-covered hills, giving them a splendor they lacked in the bright light of day. Hal and Allie paused on a small rise overlooking the Daltry ranch and watched the blood-red sun sink beyond the horizon.

"That was downright purty," Hal said, gazing at the sunset.

"That's more'n I can say for you." Allie gave him a sideways glance. "You purely do look a sight. The only spots not covered with dirt are your teeth and your green eyeballs."

"Speak for yourself, Al. You're not exactly a vision of cleanliness." He gave her the once-over and chuckled, then ran a finger down his own grimy cheek. "I'd say a face washin' or two would be in order, otherwise I doubt if your grandma Minerva will let us in the house."

"That's a fact." The sight of the large, peculiar house her pa seemed intent on spreading across Texas made Allie's lips stretch into an even larger grin. "Did you notice the latest addition?"

"Which one?"

"The widow's walk."

Hal choked. "I thought they only had those on houses by the sea."

"Grandma never let anything like that stop her. She got the idea when Persy told her about the ones they had in the East. And you know Pa. He isn't happy unless he's building something. So now we have the only house in this part of Texas with a widow's walk."

"*That* I have got to see."

"Race you to the horse trough," Allie challenged. Nudging Circe forward, she left Hal in a cloud of dust.

"That's not fair," he yelled, vowing to get even.

Minerva Daltry, matriarch of the Daltry clan and grandmother to Atalanta and the rest of the children, peered through her kitchen window to see what all the commotion in the barnyard was about.

Two sweat-caked horses and their equally dusty riders raced into the yard.

"Finally," she said with relief, recognizing one of the disreputable pair as her granddaughter. With Atalanta knowing what lay in store for her, Minerva had feared the girl might not show up for the party, but it appeared she'd worried for nothing.

"Atalanta's home," she called to her daughter-in-law, Jane, who was busy preparing the evening meal.

"It's about time," Jane said, wiping her wet hands on her apron.

"Is Hal with her?" Allie's father, Odie, rose from the table and carried the coffee he'd been drinking toward the window.

"Where else would he be? The two have been stuck together like glue since they were babes." Minerva observed the boy and girl who seemed bent on drowning each other in the water trough. Beside her, Odie chuckled.

"Odysseus Daltry, you don't seem a bit concerned that your daughter just spent the better part of a week out on the range with a man," Jane said, slamming the lid onto a pot.

"A man?" Odie looked alarmed, then his eyes crinkled at the corners. "Hal? Hal is like one of her own brothers. Now if Allie was a filly I might worry, since the boy does have an eye for horses. But I doubt if he even realizes Atalanta is a girl."

That's the problem, thought Minerva. Her gaze roamed over her granddaughter, contemplating the girl's short-cropped curly brown hair, her rail-thin build, the worn jeans and too-big shirt. Atalanta would be twenty years old tomorrow. Time she had a beau—although Allie had never shown an interest in any male, especially one that didn't have four legs. The only exception was Hal, and Allie treated him the same as she did her brothers.

Minerva remembered how the boys had flocked around Allie's sisters. From the time Venus was fourteen, the fellers had been thicker than flies after honey. Even shy Persephone had managed to have a suitor or two.

No one of the opposite sex had ever shown any interest in Allie. Watching her granddaughter, Minerva sighed. *The way she presents herself, it's no wonder.*

Minerva shifted her attention to the laughing, sandy-haired young man who'd been underfoot as long as she could remember. The boy seemed like one of her own. He and Allie had always gotten along well together, maybe because they had so much in common. Both were brought up on the range; both had a love of Texas and a passion for horses.

Minerva dropped the edge of the curtain and spryly stepped away from the window. All week the house had been bustling with preparations. And the family would be gathering from near and far. Atlas, the only exception, was still away at school.

The Daltrys considered birthdays an occasion to celebrate, and ordinarily everyone from Paradise Plains to Abilene would be stopping by to join in the festivities and offer their best wishes. But not tomorrow. On each child's twentieth birthday, the house was closed to everyone but the family. Not even Hal would be admitted.

While the family observed the usual traditions, such as favorite foods and homemade gifts, the thing that made this day so special was Minerva's own invention.

Passionately fond of anything Greek or Roman, even to the naming of her family, Minerva had chosen the twelve labors of Hercules as a test for her children and grandchildren. Using the ancient stories as a guide, she assigned each birthday child a "labor," picking one that would best develop their character and teach them whatever lesson she decided they needed to be taught. If they completed the labor before their twenty-first birthday, she would reward them with a wonderful prize. Everything pertaining to the labor was a closely guarded secret, for it was forbidden that any outsider should know of either the task or the reward.

Tomorrow Minerva would give Atalanta her labor.

The screen door slammed and the still-dripping but freshly scrubbed duo burst into the house. After boisterously greeting Jane, Odie, and Minerva, Allie and Hal headed for the cookstove to investigate the covered pots.

Minerva observed the pair for a while, then she tucked her head to hide a secret smile. *Sweet tomboy Allie, I wonder what you'll do?*

Two

"HEY, SLEEPYHEAD, TIME TO GET UP—UNLESS YOU INTEND TO spend the whole day hidin' under the covers," Allie's father yelled through the third-story attic doorway.

"Go 'way," Allie cried. She was still so stiff that her bones creaked and her muscles screamed every time she moved. Who would have believed she'd feel so bad, especially since she'd spent the night in the comfort of her own feather bed? But after a week on the range, even in her dreams she'd chased horses—most of the time on foot. The rest of the night she'd lain awake, staring at the ceiling.

"All right, but you are going to miss your birthday," Odie said in a singsong voice. Then he pulled the door shut and she heard his footsteps going back down the stairs.

Allie sighed and pulled the covers over her head to block the glare of the early-morning sun. She had just regained a comfortable position when her pa's words registered in her muddled brain. "Birthday?"

Her eyes flew open. How could she have forgotten! *The*

labor! Recalling her siblings' various tasks, she felt a queasy sensation start in her middle, and she truly wondered if she was going to be sick.

I wonder what she will give me to do. She prayed her labor would be something simple, like breaking that pair of bays that Grandma had wanted to pull her carriage.

Ha! That would be the day. She hadn't forgotten her brothers' and sisters' wails of despair when Minerva had announced their particular labor, and Allie doubted her own task would be easy, either.

It had been eight years since Hercules, Allie's oldest brother, had received his labor. Lee, who had always had a hard time with his studies and couldn't wait until he was out of school, had been forced to teach for a year, even though he was about as much at home with kids and a classroom as a bull would have been in a playpen full of baby chicks. Although he claimed it had been like spending a year in purgatory, at the end of that time he'd ended up married to the teacher whose job he'd stolen. And wonder of all wonders, he now had a teaching certificate of his own. For his prize, Grandma had built the town a library and named it in his honor.

Persephone had been next in line. So shy she would blush crimson and run for her room when any male outside of the family entered the house, Persy had been sent to their New York cousins for a season as a debutante. Their ma had a fit when Persy announced she would be marrying the owner of a saloon. But Jake had been such an engaging rascal, he soon had their mother convinced that marrying him was the smartest thing Persy had ever done. Minerva had given Persy a house.

Cupid, whose good looks had never allowed him to have less than three girlfriends at any one time, had been dumped by his fiancée and had given up on love—until Minerva gave him the labor of finding a husband for Lizzie Colepepper. Lizzie's scarred face and cantankerous personality had held men at bay for years. C. J. solved his problem by falling in love with and marrying Lizzie himself. Cupid had received a full-sized looking glass, set in a frame that Odie had created and carved with their initials.

Venus, the great beauty of the family, had had men fawning over her since she'd first appeared in long skirts. Venus, who guarded her complexion so diligently that she never went outside as long as the sun was up, had to accompany a blind writer to the Nevada desert and help him assemble material for his ten-cent novels. She'd ended up married to him, although Buck Buchanan was the one man who couldn't bear witness to her blond perfection. Minerva had given Venus and Buck a trip to India.

Allie took heart from the fact that all of her brothers and sisters had accomplished their feats, no matter how difficult they had been, and each had obtained *the prize*.

After Allie would come Atlas. Bub, as she'd nicknamed him, was a year younger than she was, the baby of the family. She solemnly considered her brother's almost obsessively orderly personality. Since she'd never known Atlas to be without a plan of action, she couldn't imagine him having a problem with anything their grandmother could dream up.

A sinking feeling clutched Allie's heart. She wasn't as big as Lee, as charming as C. J., as smart as Persy, or as pretty as Venus, and never could she be as organized as Bub.

She had always been the ugly duckling of the family. Instead of having anything that resembled Venus's or Persy's shining locks, she'd been born with hair that resembled a coil of fence wire, and eyes so pale a gray that some kids claimed she looked downright spooky. She'd always been short, skinny as a stick, and never especially bright.

When she was little, she'd looked at the rest of the clan and wondered if someone had dumped her on their doorstep late one night and disappeared, leaving the Daltrys to raise her.

Her grandma had assured her that hadn't been the case and said that Allie reminded her of herself when she'd been that age. Allie had taken comfort from her grandma's words, but unlike the ugly duckling who turned into a swan at the end of the story, the years had left Allie pretty much unchanged.

She had grown taller, but not much, and she was still thin. Her eyes were more silver than gray and her hair— what she hadn't hacked off—still stuck out like wire springs on a worn-out buggy seat.

While her brothers and sisters all excelled at one thing or another, the only thing Allie was truly good at was her ability with horses.

A fear unlike any she had ever known crawled up her spine. What if she couldn't do the task her grandmother gave her? What if she would be the only one to fail?

That disturbing thought sent all inclination to get more sleep flying out the window. Allie bolted from her bed. After a quick wash, she cast a long look at her shirt and breeches. No, she decided reluctantly. Grandma would never let her get away with wearing them, especially today.

She rummaged through her dresser until she found a chemise and underdrawers. Scowling, she lifted another item of apparel, one that Venus had left behind. Danged if anybody would ever get *her* into that thing, she thought, tossing the corset into the back of the closet. Her nose wrinkled in disgust, Allie yanked on a layer of petticoats, then put on a simple gray skirt and white blouse. After discovering the skirt would be long enough to hide her feet, she ignored the stockings and kid slippers and instead put on a pair of soft leather boots. Her only concession to any kind of primping was to run a brush through her unruly mop of curls.

When she opened her bedroom door, the downstairs noise of a fully awake household—what with the family and their spouses arriving for the big occasion—threatened to send her into swift retreat. But the thought that any one—or all—of them would soon appear to rout her made her close the door behind her, square her shoulders, and head for the kitchen.

As she made her way through the house, the absence of one particular sound, however, gave her pause. Today, in honor of the occasion, Pa wasn't building something.

One of her earliest memories was the ever-present sawing and hammering that had gone on 'most every day, except Christmas and birthdays. She always approached any area in the house that she hadn't frequented a day or two before with caution for fear a wall or stairway would have been added—or removed. With her father and grandmother's constant changes and additions, she never knew what she might come across.

The year before last, Grandma had decided she wanted a sunporch so she could warm her bones. Then last year she decided she wanted a veranda on the other side of the house so she could sit in the shade. At least they were covered for all seasons.

With the additions on both sides and the widow's walk on top, Allie didn't see how they could expand the house any more, but as long as her pa's health—and her grandma's money—held out, she had no doubt they'd try.

People rode all the way from Abilene just to take a look at the gazebo. And anyone viewing it grew slack-jawed with awe. Of course, nobody expected to see a Grecian temple smack in the middle of Texas, especially one with naked, busty maidens for fountains. Women seeing it for the first time cried that it was indecent, but when their wives weren't looking, the husbands snuck back for another peek. Her ma had given thanks that Grandma hadn't gotten that statue of David she wanted.

Even without the house, or the gazebo, the whole Daltry clan was thought to be a bit eccentric. But Allie didn't care what anybody else thought—they were her family and she liked them just the way they were.

"Hello, birthday girl," came a soft voice from behind her.

Recognizing it as that of her older sister Persephone she whirled to greet her and was immediately clasped in a bear hug. When Persy released her, Allie took a look at her sister and gasped with delight. "Persy, you're pregnant!"

"Well, I surely hope so," Persy replied with a grin, patting her rounded middle. "I'd hate to think I'd gained all this weight for nothing."

"Was it safe for you to travel all that way from New York?" Allie asked with concern, remembering Persy's difficult pregnancy with her first child, Diana, who was now four. "Do you feel all right?"

"We couldn't wait to share our good news with the family, and I couldn't miss your birthday. Don't worry," she said, touching Allie's cheek. "It's months yet before the baby will be born. Besides, I feel wonderful."

"You look great," Allie agreed. "When are you due?"

"Not for six more months."

"But—"

"I know," she giggled. "Jake thinks we might be expecting twins this time."

"Persy could be big as a barn and I have no doubt she'd still be traipsin' around in public."

Allie whirled to see her sister Venus coming toward them. "I thought you'd still be in India."

"That awful place," Venus said with a shudder.

Allie held out her arms in welcome, but after a quick peck on the cheek Venus withdrew.

"Careful of my dress, deah," she said, smoothing an imaginary wrinkle from the front of her pale yellow confection. Then she gave Allie a critical look and shook her head. "You really should do somethin' about your skin. My stahs, Atalanta, you are as brown as a pine nut. I was afraid I'd look the same way before we left India," she said, twisting a golden curl so that it lay just so against her cheek. "I'm glad Buck's next book will be done in Oregon. I hear tell the sun hardly evah shines up theah."

Allie shot Persy a mischievous look, then she leaned close to Venus and frowned. "You did get tan, didn't you? And—oh, my, Persy, look here. Isn't that a freckle?" Allie said, touching a spot on Venus's flawless, milk-white skin.

"A freckle?" Venus's blue eyes widened in horror. "I knew it. I knew it. That awful sun." She clamped her palm over the imaginary blemish and ran down the hall.

"Allie, you devil. You haven't changed a bit," Persy said, convulsing with laughter. "She'll spend the rest of the visit in her room with her face plastered with buttermilk."

"I wonder how Buck puts up with her."

"Being sightless is a help. He doesn't know how many hours she spends in front of the mirror primping." Persy sighed. "And as for all the rest, he's so wrapped up in his own fantasy world, I doubt if he'd notice anyway."

"The perfect couple," Allie quipped.

"Any idea what your labor will be?" Persy asked in a hushed voice.

Allie's smile instantly vanished. She worriedly shook her head.

"Remember how Venus pitched a fit when she heard hers? She was sure her tantrum would cause Grandma to change her mind and give her something easier to do."

"She should have known better than that. Grandma's the most stubborn Daltry in the bunch. It couldn't have worked out better in the end, though." Allie peered at Persy. "How did you feel when you heard yours?"

"Oh, Lord. I wanted to crawl under the table and die. And then after I got to New York, I ruined that expensive dress and had to go to work in the saloon to buy another. But it was worth all the trouble. I did meet and marry Jake. And Grandma gave us our house for the prize. Then we were blessed with Diana. And now—" She patted her stomach and gave Allie a dreamy look. "I wonder what's in store for you?"

"I couldn't begin to guess," Allie said solemnly.

Persy laughed, then looped her arm around Allie's shoulders and escorted her to the dining room, where the rest of the family had gathered for breakfast. The only ones not there were Lee and Meredith and their children, and C. J. and Lizzie and two-year-old Thalia, who would arrive later in the day. And Atlas was still away at school. The empty chair beside Buck told her Venus was hiding in her room.

After giving a special hug and kiss to her little niece Diana, Allie made her way around the long table, greeting each family member in turn. When she was finished she had been hugged and pummeled until she felt like a batch of day-old bread dough. Both her brothers-in-law were very dear and she knew they loved her sisters to distraction, and Allie hoped that if she ever married, she would be half as lucky.

"Where did Mama go?" Persy asked her husband.

"She took a glass of buttermilk up to your sister. Venus thought that might help her headache."

Allie choked on her coffee and kept her attention on her plate. She knew if she met Persy's eyes they'd both collapse in a fit of the giggles.

After breakfast Persy went to her room to take a nap, while the men left for the barn to look at the horses.

Her ma and grandma conspired in quiet whispers, but became silent every time Allie entered the room. Finally Minerva spoke up. "Allie, dear, we are never going to get anything done with you underfoot. Why don't you go read a book or something?"

"Guess I can take a hint," Allie said, heading for her room. But despite the mess she'd left earlier that morning, all too soon everything was in order and once again she had nothing to do. Nothing but worry, that is.

For Allie each hour seemed like ten, each determined to tune her nerves to a higher pitch. She wished Hal were there, but twentieth birthdays were for family only; not even Hal was allowed. Finally, when she couldn't stand any more, she went downstairs, but all the whispers and giggles sent her fleeing to the gazebo. Even there, she was still aware of the hustle and bustle, especially when Lee and Meredith and their noisy brood arrived—five-year-old Jupiter, three-year-old Cynthia, and the baby, Athena. C. J., Lizzie, and Thalia came a little later.

Being the first grandchild to be given a labor, Lee's birthday had been anything but a quiet affair. But now, with all the additions to the family, Allie thought it purely resembled a circus.

"Allie, you can't hide any longer," Lee called out, parting the veil of leaves that hid her from view. "Dinner's awaitin' and I'm hungry enough to eat a cow all by myself —hide, horns, and all."

"Guess I may as well get it over with." She flashed her brother an anemic smile and winced when he gave her an exuberant slap on the back.

"It won't be so bad, Allie. Besides, look at the good side. You're only twenty once."

"Once is enough," she muttered softly.

The family had gathered in the dining room, and once again in celebration the oil lights had been extinguished and twenty candles had been lit and placed around the room.

"There's my girl," her pa said, coming to take her hand. "Happy birthday, honey." He brushed her cheek with a kiss.

Allie felt like a calf being led to slaughter when he escorted her to the place of honor at the head of the table and pulled out her chair. After she was settled, he took the seat to her right. For this one night, as soon as the food was served, her grandma would occupy the seat at the opposite end of the table and her ma would sit to Minerva's right.

Her eyes brimming, Allie blinked to hold back the tears as she glanced from one beloved face to another. All smiling, all confident that she, too, would succeed. What would they think of her if she failed? She swallowed her fear when Lee winked and broke the spell.

"Hey, Persy. What did you fix to eat?" he called out, causing everyone to giggle. Meredith, for all her brains, still hadn't managed to master the art of cooking. They had a housekeeper who did the best she could, but more times than not, Lee showed up at the Daltry table, especially if Persy was around.

"How about roast quail with pecan dressing, new baby peas, whipped potatoes, candied yams, and a dozen other dishes I want to try out on you?" Persy teased, carrying a dish to the table. "I also made some of my special rolls."

"If you weren't my sister, and I wasn't already married, I'd marry you myself," Lee said, groaning in appreciation.

He groaned even louder when Meredith gave him a kick under the table, much to everyone else's delight.

"Don't feel bad, Meredith. He says the same thing to Bo Jack," her father said.

"Where is the old coot?" Jake asked.

"He's down at the bunkhouse. After he says hello to y'all, he plans to spend a few days in Abilene, sort of a vacation," her ma said.

Persy had found Bo Jack in back of Jake's saloon, where he had been run over by a whiskey wagon. Badly injured, crippled in one leg and missing an eye, the old man's appearance was enough to put anyone off, but she and Jake had nursed him back to health and given him a job. Persy discovered Bo Jack had a talent for cooking, and after they sold the saloon, he'd traveled with them to Paradise Plains where he had been cooking for the Daltrys ever since.

Allie dutifully filled her plate, then spent the rest of the meal rearranging her food. Even though the bounty was all of her favorites, she wasn't able to swallow a bite. She noticed the others ate heartily, though, making up for her lack of appetite.

Finally, when the last crumb had been eaten and the dinner dishes had been cleared away, under Persephone's directions Jake and Lee carried a magnificent birthday cake ablaze with candles into the dining room and set it on the table in front of Allie.

This was the cue for their father, Odie, to lead the others in a rousing chorus of "Happy Birthday" that fairly shook the rafters of the big old house. When the last note died, every eye seemed suspiciously bright.

Allie sniffed and wiped her own face with her napkin.

"Don't just sit there. Blow! Before the frosting melts," Lee commanded.

Allie managed a weak grin, then sucked in a deep

breath. With the help of two-year-old Thalia, who had more enthusiasm than wind, she blew out the candles. Then, her hand trembling, Allie cut and served the cake, a seven-layer confection that looked light as air and which everyone agreed was mouthwateringly delicious. Lee and C. J. dipped up bowlfuls of fresh-churned ice cream to go along with it.

Although the cake was a Daltry tradition and was served at every twentieth birthday celebration, Allie told Persy that she had never tasted a more delicious version.

Persy graciously accepted compliments on her baking, saying, "Great-grandma Daltry created it. My part was easy. I only followed the recipe."

When the last bite was devoured, Minerva got to her feet and went to stand by Allie. She bent and gave her granddaughter a kiss. "Happy birthday, child."

"Thank you, Grandma," Allie whispered. Now that the moment she had dreaded was at hand, butterflies were going berserk in her stomach. She only hoped she didn't disgrace herself by getting sick.

Her gray eyes bright, Minerva straightened and glanced around the table. "And now it's time for me to give Atalanta her labor."

As every eye fastened on her, Allie felt the blood drain from her face. She closed her eyes in a silent prayer. *Please, God. Let it be something easy, like breaking wild horses—or running barefoot from here to Paradise Plains.*

"I have thought long and hard on this, Atalanta, and I have decided that your labor shall be divided into three parts. The first: You will bake a seven-layer cake from the Daltry recipe—and let the local men bid on it at the box social at the Fourth of July celebration."

Allie's eyes flew open, only to widen in horror. The famous Daltry cake? In little more than a month? When she had never cooked a thing in her life?

"The second part of the task will be for you to sew a special dress to wear to the Harvest Ball."

Sew? Me? It was getting worse and worse and there was still more to come.

"And the third part"—Minerva lifted her hand to brush a stray curl from Thalia's chubby face—"You shall take care of Thalia for a week while C. J. and Lizzie take me to visit San Francisco."

Allie stared at her rambunctious little niece, who grinned back at her angelically. *Oh, Lord.* Even on the best of days that child could try the patience of a saint. Swallowing, Allie gazed at the beaming faces of her father and mother, her brothers, sisters, and their spouses. "Well, now, is that all?" she said dryly. She forced a smile, as if hoping to quell the feeling of doom that had settled like a heavy buffalo robe over her shoulders.

Now that she had heard the labors, all *three* of them, she knew that unless a miracle happened, she hadn't a prayer in the world of completing even one—let alone obtaining the prize.

Three

AWAKENED BY THE TRILL OF A MOCKINGBIRD, ALLIE SCOWLED and pulled the covers over her head to drown out the bird's bright call. Ordinarily she loved the sound, but now it only served to remind her of everything she was missing.

"Allie. Time to get up, dear," her mother called through the closed door.

"All right," she muttered. Before her birthday she'd always been the first one up, usually leaving for the range before anyone else was out of bed. Now she had nothing to get up for. She raised herself up onto her elbow and pounded a fist into her pillow.

She felt like a prisoner. A prisoner in her own home. The last time she'd spent this much time indoors, she'd had the measles. As miserable as they had been, the measles had been a pleasure compared to the labor.

Yesterday she had baked two more cakes, and even though she had followed the recipe carefully, both had been disasters. It had taken her the rest of the day and night to clean up the kitchen.

Today she would try again. She had no choice. Ordinarily she would have a year to complete the labor, a year where she would be expected to keep trying until she finished her task, but her grandma hadn't given her a year. Allie had to have that cake by the Fourth of July. She counted the days on her fingers. She'd never make it. And if today went anything like the last two weeks, the next few days would be the longest time in her entire life.

She reluctantly rose from the bed and pulled on her pants and shirt. She and Hal were supposed to start breaking the horses today. *But I won't be able to because I'll never get out of that danged kitchen.* She impatiently tugged on her worn footwear and thought of the new boots she'd planned to buy. She wouldn't feel right about taking any money now. Not if she couldn't finish what she had started. *It isn't fair! Not after all the work I did to help catch those nags!* She considered riding to the canyon today and working on the cake tomorrow, then she reluctantly abandoned the idea. It would take every minute she had, and then some, to master that cake.

Still grumbling, Allie splashed water over her face and washed her hands, then raised her brush to take a swipe or two at her hair. Satisfied that she looked halfway presentable, she headed downstairs.

She was surprised to find the kitchen empty, then remembered everyone else had planned to spend the day in town. That suited Allie just fine. At least today she wouldn't have to put up with her brothers' teasing.

She poured herself a steaming cup of coffee from the big enameled pot that simmered on one side of the nickel-plated cookstove, then carried the brew to the planked table. *If I could just figure this thing out.* She opened the bulky family cookbook, unfolded the recipe, and smoothed it against the tabletop. She ran her finger down the list and studied each ingredient, each step. Where had she gone wrong? Probably in her interpretation of a fistful, a pinch, a smidgen, and a dab. After a while, she shook her head. She could stare at the paper all day and wouldn't know any more than she did right now. Well, nothing to do but try it again.

She rose to her feet and wrapped an apron around her middle, then, her mouth set in a grim line, she stalked toward the stove. She painstakingly measured then beat the ingredients. When she was certain she'd done everything she was supposed to, she carefully poured the mixture into seven different pans and placed them in the oven. The batter didn't look any different today than it had yesterday, but she prayed the result wouldn't be the same.

Wiping her flour-coated hands on the front of her apron, she surveyed the rest of the kitchen. It couldn't have looked worse if it had been hit by a tornado. Dirty bowls and pans of every size and shape littered the counters. An egg that had cracked before she got it to the bowl made a trail of yellow down the table leg before it congealed on the floor. Ants were already making their way toward the sugar she'd spilled, and on top of that, a layer of flour covered everything in sight.

"You wouldn't think one cake would take so much doing," she fumed out loud. "I don't know how Persy stands it. All that cooking every day, and then having to clean up the mess to boot."

Using water she'd heated earlier, Allie washed the mixing bowls and utensils, then cleaned the tops of the cabinets. She dumped the dishwater in the flower bed outside, then filled the bucket with clean water and added a few soap chips. It was early yet—maybe she could ride out to the canyon. Her mind on Hal and the horses, she knelt and began to scrub the kitchen floor. She raised her head when a whiff of smoke drifted past her nostrils.

"Jehoshaphat! The damned cake!" She jumped to her feet.

She dashed toward the stove, where black smoke curled insidiously around the edges of the nickel-plated door. She yanked the latch open and, ignoring the blistering heat that belched into her face, grabbed for the first pan. "Oww! Damn and double damn!" She jerked her hand back and stared at her seared fingers.

"Allie?"

She whirled and saw Hal peering cautiously around the doorway. "What are you doing here?" she muttered, snatching up a pot holder.

"Good morning to you, too." He stepped into the room. "I came to see if you might be sick or something." He sailed his battered hat toward the deer antler rack, then hooked his thumbs in the back pockets of his jeans. "In case you forgot, we're supposed to start breaking those mustangs today."

"I'm not sick, and I didn't forget," she snapped, retrieving the last of the pans from the oven. "I'm busy—cooking."

"I figured as much." He drew a finger down her cheek. "Either that or you fell into the flour barrel." He leaned around her and peered at the blackened mess. "Ugh!" he said, shuddering. "What is that?" He gingerly poked a finger at it as if he fully expected it to bite.

"That is a cake. A *seven-layer* cake," she said between gritted teeth.

"It don't look like any cake I ever saw," he said, waving a hand to fan the acrid smoke from his eyes.

It didn't look like any cake she had ever seen, either, and no matter how hard she tried or how many times she made it, the results were likely to be the same. Tears of frustration filling her eyes, she turned away from Hal's sympathetic gaze.

Hal awkwardly gave her a pat on the shoulder. The touch, intending to comfort, made her cry all the harder. "Aww. Don't bawl, Allie. I didn't mean to hurt your feelings."

Embarrassed, she shrugged his hand away. "You didn't hurt my feelings. And you know I never cry. I'm just so danged mad," she said, swallowing a sob. She couldn't tell him how important this cake was to her. Or what her failure to make it would mean. She couldn't. Not only because no one outside of the family could know of the labor, but also because it went against her grain to admit anything as innocent looking as a cake could mean her defeat.

"Well, not everybody can cook." He removed the bandanna from his neck and stuffed it into her hand.

Inhaling Hal's familiar scent, a mixture of soap, clean sweat, and saddle leather, she lifted the scarf and swiped at her swollen eyes; then, because she had nothing else, she used it to noisily blow her nose.

"Why don't you get out of that rig?" He motioned to the apron she wore. "I'll help you clean up this mess, then we can get started on those horses."

"I can't." Her lip trembled. "I am not going anywhere until I make this dangblasted cake," she said, dumping the burned cake into a washtub so she could clean the pans and start again.

"Why are you so set on baking a cake? I never even knew you liked to cook."

"I don't like to cook," she said grimly. "In fact I hate it."

"Then why?" Plainly bewildered, Hal gazed down at her.

"I just have to, that's why."

He let out a long breath and shook his head. "Well, since you're bound to do it, maybe I can give you a hand."

"What makes you think you can do any better?" she asked, eyeing him dubiously. "You don't know how to cook, either."

He shrugged. "I know. But I couldn't do any worse than that," he said, dodging the pot holder she threw at him. "Besides, it looks like you've got directions"—he motioned toward the piece of flour-drenched paper on the cabinet—"and I can read. And I was always underfoot when my ma was cookin'."

"Watchin' and cookin' ain't the same. If it was that easy, don't you think I would have already done it?" Allie yanked up the paper and shoved it into his hands. "Look at this. It may as well be written in one of them foreign tongues."

Hal studied the list, then scratched his head. "A scoop of this, a dab of that, a pinch of something else. I see what you mean." He glanced around the room, then pointed to Minerva's big old cookbook. "Maybe it tells you in there."

"Not likely. I looked on every page."

"Maybe Persy could help you. She's a good cook."

"I already asked. Besides, she's not allowed to help. She only told me 'to ask and ye shall receive.' Now don't that make a lot of sense? I did ask, and she didn't tell me a thing."

"Ask and ye shall receive?" He looked thoughtful for a minute. "Doesn't it say that somewhere in the Bible?"

"The Bible?" A small seedling of hope blossoming in her chest, Allie darted into the parlor. A moment later, the Good Book tucked under her arm, she returned to the kitchen. "Let's sit out on the veranda; it's hot enough to fry eggs on the floor in here."

Hal followed her out the door and sat beside her on the wicker seat.

"This is the only place I never thought to look." Allie thumbed through the book and found a slip of paper tucked between the leaves. Written in Persy's faded script, it told exactly how to decipher the measurements listed in their ancestor's recipe. Apparently Allie hadn't been the only one to have the problem. "Hallelujah. Now maybe I can do it." Jubilant, she closed the volume with a resounding slap; then, after putting it back in its customary position on the table by the fireplace, she went back into the kitchen and dusted the flour off the original recipe. She peered first at it and then at Persy's paper.

"First the directions say to separate the eggs." She got out the same little bowls she'd used before. She cracked one egg and dumped it into the bowl. Then, moving the second bowl some distance away, she took another egg and cracked it. "Think that's far enough apart?"

"Hell, that's not the way," Hal said, his tanned face crinkling with laughter. "Even I know that much." He took the egg out of her hands. "Here, this is what it means." He cracked the egg, deftly depositing the yoke in one bowl, the white in another. He picked up another and did the same. "You only need two bowls—one for the yellows and one for the whites."

"Well, 'pears you did learn something after all." She gave him a broad grin. "I reckon I can take it from here."

Hal sighed and handed her the egg he was holding. "Well, I can tell you've got no intention of breaking horses today."

"I know I promised and I'm sorry. But it looks like the only thing I'm going to be breaking today is eggs."

Hal poured himself a cup of coffee and sat down at the table. "You never did tell me why you're so set on baking that cake."

"That's my business," Allie said pertly, dashing a large measure of flour into a big wooden bowl.

"Maybe you've got your cap set for one of those town

fellers," Hal drawled. "Everybody knows the way to a man's heart is through his stomach."

"Oh, they do, do they?" Was that the way to Hal's heart? Remembering what Venus had told her about Hal and the redhead from the saloon, Allie doubted cooking had anything to do with it. She hesitated, then knowing Hal wasn't about to give up, she answered his question. "Well, I guess you've found me out," she lied. "I am interested in a man."

"You are?" Hal frowned. "Who?"

Who? Now why did he have to ask that? Allie mentally scanned her list of suitable unattached males. One of the twins who ran the livery? He would never believe it; they were much too old. Besides, how could she tell him which one? Both were big, brawny, and redheaded. Nobody, including her, could tell them apart. There was always the deputy, Dudley Jones. Or one of the cowboys.

No. It had to be somebody special. Somebody who would make him sit up and take notice. Who was the most eligible bachelor in town? "Clay Masterson," she said softly.

"Who?"

Allie turned with a smile. "Clay Masterson. You know. He owns the Paradise Plains *Gazette.*"

"Yeah, I know him." Hal scowled. "But I didn't know you did."

"Well, I do," Allie said smoothly. "That's why I'm baking this cake. I'm hoping Clay will bid on it at the box social on the Fourth of July."

"Well, that cuts it," Hal said, scraping the chair back from the table. "Since you're so busy baking a cake for Clay Masterson, I guess you don't need me around anymore." Without another word, he slammed his hat on his head and stormed out.

"Well, I'll be," she said, gazing after him in amazement. "Wonder who put the burr under his saddle?"

Watching Hal ride out of the ranchyard, she felt a little ashamed that she'd told such a whopper. She barely knew Clay Masterson, having spoken to him only once when her grandmother had introduced her. She was quite sure the man wouldn't remember her at all.

But Hal didn't know that. *By the way he acted, I might think he was jealous if I didn't know better.* She shook her head, rejecting the notion. *He's just upset because I can't help him with the horses.*

She stepped away from the window and went back to the cake. After she'd added the rest of the ingredients, she vigorously mixed the batter, then carefully poured a measure into each cake pan, making sure they were as near the same size as she could get them. Then slowly, cautiously, she carried each pan to the oven and set it inside. "There." Breathing a sigh of relief, she closed the heavy door.

She glanced at the kitchen. Should she clean it up now? "Not on your life," she thought. She'd found out the hard way that this cooking business required serious concentration. Despite the fact that the heat was nearly intolerable, she tugged a ladder-backed chair to within a few feet of the stove and plopped down in it, determined not to move an inch until the cake was done. She watched the hands on the mantel clock until sufficient time had elapsed for her to check her pans. Almost afraid to look, she opened the oven door. To her delight, she saw that each cake had risen into a delicate light-gold layer. They looked absolutely perfect. But she had to figure out if they were done.

Using a clean broom straw she'd plucked and washed earlier, she gently inserted it into the middle of the first pan. When she pulled it out, the puddinglike batter on the end of the straw told her the cakes still had a way to go.

She carefully eased the pan back into place. Eyeing the batch, she couldn't hold back the grin that spread across her face. "I did it!" she cried, shutting the oven door. Using her shirtsleeve, she wiped the beads of perspiration from her forehead and resumed her place in the chair. "Wasn't hard a'tall, once I got the hang of it."

Just to make sure she had it right, she'd try a few more on the family. By the time of the social, she should be able to bake a cake almost as perfect as Persy's. *Who knows,* she thought smugly, *if the cake did turn out good, that fancy newspaperman might decide to bid on it.*

If he didn't, she knew Hal would—unless he was still mad about the horses.

And if he didn't? Well, there were always the twins. They'd eat anything that didn't bite back.

She closed her eyes, then just as quickly opened them. What would she do if Clay Masterson did buy her cake? She'd have to help him eat it. She'd also have to talk to him. The idea filled her with trepidation. What would she say? She always grew tongue-tied around men. It was different when she was with Hal or the twins, since all they ever talked about was horses. Somehow she was quite sure Clay would expect his supper companion to discuss more than breeding lines or gaits.

Heck, she was probably worrying for nothing. He probably wouldn't want to eat with her anyway, no matter how good a cake she could bake. She had a mirror and the mirror didn't lie. She was no great shakes to look at, nothing compared to the women she'd seen on *his* arm. The kindest thing she'd ever heard anyone say about her appearance was that she looked pleasant. She might have been content with that, except she'd heard them say the same thing about Lilly Mae Sutton, who could eat the corn off the cob through the slats of a picket fence. She lifted a finger to her mouth and ran it across her lips. *At least I don't have buckteeth.*

Allie heard a wagon rumble into the yard and knew her family had returned from town. She stood, calling out a greeting as her ma, grandma, and Persy came through the door.

"Oh, my," her mother gasped, catching sight of the room.

"Don't worry, Ma. I'll clean it up." Allie motioned toward the table. "Y'all are just in time for a piece of cake." She whisked up a pot holder and proudly opened the stove door. She pulled the first pan out. "What happened? Where'd they go?" She yanked out another. It looked the same. Allie whirled toward her sister. "I don't understand it. They were this high." She held up her thumb and finger, showing a large gap between. "Now look. They're flatter than sourdough pancakes."

"Allie, you didn't—?" Persy glanced at Minerva.

When her grandma shook her head, Allie knew she'd have to figure this one out on her own.

"What's the matter?" Her pa carried a large sack of flour through the doorway. "Y'all look like somebody died."

"Allie's cake fell," Jane said, pointing to the pans.

"Somebody must have slammed the door," Pa said, his face wreathed in sympathy. "Don't worry, daughter. I bought three more sacks of flour and two sacks of sugar. That ought to be enough to get you started again."

Started again? Allie groaned. Then, remembering what he had said about the door, she grew thoughtful. Hal hadn't slammed the door. But she had. She'd been so proud of herself she'd fairly let that oven door fly shut.

How could she have forgotten? How many times during her childhood had she heard her ma yell, *"Don't you kids slam that door. I've got a cake in the oven."* At the time

Allie had thought her mother didn't like the noise. Now she knew the real reason. Allie eyed her grandma. "When is that social, anyhow?"

"A week from Saturday," Minerva answered, giving her a smile.

"It'll take that long to get the kitchen clean," her pa teased.

"Well, now, that's something we can help with." Her mother set down the basket she carried and tied on an apron.

"What are you gonna do with them?" Odie pointed at the cakes.

Allie dumped them all into the washtub and handed one to him. "Feed it to the dogs."

Odie hefted the flattened layer and grinned. "I've got a better idea. We can use this batch for target practice. Let me know when you make more."

"Well, it won't be today, so git," her grandma said, shooing him toward the door.

Allie looked around at the mess. She was bone-weary, and this was all she had to show for her efforts.

Reading her thoughts, Persy gently touched her arm. "You'll get the hang of it. It just takes practice."

Allie managed a feeble smile. A week. A week to make a cake that a body could eat.

And in that same period of time, she had to learn something about social graces.

Four

"*WHAT THE HECK IS WRONG WITH HER?*" HAL WONDERED, AS he reined his horse around a pile of rocks. He thought he knew Allie better than anybody, but after this morning he felt as if he didn't know her at all. For one thing, he'd never seen her cry, not even that time she fell off the top of the gazebo and broke her arm. And this morning she'd cried over a cake.

A cake she was making for Clay Masterson.

Since they'd shared a bottle more than once, Hal knew Clay well enough to know that Allie didn't stand a chance with the man. Clay preferred his women sophisticated and feminine. And beautiful. More like Allie's sister Venus.

Even when she did try to look her best—which wasn't often, for she had never been one to primp—Allie wasn't anything special to look at. All she had going for her were those big gray eyes, and they had a way of seeing through a man that made most of them feel uncomfortable. It was like she could see clean to their souls.

Every girl in the area had her cap set for the newspaperman, including some who weren't single. And while

Hal personally had nothing against him, Clay wasn't the sort he'd choose for Allie.

But Clay was the one she had set her sights on, and Hal couldn't tell Allie she didn't have a chance with the man without hurting her feelings.

And what if Clay didn't bid on that cake after all the trouble she'd gone through to make it? Hell, he didn't even want to think about that.

"Hey, Anderson."

Hal lifted his head, surprised to find himself on the main street of Paradise Plains. He turned toward the voice and smiled. "Howdy, Clay. You're just the man I wanted to see." He pulled his horse to a stop at the hitching rail and dismounted.

Clay grinned from the boardwalk, then ran a hand through his thick, dark hair. "I kind of wanted to see you, too. Come on in and have some coffee."

Hal followed him inside the office and plopped down in a chair in front of the massive oak desk.

Clay poured them each a cup of coffee. "A little hair of the dog?" he asked, pouring a measure of whiskey from an amber flask into his own cup.

"Naw. Too early for me." Hal studied the man across from him and wondered why all the women found him so fascinating. Granted, Clay was tall, well over six feet, compared to Hal's own five feet ten. And while most men in town wore cotton shirts and denim jeans, Clay always wore a dark suit, white shirt, and string tie.

Could it be the mustache? Hal eyed the slender arch of hair above Clay's upper lip. The man was almost prissy about his appearance, even going so far as to have his hair cut once a week instead of once every three or four months like most fellers. When Clay set his cup in front of him, Hal caught the aroma of bay rum that told him today had been the day Clay had visited Miss Sally's Tonsorial Parlor.

"Am I growing horns?" Clay asked, settling into his own chair.

"What?"

"From the way you've been staring at me, I wondered if I had egg on my face or something."

"No. You look fine." Fine was the truth. As far as the man's appearance was concerned, Hal couldn't find a thing to criticize. Somehow that bothered him more than he cared to admit.

"Well, I wanted to thank you for the other night," Clay said with a wry grin. "If you hadn't warned me her pa was on the way back to that wagon, I might be the guest of honor at a shotgun wedding about now." His chocolate-brown eyes danced with devilment. He laughed, showing a dimple and a flash of white teeth. "I'd say I owe you one."

Hal took a sip of coffee to hide his surprise. The farmer and his daughter came into town about once a month, and while her daddy bartered his corn for supplies at the mercantile, that little gal spent her time in the hayloft of the livery doing some swapping of her own. Last night when he'd spotted the farmer heading back to the barn, Hal had stepped into the livery and called out a warning to whoever was in the loft. He hadn't known it was Clay—until now. Under ordinary circumstances, Hal would have told him to forget it, but that was before he knew about the cake and Allie. "Now that you mention it," Hal said smoothly, "I do need a favor."

Clay glanced up, then shrugged. "Name it."

"Do you know Allie Daltry?"

Clay thought a moment. "No, not that I recall. What's she look like?"

Allie had lied! Clay didn't even know her. And that made the situation even worse. She didn't stand a chance. Hal sighed and set his cup back on the desk. "She's little, with short, curly brown hair. She's Minerva Daltry's youngest granddaughter."

"Minerva. Doesn't she own Mount Olympus?" Clay asked, mentioning the nickname the townsfolk had given the Daltry ranch.

"Yes. That's Minerva all right."

"I think I did meet the girl once." He arched a brow. "What about her?"

"You know that box social that's coming up on the Fourth?"

"Yeah?"

"Allie's baking a cake and I want you to bid on it."

"Why?"

"Because she's set on eating with you, that's why." Hal leaned across the desk. "You owe me one, remember? And now I'm callin' in my marker."

Clay held up his hands. "Okay, you win. I'll buy the damned cake. I just hope she can cook."

Deciding it would be best if he didn't comment on that issue, Hal stood and held out his hand. "Well, I've got horses to break. See you a week from Saturday?"

Clay shook his hand, then said wryly, "Wouldn't miss it for the world."

"Don't sit spraddle-legged," Venus said with disgust. "Mercy sakes, Allie, how do you expect us to help you if you don't listen to a thing we say?"

"Jehoshaphat! There's just too dad-blamed much to remember," Allie said with dismay. "Do this. Don't do that. I've heard so many do's and don't's my head is fair to spinning. And besides, all this buttermilk and honey mess you put on my face is makin' me itch."

"Don't cuss and quit pickin' at your face or I'll have to smear more on you," Venus threatened. "You don't want to end up spotted, do you?"

"Don't worry, little sister," Persy said softly. "You'll do just fine. Be yourself and smile."

"And don't talk about horses," Venus ordered.

"I don't know anything else to talk about," Allie grumbled.

"Well, there's always the weather," Persy said helpfully.

Allie released a very unladylike snort. "What weather? Every day it's the same old thing. Dust and wind. It hasn't rained in so long even the mosquitos have their tongues hanging out."

"Oh!" Venus rolled her eyes at Persy. "I give up. She's hopeless." Shaking her blond curls, she gathered her skirts and marched from the room.

When Persy eyed the doorway wistfully, Allie decided to take matters into her own hands. "From the little I've learned about men—mostly Hal, and of course Pa and the boys—they like it better if you don't say much at all. That way they get a chance to talk about themselves."

Persy let out a peal of laughter. "Oh, Allie. How right you are. You may not have much experience, but you hit the nail right on the head. I've never known a man who didn't like to brag a little if given the opportunity."

"Well, since we've solved that problem, maybe you ought to take a nap, too. You're lookin' a little weary," Allie said, watching Persy attempt to smother a yawn.

"I am a bit tired at that." She bent and gave Allie a hug. "I'm sure you'll do just fine, honey. See you at supper."

When her sisters had left the room, Allie removed her coverlet so she wouldn't get the buttermilk mixture on it, then she too stretched out on her bed to rest for a bit. What with the cooking and primping and lessons in deportment, she was fairly worn to a frazzle.

She twitched her itching nose and fought the impulse to rub it, knowing that if she did a chunk of the face goo would come off on her hand.

She was hot.

She was also as thirsty as a bullfrog in a dried-up pond.

She considered sneaking downstairs to get a drink, but reluctantly decided against it. If one of her brothers spotted her wearing this stuff, she'd never live it down. If they did tease her, she could threaten to bake them another cake, but she didn't want to alienate them completely. They might be the only ones she could depend on to bid on the blasted thing.

The cowboys wouldn't do it. Most of them, even the ones with a craving for sweets, threatened to quit if she darkened the cook shack doorway with another of her creations. Even the dogs hid when she stepped out the door.

What if nobody bought it? She was afraid word might have already gotten out, especially since Hank had to send to Abilene for another shipment of flour just so he could supply the other patrons of his mercantile.

After the box social was over, she swore it would be a cold day in hell before she ever made another of the blasted things.

She groaned and licked her dry lips. Compared to her labor, rounding up wild horses was like going to an afternoon tea.

Thinking of the horses reminded her of Hal, and she wondered how he was getting along without her. Breaking the horses was important. He needed the money to repay the loan Minerva had given him. Even though she had done more than her fair share by just catching the mustangs, Allie felt she had let Hal down. Did he feel the same way? Is that why he hadn't come by? She hadn't seen him since the day he'd left in such a temper.

The social would be the day after tomorrow. Would he even be there?

Five

THE WEATHER ON THE AFTERNOON OF THE FOURTH OF JULY WAS Texas-hot and muggy, and the tempers of those waiting in the Daltry wagon were stretched to the limit.

"She's been up since dawn. How much longer can one woman take?" Jake complained, removing his derby to wipe his perspiring forehead.

"Knowing Venus, it could be hours yet," Persy said with a sigh.

"It had better not be. My frosting's starting to run." Allie frantically waved a fly away from the icing on her precious cake, then examined the frosting for any other insect that might have been drawn to the sweetness.

The Daltry wagon was another of her father's projects, built with two long padded benches that ran lengthwise opposite each other, then one up front for the driver and his companions. It had a fringed canopy top, with canvas sides that could be raised or lowered, depending on the weather—Minerva's idea. Today the curtains had been left up to give the shaded side of the wagon the benefit of a faint breeze. Allie noted with satisfaction that the empty seat opposite hers looked hot enough to pop corn.

"It's a good thing Lee and Meredith came by early to fetch the children or we'd really have a problem on our hands," Persy said, fluttering a palm leaf fan.

"Ma, tell that girl if she doesn't get out here, she'll have to walk to town," Odie ordered.

Jane had just reached the doorway when Buck and a veil-swathed Venus appeared on the threshold.

"Get a move on before the horses die of sunstroke," Minerva called out, vigorously waving her oriental paper fan.

"I couldn't find my good parasol," Venus complained. She placed her gloved hand on her husband's arm and led the way to the wagon. Then, after they were seated, she managed to take up the room that was left to arrange her skirts.

"With all that riggin' I'd say you didn't need it," Allie said, eyeing the multitude of gauze that covered her sister. "I don't know how you can see," she said before she remembered her brother-in-law's blindness.

"One of us better be able to," Buck quipped with a smile.

"At least *my* skin is protected," Venus said, adjusting the frilly parasol she had managed to find. "In spite of the fact that y'all left me and Buck the seat in the sun."

With all her petticoats, Allie doubted if Venus could feel the seat, but she noticed guiltily that Buck seemed more than a little uncomfortable.

"If you had hurried up, your bench wouldn't be so hot. Waiting on you, the rest of us are burned to a crisp," Persy said impatiently.

"I 'spect I'll be the same way presently," Venus snapped back.

"Just lower the curtain, Venus," Buck said soothingly. "I'm sure you'll cool off in a minute or two."

Venus sniffed but rolled down the curtain. While it protected her and Buck from the sun, it also blocked off any air that might have entered from that side of the wagon.

"All right, now that we're finally all here, let's get going." Odie lifted the reins and the team lurched forward, sending the fringe on the top edges of the conveyance into a wild dance.

"Oh, no," Allie cried when the cake skidded along with it.

"Odie, watch your driving." Minerva reached over and grabbed one side of the metal platter. "I'd hate to see Allie's cake spoiled after all the hard work she went through. Besides, we sure wouldn't want to have to wait while she made another."

Jake chuckled. "Amen to that."

When the team settled into a steady walk, Allie released the breath she'd been holding and peered at the cake. It was all right so far. Now, if it didn't melt, she had a chance of getting it there in one piece.

The cake had turned out better than expected, and even though it couldn't compare with the one Persy had made for her birthday, Allie was quite pleased with the result. The thick, pink, sticky frosting glued the layers together and hid any unevenness. The tiny white rosebuds and baby fern leaves from her mother's flower garden she'd arranged in a circle on the top and around the base hid the rest. All together, the cake looked pretty impressive, she thought proudly.

She couldn't wait for Hal to see it.

The sun and the soft clop-clop of the horses' feet in the soft dust, along with the steady whir of cicadas, soon lulled some of the family into sleep. Persy and Jake rested with eyes closed, and Minerva slumped against a cushion she had propped against the back of the front seat.

Although Allie nodded drowsily, she dared not close her eyes. Instead she concentrated on Venus, who gave a commentary on various things along the way: a jackrabbit under a clump of sage; a coyote watching from the distance. Listening as Venus patiently answered her inquisitive husband's questions, Allie was oddly touched by the scene. It was clear that Venus adored Buck, and while she could be quite selfish and thoughtless around everyone else, she certainly wasn't that way with him.

The wagon rumbled into the outskirts of Paradise Plains. Allie craned her neck when they approached one small house, but saw neither Hal nor his father. They passed a few more homes and the Daltry Library—Hercules's prize from Minerva—which had one main book-lined reading room, plus an office and private sitting area in the back. Up ahead she saw the church, and to the right of that sat the one-room schoolhouse where both Lee and Meredith had taught.

As Allie gazed down the long, dusty street, she thought Paradise Plains could have been almost any small cattle town. A few false-fronted buildings, housing Miss Sallie's barber/dentist shop, Clay Masterson's Paradise *Gazette,* Hank and Maybelle's general mercantile, and the Horse Hotel livery stable, lined one side of the thoroughfare. The sheriff's office, Buccaneer Restaurant, Mrs. Bennet's boardinghouse, and Miss Lavender's Hatbox edged the other.

The railroad track—a whistle-stop—separated the town from the more unsavory elements, including Lucky's saloon and whorehouse.

They were at the opposite, more respectable end of the street, at the combination community hall/church building, where most of the town's functions were held. With everyone gathered for the Independence Day celebration, the churchyard was a beehive of activity.

"We're here," Odie called over his shoulder.

Minerva smothered a yawn, then sat up and adjusted her bonnet.

Persy and Jake opened sleep-lidded eyes and gazed around them.

Venus, who had removed her veils before any of the townsfolk could see them, anchored her stylish hat into place.

"There they are," her ma called out, directing Odie toward the small group that frantically waved their hands in order to get his attention. Leaning forward, Allie saw her brothers Lee and C. J. and their families sitting on a blanket they'd spread on a patch of dried grass in the shade of an old oak tree.

Her pa guided the buckboard near them and pulled the team to a stop. "Howdy, boys and hel–lo, ladies," he said, greeting Meredith and Lizzie, who had her arms wrapped tightly around Thalia to keep the toddler from running under the hooves of the horses.

Odie jumped down, then helped Jane, Minerva, and Allie to the ground. "That little one looks cooked fair to a frazzle. You boys tend to the horses and give that baby to me." He reached out for the squirming Thalia. "Come to Grandpa, little darlin'."

"Little devil is more like it," Lizzie said in exasperation, relinquishing her hold.

"Now, dear, she wouldn't be a Daltry if she wasn't full of spirit," Jane said, smiling as she watched the large man bounce about the grounds with the laughing child perched on his shoulders.

"She's got enough spirit for a dozen Daltrys, and then some." Sighing, Lizzie attempted to tuck a stray lock of midnight-black hair into place. "She's got me plumb tuck-ered and the day's hardly started."

"Lizzie can hardly wait for that train trip, but she is wondering how Allie is going to manage that wild child of hers," Meredith said, grinning at Allie.

Allie wondered that herself. Thalia was so lively she regularly wore out the whole clan and was still raring to go when everybody else was pleading for mercy.

"Where's Jupiter?" Minerva asked, shading her eyes to peer at the throng of people who had come to the picnic.

"He and Diana are helping decorate the bandstand. I swear they'd hang red, white, and blue streamers on us if we'd stand still long enough. Cynthia and the baby are at the library, taking a nap under Mrs. Cooper's watchful eye," Meredith added.

"That woman is an absolute jewel. You're lucky you have her," Jane said, referring to the rawboned widow who had been housekeeper and cook for Lee and Mere-dith the past couple of years.

"I don't know when I've seen so many decorations," Minerva said, gazing at the colorful display.

"My fingers are plumb crampy from cutting so much paper, but it does look festive," Lizzie admitted. "And wait till you see the fireworks. A whole boxcarload. The brigade has been filling pails of water all morning, just in case the thing gets out of hand."

"Lee did go overboard a little this year, but he wanted to keep people's minds off the drought," Meredith said in her husband's defense.

"I thought he did it because he wanted to celebrate my and C. J.'s anniversary," Lizzie teased, her sapphire eyes sparkling.

"It *is* your anniversary. Congratulations. What with ev-erything else going on, I'd almost forgotten," Jane mur-mured.

"I doubt if anything could make people forget the drought," Minerva said. "Old man Spence over Buffalo Gap way claims it's so dry he doesn't have to do much churning to get his butter, because his cow's givin' curdled milk."

"Now, Ma, you know that old coot's been known to exaggerate," Jane said, laughing. "But I do know my flowers are going to be sticks if it doesn't rain soon."

"Our well is getting mighty low," Lizzie said solemnly. "C. J. plans to ask his pa and Lee to come over and help him deepen it."

"I'm sure they'd be happy to." Minerva took a deep breath and rolled her shoulders as if to shrug off any problems. "I don't know what we're all looking so glum for; we'll get by just like we always have," she said brightly. "This is a celebration—did you girls notice Allie's cake? She made it all by herself to sell at the box social."

"So you did it! Congratulations!" Meredith said with a warm smile.

Allie proudly removed her cake from the wagon, and after all had admired it, she carefully made her way toward the long table where other cakes and delicacies of all kinds were on display.

She felt a twinge of misgiving when a tall, gangling youth left the group he was with and sauntered in her direction. The darling of his grandma's eye, Simon Bennet had been the town terror since he'd been old enough to walk. Now in his early teens, his behavior had gone from bad to worse.

"Whatcha got there, Allie?" Simon asked, his tone telling her he was bent on mischief.

"A cake for the auction." Eyeing him warily, she'd moved to go around him when he suddenly threw up his hand. Afraid he intended to upend her cake, she jerked it away.

The cake tilted, and the heat, along with the slick icing, sent each section into a skid. All seven layers came to a halt against the front of her dress.

"Dang you, Simon. Now look what you made me do." Filled with fury, she stared down at her misshapen cake and the mess down the front of her shirtwaist.

"Ha, ha. You're supposed to eat it, not wear it," Simon said, pointing at her.

"Is he causing you a problem, Miss Daltry?"

Allie gazed into chocolate-brown eyes that glittered in anger. "I think you owe the young lady an apology," Clay Masterson said, glaring down at the boy.

Simon's Adam's apple bobbed and he swallowed nervously. "Sorry, Allie," he squeaked, his voice breaking in his agitation. Before Clay could stop him, he darted away into the crowd.

"Here, let me help you with that." Clay removed the cake from her hands, carried it to one end of the table, and set it down. "I think if you smooth the icing here—and here—it will be just fine." He smiled down at her. "It's a lovely creation. The man who gets it will have quite a prize."

His words and the way he looked at her when he said them made Allie weak in the knees. "Th–thank you for being so kind as to say so," she stammered, a rush of heat painting her cheeks.

He removed an immaculate white linen handkerchief from his coat pocket and held it out to her. "Maybe this might help remove part of the frosting." His eyes darkened. "I think it's about time someone gave Simon Bennet the thrashing he deserves. If you will excuse me, Miss Daltry?"

"Allie," she said shyly. "Nobody calls me Miss."

"Allie. A lovely name. It suits you." He lifted her hand to his mouth and kissed it. "Until later?" His gaze fastened on hers for a moment, then when she nodded he smiled and walked away.

"I must be dreamin'," Allie said, staring after him. She glanced down at the monogrammed handkerchief he'd given her. Nope. It was real, all right. She pulled her sticky dress front away from her skin, then turned to see Venus standing behind her.

"Well, Atalanta, ah see you've managed to get yourself in a mess already," Venus said, eyeing her up and down. "Come on, let's see if we can't get you cleaned up befoah anyone notices."

"Did you see him?" Allie asked, looking back over her shoulder.

"Did ah see who?" Venus rolled her eyes impatiently. "Are you referrin' to that Anderson boy?"

"No. Clay Masterson." Since arriving, she hadn't even thought of Hal, but now she scanned the crowd.

"Clay Masterson." Venus grimaced. "Allie, take mah advice and stay away from that man."

"Why? Mama likes him and he just saved my cake from Simon. He seems like a perfect gentleman."

"That is the impression he tries to convey."

Allie hoped she would say more, but Venus turned and led the way to a small anteroom where she instructed Allie to remove her dress. While Allie washed the sticky residue from her skin, Venus sponged the rest from the front of the garment.

"There. It's a bit damp, but in this heat it should dry quickly."

"You never did explain about Clay," Allie said.

Venus hesitated. "Mama tried to match me up with him, too. At first ah was flattered by his attentions. What girl wouldn't be? He is the handsomest man in town.

Then he began to get possessive. Ah didn't like it and told him so, then, when he persisted, ah refused to see him. Although he never said or did anything ah could really object to, some sixth sense told me he couldn't be trusted."

"Maybe it was your imagination," Allie said, feeling a need to defend the man, since he had been the one to come to her rescue.

"Maybe so." Venus shrugged. "Ah just thought you should be warned." She examined herself in the cracked mirror and smiled. "After all, what can you expect from a man who earns his living printin' outright lies, half-truths, and innuendos?" With that, she tossed her head and pranced out of the room.

Following along behind, Allie pondered her sister's words. Clay acted like a gentleman with her, and until he proved himself to be otherwise, she intended to give him the benefit of the doubt.

Still thoughtful, she headed for the table to ascertain if any other disasters had befallen her cake. Flat on one side where it had skidded into her, it now appeared more like rounded stair steps than equal layers. The icing had melted in spots, leaving bare patches that reminded her of snow-covered ground on a hot spring day. A couple of the roses had slid into a shallow trench where somebody had apparently sampled the icing. Taking a knife someone had left on the end of the table, she attempted to repair the damage; then, when it was as presentable as she could make it, she decided to examine the competition. She strolled the length of the long table and studied the other baked goods, finding most all of them perfect—except the widow Bennet's. Apparently Simon had helped himself to a chunk of his grandmother's cake ahead of time.

Compared to the others, Allie knew her cake was nothing to brag about. Would it be good enough for anyone to bid on it?

She had boasted to Hal that she was making the cake for Clay Masterson. Now she wondered why on earth she had said such a thing. As kind as the man had been, he certainly had given her no indication that he intended to bid on her cake. In fact, the first opportunity he'd had, he'd rushed away.

Hal might buy it—if he was here—but Venus said she hadn't seen him. After she'd rejoined her family, Allie anxiously surveyed the crowd, hoping to spot Hal's familiar battered hat.

She didn't see it or him.

Maybe he was still mad about the horses.

Maybe he wouldn't even come.

"Looks like they're getting ready to run the footraces," her ma said.

The footraces. This would be the first year she would miss them. It was also the first year she'd worn anything but pants. Allie glanced down at her dress, then reluctantly shook her head. No, she didn't dare try to run in it. Her ma would have a fit. Besides, the garment was so blamed hot she'd probably die of heatstroke before she ran twenty steps.

"Girls, I think it's time we took these to the tables," Minerva said, lifting one of several wicker containers they'd brought from home. "We'll surely have some hungry people by the time they are through."

"Thirsty, too," a red-faced Odie said, returning the still-energetic Thalia to her mother. "Hey, boys," he called to Lee and C. J., who were rejoining the group. "Y'all know where they hid the liquid refreshments?"

"Follow me," C. J. said, leading the way.

"Mama. Play," Thalia demanded, trying to free herself from her mother's staying hand. The little girl extended a chubby finger and pointed to a bunch of older children who were engaged in a boisterous game of tag.

"No, dear. You are too little. Yum, yum. See what Grandma brought?" Lizzie handed the pouting child a cookie.

"Hey, Ma. Look," Lee and Meredith's son, Jupiter, yelled from the dance platform. He and two other boys were attaching red, white, and blue paper streamers to a railing that ran on two sides of a large wooden area the men had constructed earlier in the week. To take advantage of the cooler air outside, the floor would remain until after the Harvest Dance in the fall. After that, it would be dismantled and sold to the highest bidder and another would be built in the spring.

Allie helped her mother and grandma carry the large baskets of fried chicken, corn on the cob, fresh vegetables, cornbread, and cookies to the long row of muslin-draped tables that sat in the shade of two large black-walnut trees. After that, they joined other women who sought relief from the heat by relaxing on shade-dappled pallets and sipping iced lemonade while they fanned themselves with palm leaf or printed cardboard fans. When she became bored with the talk of canning and children, Allie left the group and strolled about the grounds. She saw Clay, surrounded by a bevy of unmarried girls, but Hal was nowhere in sight. Deciding that he had probably entered the footrace, she joined the rest of the cheering crowd that waited for the winners to come in. Standing on her tiptoes, she spotted his familiar figure.

Shirtless and barefoot, his bronzed skin slick with sweat, Hal and another taller young man fought for the lead.

"Come on, Hal, you can do it," she cried, her own shout lost in the midst of others.

"Here they come. It's Anderson. Now it's Foley. Gonna

be a close one, folks," Fritz Tittle, the owner of the Buccaneer Restaurant, yelled. "It's Anderson. Hal Anderson is the winner."

A broad grin on her face, Allie edged her way through the crowd to congratulate Hal, but stopped short when she saw that someone else had gotten there first.

A gaudily dressed redhead clung to Hal like a freshly laundered, still-wet shirt. Egged on by the jeers and catcalls of the onlookers, the woman busily dotted Hal's already red face with crimson kisses, which, Allie noticed, he was not in the least shy about returning.

"Well, I never. And in broad daylight." Unable to bear the sight any longer, Allie gathered her skirts and walked swiftly away.

How could he do such a thing? Of course she'd heard rumors, but she'd never thought they were true. She told herself he was a grown man and as such had a right to do whatever he pleased. She surely had no strings attached to him. They were friends, nothing more.

Then why did she feel so betrayed?

Surprised to find tears on her cheeks, she retreated behind a large tree, angry that anything Hal could do would make her cry. She never cried.

Yes, she did. She'd cried over that damned cake. Thinking these were two of the silliest reasons she'd ever heard for shedding tears, she was more furious at herself when they continued to fall.

"Something wrong, Allie?"

"What?" She blinked to clear her vision and saw Hal standing by her side. Never in a million years would she admit he'd found her crying. "I got caught in a dust devil. I think I got some dirt in my eye," she said, flushing crimson.

"Let me see." He whipped out a wrinkled bandanna and leaned close. His green eyes stared into hers and she felt his hot breath on her still-damp cheek. "I can't see anything," he said, drawing back with a frown.

"It's all right now," she said quickly. Noticing the curious stares that were directed their way, she took a step backward. "By the way, congratulations on winning the race. I wanted to tell you when you won, but you seemed to be busy." She peered around him. "Where is your friend?"

"Friend?" He shifted uneasily. "Yeah. I guess a lot of fellers wanted to slap me on the back."

Fellers? He knew exactly who she was talking about, and he didn't even have the good grace to look embarrassed. She leaned forward and ran a fingertip by the corner of his mouth. "Oh, my, are you bleeding?" She rubbed her fingers together. "No. Too greasy for blood. It feels more like paint." She waited to see how he'd get out of that one.

"Uh . . . If you are sure you're all right, I think I'll get some lemonade," he said, managing a sickly grin.

"I'm fine," she snapped. "In fact, I'm just dandy. So you can run along and quench your thirst."

His eyes narrowed, then without another word, he turned on his heel and strode away.

"The lemonade's that way," she yelled, pointing toward the trees, but Hal kept on walking—toward Main Street and Lucky's saloon.

The rest of the day passed without Allie catching a glimpse of him, which was all right with her—until she remembered she hadn't seen the dance hall girl, either. The thought that the two of them might be together didn't bother her as much as it might have if she hadn't been so worried about the cake auction. Now that Hal had left in a snit, who would bid on her cake?

Six

HURRYING INTO THE CHURCHYARD, WHERE HANK, THE CHUBBY, middle-aged owner of the mercantile, was auctioning off the remaining cakes, Hal paused by the linen-swathed table to catch his breath. Only two cakes remained, he noticed, and by the multiple layers, he knew one of them belonged to Allie.

Well, she wouldn't have to shed any more tears. Even if she wouldn't admit it, he knew that's why she'd been crying. The two dollars he had earned repairing fence for a ranch north of town jingled in his pants pocket. At least now *he* had the money to buy her cake—if Clay didn't keep his word.

Hal had wanted to tell Allie where he was going, but then she'd gotten so mad about Sadie kissing him that he hadn't bothered. He and the dance hall woman were friends, nothing more, but he figured he didn't owe Allie any explanations. Hell, they were pards—not married! But it did sorta please him that she'd actually been jealous.

He leaned against the trunk of an oak tree and

searched the crowd seated in front of the platform for the Daltrys. He spotted Allie on a third-row bench, next to her grandma. Her tanned hands were clenched in her lap. He longed to tell her not to worry, that everything would be all right, but her gaze was riveted on the auctioneer.

Frowning, he scanned the sea of faces until he saw Clay Masterson, who as usual had himself surrounded by a bevy of the town's unattached women. *Pay attention, damn it,* he silently ordered.

As if in response to Hal's unspoken command, Clay looked his way; then, meeting his eyes, the newspaper owner nodded.

Now that he knew Clay intended to bid, he should have been relieved. Instead, he felt irritated. Even knowing he wouldn't be Allie's first choice, Hal had secretly hoped they could eat together; but now he knew there would be scant chance of that. Besides, she was probably still mad about Sadie's kiss.

"And now, gentlemen, we have this lovely multilayered confection." Hank held up the lopsided cake. The pink icing sagged around the edge of the platter, and a wilted rose dangled precariously from the bottom layer. "Who will be the first bidder?"

"Two bits." A brawny redheaded man held up a hand. Next to him another man who looked exactly like him nodded.

"That's a start. Twin bids two bits."

Hal grinned. Nobody remembered the redheaded brothers' names. It wouldn't have done any good if they had, since nobody could tell them apart. To simplify matters, everyone called both of them Twin. And since they did everything together, the person whose cake they bought would have both of them for dinner partners.

"Fifty cents," Clay said.

A prosperous man like him ought to do better than that, Hal thought, ready to add his own bid.

"One dollar," Twin said solemnly, before he could do it.

"Dollar fifty." A long-faced cowboy whom Hal recognized as Charlie Simmons held up his hand.

"Dollar six bits," Twin said, punctuating the last with nods of his head.

"Two dollars," the lean puncher drawled, beating Hal to the bid.

"Five dollars," Clay said smoothly. Getting to his feet, he faced the crowd as if letting them know that whatever it took, he intended to have that particular cake.

Hal glanced at Allie and saw her face light with amazement.

"Any more bids?" Hank queried, mopping his balding head.

The twins shook their heads.

Charlie gave Allie a mournful look, then, his shoulders sagging in defeat, he ambled away.

Hank smiled at Allie. "Well, now, it looks like our illustrious newsman has just bought Allie Daltry's cake."

A dozen or so people craned their necks to get a better look. Embarrassed by their attention, heat flushed Allie's cheeks and she ducked her head.

"Come collect your prize, Clay."

"I fully intend to." Carrying the crooked pink cake, Clay made his way toward Allie.

"Doggone it," Hal said, shoving his hands into his back pockets. Uncertain how to feel, he watched Clay lead Allie toward a table that sat apart from the others in the shade of a spreading elm tree.

"Come on, men. This looks like a fine cake, too. Who will give me the first bid?" Hank called, holding up the last cake of the sale.

Apparently nobody was interested. Most of the crowd

had wandered toward the tables where boxes and baskets were being opened and shared, so that everyone might have a taste of what everyone else had brought. After filling their plates, families settled on blankets spread here and there on the grass.

When his own rumbling stomach reminded him that he hadn't had a bite to eat all day, Hal gazed longingly at the table of food. Although nobody would say anything, he'd feel guilty about partaking of theirs when he had contributed nothing in return. He looked back at the platform, where Hank still held the forlorn little cake.

Her thin, wrinkled face twisted with anxiety, the widow Bibble sat alone on the end of a bench.

"Fifty cents," Hal called out, wondering why the twins didn't stay to bid.

The elderly woman flashed him a grateful smile.

"Hal bids fifty cents. Anyone want to go higher?"

A couple of fellows lounged in the shade of a nearby tree, but they didn't seem interested in bidding. Hal looked at the old woman. Nobody ought to have their cake go with only one bid. Hal put his hand close to his mouth and projected his voice to the side to simulate a second bidder. "A dollar."

The auctioneer looked around, confused, then his gaze drifted back to Hal in understanding. "Any more bids?"

"Two dollars," Hal said, emptying his pockets.

Raising an eyebrow, the auctioneer chuckled and shook his head. He surveyed the area, then banged his gavel. "Sold to Hal Anderson for two dollars." His shiny face wreathed in a smile, Hank motioned him forward. "Come get your cake, son."

Hal strode forward and handed him the money. "Looks mighty good," he praised the old lady. In reality the cake didn't look as good as Allie's, and it was a whole lot smaller. But he was hungry enough to eat almost anything, and at least this way he had some excuse to stay.

The little cake balanced in one hand, he extended his arm to the widow. "I think I see a table right over there. I'll pull it into the shade and we can set a spell and visit while we eat."

"That would be delightful." She smiled up at him. "I haven't seen you in quite some time," she said, settling her small, spare frame on the bench he'd provided.

"Been awful busy," he said, biting into the cake. Immediately, his question about why the twins hadn't bid had been answered. They apparently had sampled one of the widow's cakes before. Part of his mouth felt as if he had been eating sawdust, and his tongue felt plumb slick from the lard she'd used in the icing. Still, he forced himself to finish and politely listened as she talked . . . and talked. His ears ringing from her endless chatter, Hal finally excused himself to fetch a couple of glasses of lemonade.

Even though it was in the opposite direction, he ambled toward the table where Allie and Clay sat engaged in conversation. Allie's face fairly glowed with pleasure and he heard her laughing clear across the churchyard. At least *she* seemed to be having a good time.

He saw Clay bend close to her curly head and whisper something in her ear. Smiling, her gray eyes sparkling, Allie gazed intently into the newsman's face.

The cake, Hal noticed, except for the small pieces that decorated each of their plates, seemed to have remained untouched. That more than anything else irritated him. After all the trouble she'd gone through to make the blasted thing, why weren't they eating it? His eyes narrowed. And if they hadn't been eating cake, what had they been doing?

The two were so engrossed in each other they seemed oblivious to anything else. In all the years he'd known her,

Allie had never been one to say more than a few words at a time. But around the handsome bachelor, she appeared to be dang near as gabby as the widow Bibble.

Even though he kept his distance, Hal had the feeling he could climb on their table and dance a jig and she wouldn't even know he was there. Allie looked different today, prettier somehow. Was that because of Clay? Or the dress? He studied her, taking notice of the soft feminine curves. Funny, he didn't remember her being so—so—rounded. He saw some of the other men stare at her in a speculative way and figured they'd noticed, too.

When Clay slid his arm around Allie's waist, Hal bristled. He was only supposed to bid on the cake, and he damned sure didn't have to be that accommodating. From where he stood, Clay and Allie looked like two lovers, instead of two people who barely knew each other.

"Hal, dear. Did you find the lemonade?" the widow asked, touching his sleeve.

"Uh, no, ma'am, I didn't." The truth was he'd forgotten all about it.

She patted his arm. "Well, don't worry about it. It's time I went home anyway. My poor cats will think I've gotten lost. This is the time I always feed them, although they're probably still full of cake batter. I can't keep the little darlings out of anything," she said with a high-pitched giggle.

He helped her into her buggy, and when she was on her way, he recalled what she'd said. *Cats?* How could he have forgotten? The widow's yard was always full of the critters, and they peered from every window in the small house.

They ate the batter. That's why the cake was so small.

And he'd eaten the cake. His stomach lurched—then rolled.

He'd been eating cat slop while Clay had been flirting with Allie.

Hal started toward the lemonade stand, then shook his head. It would take something a lot stronger than lemonade to get that taste out of his mouth. He shot a resentful look toward the couple at the table, then lengthening his stride, he headed down Main Street and across the tracks to Lucky's saloon.

After they had sampled the cake, Clay had brought Allie a plate laden with a crispy breast of chicken and a slice of pink roast beef, along with potato salad, and crunchy bread-and-butter pickles. Later, even though she told him that she was capable of eating by herself, he had insisted on feeding her grapes, still wet from the ice, and sweet strawberries that he dipped in whipping cream.

As she ate the morsels from his fingertips, Allie felt beautiful, almost seductive. It gave her a sensation of power. She imagined that if they were alone, Clay would have attempted to kiss her, for all day he had behaved as if they were sweethearts.

Basking in his attention, she found herself wondering what his kisses would be like. Would they be the same as Hal's? She really couldn't compare that, either, for outside of a brotherly peck on the cheek, no man had ever kissed her. From there she found herself fantasizing about what kind of husband Clay would make, which in itself was strange, for she hadn't the slightest intention in the world of getting married to anybody. Even *if* somebody like Clay would ask her, which of course he wouldn't . . .

Twilight came, along with an audible sigh of relief from the crowd. While it had cooled some, Allie likened it to the kitchen after she had taken the cake out of the oven. Even though the fire was banked, enough heat remained to remind you of the inferno it had been just a short time before.

After they'd finished eating, Clay explained that since he was on the fire brigade, he wouldn't be able to watch the fireworks display with her. When it was time for him to leave, he took her hand and helped her to her feet.

Her emotions were in such a muddle by that time, she felt a sense of relief when he returned her to her family. Apparently her ma or grandma had told the rest of them not to ask her any questions, because although they eyed her with curiosity, nobody said a word about Clay Masterson.

Uneasy under their scrutiny, Allie was glad when the fireworks started, because their attention would be diverted to something else.

When a mantle of darkness settled over the churchyard, a thrill of eager anticipation lit every eye. Lanterns were lit and placed around the platform. Benches and blankets were arranged in a half circle, and after everyone was settled, Meredith's students gave short recitations on what Independence Day meant to them. Then as a rousing rendition of "The Star Spangled Banner" echoed through the air, C. J. lit the first of the fireworks. With the sky ablaze in starbursts of every color, smoke and the acrid scent of gunpowder hung heavy in the humid air.

Allie, sitting with her family, noticed the children, who were always in perpetual motion, had settled down to watch the display. Her blue eyes wide with delight, Thalia clapped her chubby hands together and cried, "Purty. Purty." Allie thought about the week when her niece would be in her care, and decided all she'd need was a boxcarful of fireworks.

While the ladies oohed and aahed about the spangled sky, the men and boys seemed to enjoy the ones that made the loudest racket. Allie agreed with her grandma that there was enough of that to arouse the dead. When the last fuse was lit, they breathed a sigh of relief, as did the volunteer fire brigade, who'd had to douse numerous small grass fires as well as extinguish sparks that had landed on several blankets.

"Ladies and gentlemen, that concludes our fireworks display for this glorious Fourth of July," Sheriff Tommy Sampson announced from the platform. "Let's give a hand to our fireworks experts—especially Lee Daltry, who so generously provided this lavish display."

Lee took a bow and flashed one of his famous smiles to the cheering audience.

"And," the sheriff added, inclining his silver-topped head toward another group, "let's not forget our trusty firemen, whom Lee kept busy all night."

The smoke-blackened brigade also took a bow to another clapping of hands.

"And to the ladies, who provided not only the cakes, but all the wonderful food that went along with them." Sheriff Tommy and all the men bowed to their respective female cohorts.

The ladies giggled and clapped in delight.

"Now I have a special announcement. Y'all know the Harvest Ball we usually hold every August? Well, this time it will be a real special occasion because we are going to hold a contest." He gave them a smug smile and twirled his long mustache between the tips of his fingers.

"Well? What is it?" a man shouted.

"A rainmaking contest."

"A what?" a number of the audience said, not certain they had heard him right.

"You all know about the drought we've been having. Well, a few of the fellers and me decided we would do something about it. We hired a rainmaker. Professor Ambrose Ledbetter. But we intend to let all of you have a stab at it first. Lee Daltry has put up *one hundred dollars* to the first person who can make it rain."

"Now how can we do that? Only God can make it rain," a man scoffed.

"Well, we can damned sure get his attention," another said.

"How much does it have to rain? A drop? Two? Or a downpour?"

"Enough to get wet. Anything above and beyond that and I will personally add another fifty dollars," the sheriff said.

"Hell, I would, too," Will Moore called out. "My cows are dying of thirst, and the well's gone dry. Anybody who can make it rain enough to do any good deserves sainthood as far as I'm concerned."

"I've got no interest in being made a saint, but I sure could use that money," a farmer said.

"All right. You have a little less than two months to come up with a plan. Anything goes—as long as it don't destroy the town," Sheriff Sampson added wryly, running a finger down his drooping mustache.

A steady hum of conversation filled the humid air as everyone over the age of five plotted on how to make it rain.

Knowing they would be there all night, the lawman banged the gavel to get their attention. "Now it's time to say good night. Good night!" he bellowed. Then the gray-haired man gave everybody a smile and stepped down from the stage.

While everyone agreed the fireworks display had been most impressive, and Allie knew it would be the topic of conversation for many a month to come, she also knew the event on everyone's mind was the coming Rain-maker's Ball and contest. She gave her brother Lee an admiring glance, for she had no doubt the whole thing was his idea.

Noticing, he smiled and winked.

Allie felt a sense of pride that once again, whether the town realized it or not, he had given them something to think of besides the drought.

On her way home, Allie leaned against the back of the wagon seat and gazed up at the stars, while the rest of the family, including Jake, who couldn't carry a tune if he had a bucket, joined together in song.

When they tired of singing, the group seemed content to admire the moon, which rose like a second golden sun, only without the heat.

Allie, too, stared dreamily at the landscape, which earlier had been just so much dirt, mesquite, and dried grass. Now she thought it almost magical, a land of romantic contrasts, mysterious black silhouettes against silver-coated, gently rolling hills, serenaded by a chorus of crickets and a melancholy coyote.

Everyone succumbed to its spell. Only she and her grandma sat alone.

Venus cuddled with her head on Buck's shoulder and described the scenery in a hushed voice.

Persy and her unborn child were enfolded in her husband's arms.

Even her parents were not immune.

"How do you feel now that you've completed the first part of the labor?" her grandma asked softly.

Allie looked at her in surprise. She had, and she hadn't even realized it until now. "Wonderful," she whispered, so as not to disturb the others. "But I'm not looking forward to the next."

Her grandmother simply smiled.

Later, stretched out in her own bed, Allie thought about the day's events. After spending weeks worrying about the affair, she couldn't believe she'd had such a good time. She'd be the first to admit that her cake hadn't been very good. It turned out to be tough and tasted a bit salty, but Clay said he wasn't much for sweets anyhow. Then he'd leaned close and whispered, "unless they are sweet ladies like you." He'd said some other things that made her blush to think about, although she had recognized some of them as passages from the Bible. She never knew the Songs of Solomon could sound so scandalous. She was glad her sisters hadn't witnessed her crimson cheeks, as they surely would have invited unwanted questions. The man certainly had a way with words.

Unlike someone else she knew. After Hal had returned to the social, he hadn't even bothered to say hello. When she and Clay had sat down to eat, she had seen Hal sharing a cake with the talkative widow Bibble. At the time she'd wondered what had happened to the dance hall girl. Then she'd decided he was probably hungry, and more likely than not, the floozy couldn't cook. Remembering how miserable Hal had looked, she smiled. *Serves him right for leaving the way he had.* She breathed in a sigh of contentment and closed her eyes.

Visions of Clay danced through her thoughts, only to be replaced by images of Hal. . . .

Seven

THE MORNING AFTER THE SOCIAL, HAL ROSE BEFORE DAWN AND
headed for the canyon where the mustangs were cor-
ralled. Not that he felt like breaking wild horses, especially after spending half the night in the saloon. He
usually didn't drink much, nor often, but when he did he
paid for it in spades. Maybe it was a good thing whiskey
made him so sick. After seeing what it had done to his pa,
he had reason to be grateful that he didn't like the stuff.

He hadn't intended to get drunk, only to get the taste of
that cake out of his mouth. But then he got to thinking
about Allie and Clay, and one drink led to another. Before long he couldn't even see to find his way home. He'd
spent the next few hours passed out under a tree, which
was probably for the best. At least his pa hadn't seen him
in such a pitiful condition. The old man had managed to
stay on the wagon for almost a month, and Hal wouldn't
want to jeopardize that.

When the train chugged through town at about three or
so, its whistle jolted him awake. Then a wagon rumbled
up the street. Until this morning he'd never realized how

noisy the town was, with people whistling and shouting, dogs barking, cats meowing, somebody beating on a pan —he simply couldn't take it anymore. Even if he didn't feel up to breaking horses, at least the canyon would be quiet.

Too tired to stay awake, he dozed in the saddle, trusting his buckskin gelding to not let him fall. When the horse nickered, Hal opened one eye and saw Allie. Damn. He'd thought she'd still be so mad at him she'd stay away. He sagged in the saddle, pretending to be asleep.

"Good morning, sleepyhead," she called out from her perch on the rack by the brushy fence.

He raised his head and peered at her from under his hat. "I thought you'd be sleepin' in after your big date yesterday," he replied coolly, dismounting to open the gate.

"Who, me? Why, I feel as pert as a newborn calf. I thought I might give you a hand with the horses—especially since it looks like you might have a headache," she said astutely.

"Nothing wrong with *my* head. I feel just fine." He realized too late that his bloodshot eyes told her that was far from the truth.

"Glad to hear it," she said a little more loudly than necessary. She followed him through the opening and waited while he fastened the gate. "Then you shouldn't have any problem a'tall topping off a dozen or so of those broncs."

He tried to repress a shudder.

"Did you enjoy the festivities yesterday?"

"It was dandy. Just dandy," he replied grumpily.

"That Clay kept me laughing all day. I never knew a man who could tell so many funny stories."

"Oh, he's a card all right. A real joker." He squinted at her. "I noticed you seemed to be having a good time."

"Oh, I did," she said enthusiastically. "Clay is such a fine dresser, and he says the sweetest things."

Like what? "He does have a way with the ladies." *But I never thought you'd be one of them.* "I take it he enjoyed your cake?"

"He said it was a creation to delight the eyes."

If you were blind, Hal thought. "That's nice, but I noticed he didn't eat much of it."

"Clay said he wasn't much for sweets." She tilted her head and peered at him from under the brim of her hat. "I saw you were eating with the widow Bibble. How was your cake?"

"Fine," he lied.

"Really? Twin said she invited him for dinner once and everything he tasted had cat hair in it. Claimed she had forty or so critters in the house and dozens more outside. He said he plumb enjoyed the fresh air of the stable after being at the widow's."

Reminded of the cake and the cats, his stomach gave an uncomfortable twist. Praying he wouldn't disgrace himself, he placed a hand on his middle and hurried away to unsaddle his horse. So he felt just dandy, did he? He was feeling many things right now, and dandy hadn't even made the list. He stripped off his saddle gear and placed it in the dappled shade of a sycamore tree. He eyed the spot, wishing he could lie down and die in peace. But danged if he'd give Allie that satisfaction. Instead, he took a swig of water from the canteen and poured another measure over his aching head.

He shot a resentful glance in her direction, then gingerly placed his hat back on his head. She'd done it on purpose. *Tellin' me that about the widow when she knew I ate that danged cake.* Sometimes Allie had an almost fiendish notion of what was funny. *Probably her idea of gettin' even because I snubbed her at the social.*

Why *had* he snubbed her at the social? He hadn't intended to, at least not at first. But somehow it had irritated the hell out of him that she and Clay Masterson were having such a good time. That in itself made no sense, since he'd wanted her to have fun.

And he couldn't really fault Clay. Especially since he'd practically blackmailed the man into buying Allie's cake. But Clay didn't have to enjoy himself that much, and he certainly didn't have to put his arm around Allie. And she didn't have to act like she fancied it so much, either.

After he'd seen the way they were cuddled up, he hadn't dared stop to say hello, for fear he would end up punching Clay in the jaw.

That would have been a pretty howdy-do, he thought. He could just imagine what Allie's mother would say about him brawling on the front lawn of the churchyard. On second thought, she'd probably expect it. He'd never been one of Jane Daltry's favorite people—and that was before he'd yahooed her from the upstairs window of the Lucky Chance whorehouse. If it hadn't been for Odie and Miss Minerva, he thought glumly, he probably wouldn't be allowed on the ranch.

At least Jane hadn't told Allie, because that girl would never let a thing like that slide. She'd probably take a whip to him for embarrassing her mother in public.

Now that his stomach felt a bit more stable, he strode to the smaller corral outside which Allie had herded a dozen or so horses. He stopped for a moment to watch. Nobody could work horses like Allie. She had a sixth sense when it came to the animals, almost like she could read their minds.

A hammerheaded dun split from the others and she immediately headed it off. Enraged, it whirled and charged her mare. Only Allie's quick rein saved her horse from injury. She spun her mare and came in behind the dun. Before the horse knew what was happening, he was in the corral with the others.

"Are you going to shut that gate or are you waiting for one of them to do it?" she called.

"Wish they could. If they were that smart this job would be easy." He quickly pulled the gate into place and wired it shut.

"If they were that smart, we wouldn't have caught them in the first place," she said, jumping down beside him. "I take it you're feelin' better?" she said, mischief twinkling in her gray eyes.

"Some," he admitted, giving her a crooked grin.

"Glad to hear it." She turned away and climbed up on the corral fence. "Thought I'd work this bunch. Then when you feel up to it, you can take a turn."

"All right," he answered, not hearing a word of what she'd said. His gaze roamed up her skintight jeans to the pert little bottom bent over the fence. How could anyone so little have such long legs? A ray of sunlight caught in her wind-tossed hair, lighting it with gold. She was letting it grow, he noticed. He liked it.

"I'll start with that one," she said, pointing to the dun.

"What?"

"I'll start breaking that one," she said again, dropping down inside the corral.

"No. You can't ride him." Hal landed beside her.

"And why not?" she asked, her eyes narrowing.

"Because you might get hurt."

She planted her feet and put her hands on her hips. "I've been riding since before I could walk. I don't need anybody telling me what horses I can, or can't, ride."

"Well, you're not riding him." He took in the mutinous set to her jaw and changed his tactics. "Allie, be reasonable. See the scars?" he motioned toward the jagged slashes that marred the animal's coat. "Somebody had this horse before and beat him with a whip. Now, look at his eyes. Close together and mean. That horse plain hates the sight of us." He reached out and gripped her shoulders. "Even if we did break him, I'm not sure you could trust an animal like that. I've half a mind to turn him loose."

Allie shrugged his hands away. "That's plain foolishness. You need every horse here to make good on the loan."

"Then I'll be the one to ride him."

Allie shook her head. "If he's that ornery, it'll take both of us." She studied the horse. "I don't think he's mean. I think he's scared." She took a step toward the stallion. "Easy, boy," she crooned. "I'll have him eating out of my hand in no time," she said, turning to flash a confident smile.

Behind her the dun flattened his ears; then, without warning, the animal lunged.

"Allie! Look out!" Hal leaped forward and shoved her to one side.

The horse slid to a halt.

Hal met the stud eye to eye. This time Allie was wrong. The horse showed no fear, just pure cussedness. After making sure Allie was out of harm's way, Hal pulled the wire and opened the gate. Then, separating the animal from the others, he slid the poles on the main gate and gave the dun his freedom.

"What did you do that for?"

"That animal would have trampled you if he'd had the chance. Even if we could have broken him, I didn't want to be responsible for him injuring somebody else later on." He shoved his hands in his pockets to keep her from noticing how badly he was shaking. He turned toward the canyon where the rest of the wild bunch grazed and hoped there were no more like that outlaw.

The thud of hooves startled him, and he swung back around. Allie had her rope on another one of the horses. Suddenly he had the urge to place her, too, on the other side of the enclosure, somewhere safe and away from the mustangs. But he knew she'd never stand for that, not for one damned minute. Sometimes she could be as contrary as the horses.

He scrutinized the second horse she'd chosen, a bay mare with an intelligent look in its eye. From the way the animal responded to Allie's touch, it would be easily broken. After satisfying himself that the rest of the horses would present no problem, he forced himself to relax.

"You gonna stand there watching me all day?" she asked, scrunching up her face. "You're makin' me nervous."

"You sure are cute when you're mad," he teased, stepping closer.

"Wh–hat?" Blushing as red as a Texas sunset, Allie stared at him like he'd grown two heads.

"You're even cuter when you're all flustered." He gazed into eyes the color of moonlight on rippling water, then shyness made her drop her head. "What did you do to your hair? It looks different." He reached his hand toward the shining cap that formed a sunlit halo around her head. Soft as down, a ringlet coiled around his finger. Suddenly he wanted to bury both hands in the shining mass and kiss the mouth that gaped in amazement. He couldn't help but wonder what she would do.

Answering his own question, he decided she'd wallop him for sure. He could tell by her expression that she already thought he was crazy. Maybe he was. Whatever the problem, he sure couldn't seem to keep his mind on the job at hand. He sighed, then ruffled her curls. "Well, Miss Atalanta. Shall we get started breaking those horses?"

*   *   *

Dirty from head to foot and so tired they could hardly put one foot into the stirrup, she and Hal left the canyon and headed home.

"Good day's work," Hal said. "Some of them will make real nice saddle horses."

"That bay mare is a sweetheart. She'd make a good mount for a woman or a child."

"Are you going out with him again?" Hal blurted out before he thought. Now what had made him ask that—and just when things were getting back to normal?

Allie gave him a bewildered look. "Who?"

Hell, he'd started it, he had to finish. "Clay Masterson. I just wondered if he had asked you out again."

"Well, he did ask if I was going to the Rainmaker's Ball."

"The what?"

"I guess you'd already gone by then. Last night Sheriff Tommy announced that we're gonna have a rainmaking contest with cash money for the first person who makes it rain hard enough to get wet."

He chuckled. "Was he serious?"

"Sure. Lee put up a hundred dollars. The sheriff and Will Moore added another fifty each to that. Pa and some others hired a professional rainmaker. A Professor Ambrose Ledbetter. But everybody else gets a chance first. It's going to be a big to-do."

"Cash money." He could sure use some of that. "When?"

"The last of August. It will be the usual Harvest Dance, only with the contest beforehand."

"Are you going with *him?*" he asked, dreading the answer.

"Maybe. I had a real good time at the social. Are you going?"

To watch her and Clay again? He scowled. "Might be busy. I have been known to have a date or two myself, you know."

"Who?" she asked haughtily. "That redheaded hussy?"

"I don't think that is any of your business," he said smugly. "Besides, you don't need me hanging around as long as you have Clay Masterson."

"You've got that right," she said, sticking her nose into the air. "With Clay around, I don't need you at all."

When she kneed her horse to a faster gait, Hal reached for her bridle and pulled the horses to a stop. "Allie, don't trust Clay too far. He's a lot more experienced than you. I'd hate to see you get hurt."

"Of all the nerve," she said, her gray eyes blazing. "I'm not a child, Hal Anderson. I'm a grown woman and I can certainly take care of myself."

His gaze slow and deliberate, he eyed her from head to toe. "I've got to admit, you've filled out in all the right places, but Allie, in some ways you are as young as a newborn babe." He abruptly dropped her bridle and left the road, cutting across the valley as he headed toward town.

Too furious to speak, Allie watched him gallop across the meadow. The way he acted, you'd think he was her brother. Young as a newborn babe, indeed. Telling her to beware of Clay. He had some gall. She didn't tell him what to do, even though sometimes she would have liked to. She hadn't said, "Stay away from that redheaded floozy!" Or "Stop drinking before you end up like your pa." No, she hadn't said any of those things. Maybe next time she would.

She lifted the reins and pointed Circe toward home. There was a time when she'd known Hal as well as she knew herself. Knew his thoughts, even knew what he was going to say before he'd said it. She didn't know whether it was losing the ranch and moving to town that had done it or having to take care of his pa, but Hal had changed. His disposition had changed, too. He used to be calm, easygoing, with never a bad word for anybody. Now, most of the time he was as prickly as a spiny-thorned cactus. But she could allow some for that, knowing all he'd been through.

He'd felt awful today, but still he had managed to do his share of the work, even though she'd told him she was quite capable of handling the horses on her own. He looked thin and tired and he hadn't been getting enough sleep. He wasn't eating right, but that was understandable since neither Hal nor his pa could cook.

For that matter, neither could she. But she could learn. She had made a cake, even though she'd never make one of those again if she could help it. Before she and Jake had left, Persy had shown her how to fix a few simple dishes. Allie thought it didn't really seem that hard, once she got the hang of it. Heck, with Bo Jack's help she might even get good at it after a while. Maybe good enough to cook a meal or two for Hal and his pa.

At least she didn't look starved. Hal had said she'd filled out in all the right places—even if he hadn't seemed too happy about it. She'd been so shocked when he said it, she'd danged near fell off her horse. Then he'd touched her hair and said he liked the way she was letting it grow. And he'd actually turned pale when he'd pulled her out of the way of the horse, and even though he'd tried to hide it, she'd seen his hands were shaking. He had been scared —not for himself, but for her.

Before when they'd ridden wild ones, he'd laughed when she'd gotten tossed in the dust. Today he'd picked her up and asked if she was hurt. Once he'd held her so long, she'd thought he might kiss her.

Kiss her!

Now where in the world had that idea come from?

Then warning her about Clay. If she didn't know Hal better, she might think he was jealous.

Hal, jealous?

The idea was so ridiculous she chuckled. *Boy, Allie, I think your wits are addled. You have been out in the sun too long.*

By the time she reached the Circle D her thoughts were jumbled. She unsaddled her horse and rubbed her down; then, instead of going to the house, she walked to the gazebo. She needed time to think, to mull over Hal's odd behavior—and the strange things that were happening inside her.

Eight

IN THE STUDY OF THE DALTRY HOUSE, HAL WAITED WHILE Minerva wrote out a receipt.

"There," she said, handing him the slip of paper. "You've done good, boy. Another payment and we'll be square."

"I want to thank you, Miz Minerva. Pa wants to thank you, too."

"How is your pa? I haven't seen him in quite a spell."

"He's better. He's staying close to home these days. Hasn't had a drink in pert near two months now."

"I'm glad to hear it. Tell him to drop by and sit a spell. I'll even make him some of those sugar cookies he likes so much."

"I'll tell him." Hal rolled his hat brim in his hands. "Is Allie around anywhere?"

Minerva smiled. "In the kitchen. I know she'd like it if you'd stop by and have some lemonade."

"I'll do that," he said, trying not to appear too eager. He held out his hand and Minerva took it in her firm grasp. "Good-bye, ma'am."

The old lady nodded, her gray eyes twinkling.

Uncomfortable under her scrutiny, he headed for the kitchen and found his pard scowling over a piece of paper she had spread out on the table. "Allie?"

She raised her head and her face lit with a broad smile. "I was hoping you'd stop by." She scrambled to her feet and grabbed his hand.

"You were?" A warm glow spreading inside him, he glanced from her to the paper. "You ain't making another cake?"

"No." She hesitated. "But I am making a dress, and I could sure use your help."

"Now, hold on." He raised his hands. "I don't know anything about dressmaking." He hadn't known anything about cakemaking either, but that hadn't made no never mind.

"Your ma never made a dress?"

"Of course she did," he said indignantly. "All women know how to sew."

"I don't."

"Your ma never taught you?"

"She tried."

"How come you're so interested in sewing a dress?" he asked, afraid he already knew. "You never were before."

"I need one for the Rainmaker's Dance."

For Clay Masterson. For a moment Hal was tempted to turn his back on her and walk out the door, but then she slipped her arm into his. Her eyes dark as the sky before a storm, she gazed up at him. "Please. I can't do it without you."

The pleading look she gave him was his undoing. He could no more refuse her than he could fly. "Why don't you have your ma or grandma help you?"

"They can't."

Hal thought for a minute. How hard could it be? He

did know how to mend harness. For that matter so did Allie. A dress couldn't be much different. "Do you have the cloth goods—and some pins?"

Allie nodded. "You'll do it?"

"You helped with the horses, so maybe together we can figure out this dress."

She wrapped her arms around him and gave him a hug. "Thank you."

"You don't need to thank me, Allie," he said, touching her hair. "After all, that's what pards are for."

But he certainly wasn't feeling very pardlike when she released him and ran to fetch the cloth and pins. His rod was as hard as a river rock.

Confused by the feelings that warred within him, Hal stared after her. All their lives he and Allie had exchanged hugs and sometimes even kisses, but never before had his body responded to her the way it was reacting now. He had always thought of Allie as sort of a younger sister, but the notions he was having now definitely were not those of a brother. Her touch, her scent, the softness of her body and her hair made him aware that he was a man and she was a woman.

Embarrassed by his condition and afraid she would notice, he turned his back and walked to the window, wishing he could get on his horse and ride.

Through the glass pane he saw Allie's mother on her hands and knees working in her flower garden.

Sensing his eyes on her, she raised her head. She gazed toward the window and her face mirrored her disapproval.

That look, along with his own guilt, managed to vanquish any lustful thoughts he might have had.

"I'm ready," Allie called from behind him. On her knees, she knelt before the bolt of creamy fabric patterned with delicate bunches of blue flowers that she had spread across the dining room floor.

Hal gazed at her, then at the length of cloth. "I don't know how much help I'll be, but I guess we can cut it out by guess and by gosh."

From somewhere she had managed to produce a muslin pattern. He'd thought it might be one of Venus's, but judging by the size, he decided it must be Minerva's. He could tell it would be too big for Allie, since she was such a runt, but being a coward, he didn't say anything. If he had, Allie would have had to cut another pattern. In order for her to do that, *he* would have to measure her. Just the idea of molding that measuring tape around her breasts, her waist, and her hips made him break out in a sweat. Besides, why should he go through that torture for a dress she was making to impress Clay Masterson? No, sir, he silently declared, he wasn't about to say a word.

Three hours later, he hoisted himself off the floor and into a chair. He rubbed his sore knees and gratefully sipped from a glass of lemonade that Minerva had brought them. He smiled at Allie. "Well, now that we've got it cut out, reckon you can stitch it up?"

Allie grinned. "Like you said, it can't be much different from mending a bridle." She fingered a piece of the delicate flower-sprigged fabric. "Easier, in fact, since I won't be sewing leather."

Two days later when Hal rode into the yard he saw Allie stomping toward the corral. By the look of her something was definitely wrong, and he had a good idea what it was. "Got your sewing finished?"

She scowled, her eyes like a stormy sky. "I don't want to talk about it."

"I take it that's a no?"

"You take it right," she answered grimly, reaching toward the top rail of the corral for her saddle.

Hal hoisted the saddle from her hands and set it back on the fence. "It's too hot to ride." He took her hand and pulled her toward the gazebo. "Come on. Let's sit in the shade and you can tell me about it."

It was not until they were seated beneath a bower of leaves that she blurted out, "It doesn't fit. And the more I try the worse it gets."

"Too big," he guessed, gazing at her small figure.

She nodded. "If I was Pa's size—or bigger—it might come close."

He laughed.

"I don't think it's funny."

"I wasn't laughing at you. I was picturing your pa in that dress."

She gave him a reluctant grin. "I guess that would be a sight to see."

"Wouldn't your ma help?"

Allie hesitated. "She can't and I can't ask her."

She couldn't ask her ma, but she could ask him. Why? Then he remembered a time years ago when he'd been disappointed because he hadn't been asked to a Daltry birthday party. He had always been asked before. Allie had told him not to fret, because nobody outside of the family could come. It was one of the rules. Then she said it was because it was Lee's *twentieth* birthday and that was when her grandma would give him his labor. It was a secret. He recalled that after she'd realized what she'd said, she'd clamped her hand over her mouth. Then she'd made him promise he'd forget everything he'd heard. She'd also made him swear he'd never tell another living soul.

Since the Daltrys had always had some odd notions, he had thought nothing more about it—until now. He wondered if this had anything to do with *her* twentieth birthday. Or was she just making this dress to impress Clay Masterson? Either way it seemed she needed his help. "Let's see. The shindig is Saturday, isn't it?" He whistled. "That's two days from now!"

"I know."

"Well, we'd better get crackin'."

Once inside the house, Allie disappeared, leaving him in the sunroom with a pitcher of lemonade. When she came back she had the dress draped over her arm.

"I thought you were going to put it on."

"I am—over these," she said, motioning toward her clothes. "You'll see why in a minute." She tugged the dress over her head, then she turned to face him. "See?"

The neckline dipped well below her breasts, the waist neared her knees. Yards of fabric puddled on the floor around her feet, giving her the appearance of a small child who was attempting to wear her mother's clothes. Even though he wanted to laugh at the picture she made, his own guilt wouldn't allow him to do it. She'd worked long and hard on a dress he'd known wouldn't fit and he'd done nothing about it. Well, now he had to do something. If he didn't she'd sure as shootin' cry, and that he couldn't deal with.

He set the lemonade down on the table and got to his feet. "I think I know what's wrong." He grabbed a handful of fabric on each of her shoulders and hoisted it up. "How's that?"

She looked down and nodded. "Better. At least it's a place to start."

She took the dress off and cut off the excess fabric, then she resewed the seam. "There," she said, biting off the thread. "At least now it's decent."

"Maybe you could put it on wrong side out this time. It would be easier to pin it to the right size."

"Good idea." She disappeared into the other room, and a few minutes later she stood before him. "How is it?"

He sucked in a breath, trying to figure out how to deal with the pale white flesh she had exposed to his view. "Well . . . well . . ." Not knowing what to say, he cleared his throat.

"Well, what?" she demanded, jamming her hands on her hips, the movement baring even more of her creamy breasts.

Hal swallowed. "I think you'd better put the shirt back on."

"Oh, for pity's sake. You've seen me wearing a lot less than this."

"Yeah, but you ain't ten years old anymore."

"I didn't know you'd noticed."

Oh, he'd noticed all right. Hell, he'd have to be blind not to.

She snatched up a chunk of extra fabric and shoved it into the neckline. "There. Now you can quit blushing."

"I ain't blushing," he said, knowing by the rush of heat he felt that *that* was a flat-out lie. When he raised his head, he was grateful to see that she had managed to hide most of her bosom from his view. "You know, I think you've got the answer. Maybe you could sew that piece in sideways and fill in the gap, then you might pretty it up with lace or something."

"Could you pin it for me?" she asked, her expression so hopeful that he couldn't say no.

"I could try, provided you hand the pins to me." After all, how hard could it be? It wasn't like she was falling out of the thing anymore.

A pin in one hand, he slid the fingers of the other hand into the edge of her neckline to hold the yard goods in place. The minute he touched her soft, warm flesh he knew he'd made a mistake. He couldn't pin it. He couldn't move and he couldn't seem to take his fingers away. Hell, he couldn't even breathe.

"Hal?"

He didn't know how long he'd stood there before the sound of her voice made him realize he had to do something. He gritted his teeth, closed his eyes, and jammed the pin into place.

"Oww!"

He jumped like he'd been the one who'd been stuck. The motion made him stick her again.

"Dang it! You did it again!" Knocking his hand away, she propped her fists on her hips. "What in the world is the matter with you?" She rubbed her chest where he'd pricked her. "I think I'm bleeding." She twisted away to examine the spot. "I am. See?"

He thought he'd come near to choking when she pointed to a dot of red just above her nipple, which was in plain sight just below her fingertip. "Allie, for gawd's sake!"

She shot him a look of surprise, then a rush of crimson dotted her cheeks. "Maybe I'd better do this part myself."

"Good idea," he said, almost faint with relief.

She turned her back and pinned the front.

When she twisted toward him, he saw she was covered, but that still didn't erase the memory of that rosebud peak surrounded by firm white flesh.

"What about the rest?" She solemnly held out the sides, which looked big enough to go around her twice.

He relented. "Maybe I can pin that part."

"Are you sure? I don't want to show up at that dance looking like I've been used for a pincushion."

"I don't think you've got any choice, if you can't get anybody else to help you. Besides, nobody's got any business looking at that part of you anyhow."

"Oh," she said, arching a brow, "lots of girls wear dresses lower than that."

"Well, you're not going to." He jutted out his jaw. If he had his way, it would be filled in clear up to her chin—and then some. He sure didn't like the idea of any other man, especially Clay Masterson, seeing what he had seen.

"Are you going to help me, or do you intend to stand there gawking?"

"I'm not gawking. Just stand still." He gathered a good six inches of fabric that hung out beneath her arms and cut it off with the scissors, not realizing until he'd done it that he had also cut off the seam. Lord, he'd done it now. From where he stood she may as well not be wearing anything. He never realized how much of a bosom she had until this moment. A good handful and then some. Another uncomfortable ache slithered through his lower body.

If Allie's mother knew what he was doing . . . He desperately grabbed the gaping cloth and pulled it together, then anxiously kept it closed until he had secured it with pins.

His forehead dotted with perspiration, his knees about to fold under him, he gazed into her bewildered eyes. "Allie, I can't do this anymore." Grabbing his hat, he bolted for the door.

"What about the dress?" she called from the porch.

"Sew it where I've got it pinned," he yelled over his shoulder.

"Where are you going?"

Afraid she might decide to follow, he lengthened his stride and was at a dead run by the time he reached the corral. Where was he going? He had no idea. The only thing he was sure of was that he had to get out of that house. He untied his startled horse and leaped into the saddle.

"Where are you going?" she yelled again.

"Swimming."

"Swimming? Well, if that don't beat all." She gazed after him as he raced past, then shook her head.

Nine

WITH SUPPER FINISHED, THE REST OF THE FAMILY RETIRED TO the coolness of the gazebo, leaving Allie alone in the house. It was Friday, August twenty-ninth. One night before the dance, and despite the fact that she'd sewed from can to can't see, her dress still wasn't done.

Her fingers so sore from pinpricks that she could hardly use them, she finished attaching the last of the lace to the edge of the sleeve, then desperately needing a break, she lay the garment aside.

Rising from her chair, she rubbed her eyes to relieve the strain, then left the sunroom and walked to the kitchen to get a drink of water.

The dress, such as it was—for she had never seen another quite like it—was nearly finished. Except for the hem. And for the life of her she couldn't figure out what to do about that. She'd tried to pin it, but she couldn't do that and wear it at the same time. She'd tried to even out the bottom without wearing it and one side was now a foot shorter than the other. If she cut it off any more, that side would be near her knees. She was still pondering what to do when Hal's buckskin trotted into the yard. She rolled her eyes toward heaven. "Thank you, Lord."

She ran to the porch and leaned over the railing. "Am I ever glad to see you."

His grin showing white in his deeply tanned face, he dismounted and strode toward her. "I'm glad to hear that. After I purt near stuck you to death, I wasn't sure I'd be welcome."

"You're always welcome as far as I'm concerned," she said, tucking her arm into his and leading him toward the house.

"I wish your ma felt the same." He glanced uneasily toward the gazebo.

"Ma likes you."

"Sure."

"No, really she does. It's just that sometimes when her daughters are concerned she kind of gets a burr under her skirt."

He chuckled. "I never heard it put quite like that. How's the dress coming?"

"You would have to mention that." She took his hand and pulled him toward the sunroom.

"Whoa, now," he said, digging his heels in, bringing her spinning back toward him. "I'm not going to have to do any more pinning, am I?"

"Maybe." Pressed against his chest like she was, she had nowhere else to look but up into those green, green eyes. Taking in his worried look, she said gently. "But this time it's around the bottom."

"Bottom of what?"

"Of the dress, silly. You know, that part along the floor."

The relief on his face was so comical she couldn't help but giggle. "Come along, now. I really do need your help."

She had him turn his back until she had slipped into the

dress. Once she had it on, she glanced down at the garment, hoping that he didn't notice one sleeve was slightly longer than the other and the lace she had added to the neckline was a little crooked. "How does it look?"

He turned and studied her for a minute. "Real nice. The little blue flowers look pretty with your eyes."

"My eyes are gray."

"I know that. They still look pretty."

"I thought I might tie this around the waist." She held out a length of wide blue ribbon. "What do you think?"

"Let's try it."

When she couldn't seem to get it straight, he moved forward and smoothed the fabric around her middle. Allie gazed up at his freshly shaved cheeks and detected the spicy scent of bay rum. "My, you smell nice."

By the way he ducked his head, a body would almost think he was embarrassed.

He tied the bow, then stepped away to survey the results. He nodded. "A nice touch."

"What can I do about this?" She pointed toward the floor.

He considered the large amount of fabric pooled about her feet. "You might take a hitch in part of it. Then cut off the rest."

"What?"

He went behind her and drew the skirt smooth across her front and sides, according to the latest fashion. Then he took the material he had pulled back, wadded it up and pressed it to her backside. "Kind of like this."

"Nobody wears bustles anymore," Allie said, twisting in an effort to see the contraption.

"We'll make it more flat. They do wear those things that kind of remind me of a squashed pillow."

She caught his eye and grinned. "A pillow on my backside. Might come in handy if I fall." She bent to examine the part at the floor. "What about that?"

"Let's get this other taken care of first, then we'll cut part of it off and stitch up what's left."

"Sounds good to me."

Hours later, Allie was beginning to wish she'd never heard of either the dance or the dress. She could tell by the look on Hal's face that he felt the same. She hastily finished the bottom hem, then held it up for his inspection. "Done." She struggled to her feet and groaned, bending and arching to relieve her stiff joints.

"Try it on. I want to see how it looks."

"Again?" she said with a moan.

"You might have forgotten something. It's better to find out now than later."

"You're right." He turned his back while she quickly removed her pants and shirt and slipped the dress over her head. "You'll have to do these buttons; my fingers are too sore."

"I'll try." He carefully buttoned one after another until the dress was secure.

Her heart pounding, she turned toward him. "How do I look?"

"You have any dancing shoes? It doesn't look quite right with boots."

"Right here." She crossed the room and retrieved the kid slippers, then put them on and stood before him. "Well?"

"Pretty as a picture." He gently touched her cheek. "Clay is going to be one lucky man." He rubbed his forehead and released a weary sigh. "Guess I'd better get goin'. That clock says it's almost eleven. If you intend to dance tomorrow night, you should get some sleep."

When he turned toward the door, Allie grabbed his

arm. "Wait. I did forget something," she said with dismay. "I don't know how to dance."

"Aww, you do too," he argued. "I've seen you."

"I don't mean that galloping thing the cowboys do. I mean a refined dance—like a waltz."

"A waltz." He looked at his feet. "I've done it a couple of times. I'm no great shakes as a dancer, but I reckon I could show you enough to get by."

He slid his arm around her waist, then took her hand with his other. "Now, it's kind of like a box. One, two, three. One, two, three."

"I keep bumping into you," she said, trying to keep track of what his feet were doing.

"Maybe if I hold you a little tighter," he said, pulling her against him. "Now. One, two, three. One, two, three."

Allie closed her eyes and tried to calm the pounding of her heart. She never knew dancing could make a body so breathless. Or so dizzy. She felt like a chicken caught in a windstorm. She leaned her head against Hal's chest and was surprised his heart seemed to be beating as fast as hers. She gazed up into his earnest green eyes. The look she saw there made her breath catch in her throat, and she felt light enough to fly. "One, two, three," she whispered, trying to concentrate on what they were doing.

"One, two, three," he said just as softly, pulling her even closer. "I think you're getting the hang of it. Do you need help with anything else—like kissin'?"

"Kissin'?" Her eyes wide, she gazed into his. "I've never kissed anybody before, except you, and that was not a real grown-up kiss, anyway."

"Clay's a sophisticated man," he told her. "You ought to know how to kiss."

She bit her lip. "Well, I reckon I do need to know that. Would you be willing to help me?"

"I suppose I should—since we're such good friends and all."

Allie watched mesmerized as he closed his eyes and bent his head. The mouth that had hovered so near now pressed lightly, then molded itself to hers. The sensation it caused made her heart pound and her head so flighty she thought she might faint.

"How's that?" he said, pulling away.

"I think we better keep trying—at least till I get the hang of it." Before he had a chance to refuse, she looped her arms around his neck and drew his head down again.

He breathed tiny kisses on her forehead, her temples, her nose, even her ears. Then when she thought she would die with wanting, he returned to her lips, kissing her gently at first. Then his embrace tightened, his body fashioned itself around hers, enfolding her between his thighs as the kiss deepened.

Her heart drumming like a Comanche on the warpath, Allie moaned, the action parting her lips. Her eyes widened when he traced the outline of her mouth with his tongue; then slowly, insistently, he pushed it between her teeth. He lured, coaxed, teased her until she followed his lead. He tasted of mint and lemonade and ginger cookies, all uniquely Hal. Then he withdrew his tongue slightly, only to push it in again, in a pulsating, surging motion that sent a strange heat coiling within her.

Eager to discover more, she tasted him again, drawing him deeper. Still not satisfied, she pressed herself even closer, until she could feel the hardness of his body through the thin fabric of her dress. Her own heat was like liquid fingers of fire that spread through her blood and threatened to consume her. She trembled, desperately needing—

Suddenly, Hal loosened her hold and broke free. "I

think that's enough practice for one night," he said hoarsely.

"Did I do it right?"

He shot her a look of amazement. "If you did it any better, we'd both be in a heap of trouble."

Before Allie could ask him to explain his strange remark, he was gone. Still trembling, she went to the porch and listened to the steady drum of hoofbeats as he headed toward town. She raised a hand to her breast, where her own heart was pounding just as loudly, and leaned against a post. She closed her eyes, remembering how Hal had closed his when he'd kissed her. She thought about those kisses, from each tiny peck to the breath-robbing passion that had threatened to make her swoon. She heaved a sigh of disappointment, wondering what had made him stop. Just when she was really getting to enjoy it, too.

Hal reined the laboring buckskin to a halt, then swung to the ground and stalked toward the rippling water, removing his boots and clothes as he walked. Looking down at his swollen, throbbing staff, he wondered if anything would ever cool his heated blood. Nobody had ever put him in this kind of condition, not even the ladies at Miss Annie's. Never in a million years would he have thought it would happen with little Allie.

He'd known her since they were babies. As children they'd swum naked in this very spot. Why all of a sudden did just being around her make him as confused as a rattlesnake in a hailstorm? Just holding her in his arms made him weak in the knees, never mind what it did to another part of him.

And that kissing business? It was a good thing Odie hadn't caught him. Why in the world had he ever suggested such a thing? The very idea that Clay might decide to kiss her made Hal clench his teeth. *He'd better not lay a hand on her, or I'll flatten his uppity nose.*

Clay is the one she wants, his conscience reminded him. *To her, I'm only a friend.* Recalling the fire in that last kiss made him want to swear. *Some friend I am. I couldn't leave her sweet and innocent; I had to show her how to do it.* Feeling about as wretched as he'd ever felt in his life, he dove deep into the water, hoping that if he stayed down long enough, he would drown. At least he'd be out of his misery.

But if he died, who would watch over Allie?

Lungs bursting, he popped back to the surface. This whole thing was his own doing. Clay would never have noticed Allie if it wasn't for him.

Whatever it took, no matter how much it pained, he owed it to Allie to see she didn't get hurt.

Ten

"C. J., DON'T YOU THINK—?"

"Lizzie! Shh!" he hissed, as he carefully packed sticks of dynamite into a round metal cylinder.

With his brows knotted the way they were, she thought her husband came closer to resembling a blond devil than the innocent-looking cherub his name implied.

"Go get the cotton—and remember, not a word to anybody!"

Lizzie hesitated.

C. J. stood and gripped her arms, his gaze penetrating and stern. "Promise?"

"You aren't going to give up on this, are you?" she asked.

"Liz–zie. I know I can make it rain." He gave her a heart-melting smile. "Promise?"

Lizzie crossed her fingers behind her back. "Oh, all right," she said, hoping he would believe she had relented. "But you'd better not make me a widow, Cupid Daltry."

"As pretty as you are, you wouldn't be a widow for long," he teased.

"That's not funny, C. J.," she said, her voice breaking.

"Don't worry, love." He pulled her close and nuzzled her lips. "Everything will be all right. I know exactly what I'm doing." He grinned. "Now run along and get that cotton." Spinning her in the direction of the mercantile, he sent her on her way with a playful swat to her bottom.

Lizzie didn't look back because she was afraid if she did her resolve would falter. Instead, with head held high and vision blurred, she walked briskly toward the front of the store. Then, reaching Main Street, she bypassed the store and headed for the churchyard. Whether C. J. knew it or not, some promises were made to be broken. She'd get his damned cotton, but first she intended to find Odie. Maybe her father-in-law could talk some sense into his half-wit son.

She was so preoccupied with her thoughts she was surprised when she heard someone call out her name. She twisted, glancing back over her shoulder, and saw her husband's family seated on a quilt beneath a spreading oak tree. She waved and headed toward them. Jane, Meredith, Minerva, and Allie all waved back. Lizzie was so glad to see Odie and Lee, she almost wept with relief.

"Howdy, gal. Pull up a patch of shade and join the family," her father-in-law called out.

"I was hoping y'all had arrived." Lizzie forced a shaky smile, wondering how to tell Odie about C. J. without getting the whole family alarmed.

"You 'peared to be off in another world," Minerva noted. "Were you looking for Thalia?"

"No. She's busy wearing out Amy Moore. I was just on my way to the mercantile to buy some cotton."

"Cotton?" Allie repeated. "Why?"

"I have to get some for C. J. And some for our ears."

"Think it might be that noisy, do you?" Minerva said.

"I'm sure of it," Lizzie said grimly.

"Come to think of it, that might be a good idea," Odie said. "I hear tell some of the old-timers are gonna shoot their buffalo guns in unison, aiming them into the sky."

"Guess they think if they poke a hole in it it's bound to leak," Minerva said, chuckling.

"Have you seen that rainmaker's machine yet?" Lee asked his father.

"Nope. He's got it covered top to bottom with canvas. I tried to sneak a peek but that dog he's got tied to the contraption keeps everybody away. I hear tell that machine belches smoke and fire like nothing you've ever seen. The professor's keeping it under wraps until everybody else has had a turn and failed."

"I hope the man's able to do us some good," Lee said, fanning himself with his hat.

"If he makes it cloud up, it would be worth the price," Minerva added, wiping her brow with her handkerchief.

"It would be a blessed relief, all right," Jane agreed.

"If it does rain, it won't be because of the professor." Lee bent forward and confided in a soft voice, "Don't breathe a word of it, but a couple of fellers that I'd better not name stole an old Indian medicine man from off the reservation. He's gonna do a rain dance in exchange for a bottle of whiskey and a couple of head of beef."

"Oh, my Lord," Jane said, shaking her head. "As if the problems between the ranchers and farmers aren't enough, they'll probably end up startin' another Indian war."

"Now, if you want to hear some plain downright foolishness, listen to this," Meredith chimed in. "Some of the town ladies are going to beat on washtubs. Claim it will sound like thunder. They reason that if it thunders, it's bound to rain."

"Now that's plain silly," Jane said, laughing.

"Sounds like the heat has addled some brains," Allie agreed. "Speaking of addled brains, where's C. J.?"

"Don't ask," Lizzie said, rolling her eyes.

"Oh, no! Don't tell me—"

"What's that boy up to now?" Odie asked.

"I promised I wouldn't say anything." Lizzie glanced toward Odie and Lee. "But I surely would feel better if you two would kind of stroll down behind Hank's mercantile to that icehouse yonder." She nodded toward the hideout. "But if you should happen to come across C. J., please don't tell him you saw me. If he finds out I let the cat out of the bag, he'll pout for a week."

"He still does that, does he?" Odie looked at Lee and they both laughed.

"Don't worry, Liz, we won't say a word," Lee promised solemnly, his blue eyes dancing.

"Now you better hurry on along and get your cotton before he comes looking for you." Odie dug into his pocket and took out a dollar and gave it to her. "Might not hurt to get some for us, too."

"Be happy to," she said, tucking the coin into her reticule.

Allie watched Lizzie turn and sneak another look toward the icehouse before hurrying toward the mercantile. "She sure seems worried," Allie said thoughtfully. "Knowing C. J., maybe she's got good reason."

Her ma turned abruptly. "Odie?"

"I'm goin', honey. Don't fret." Odie lumbered to his feet and raised his hands overhead in a wide stretch. "Lee, what do you say to a little walk? Might help loosen up the limbs."

"Yeah, I'm kind of cramped up, too."

The two men casually ambled toward the general area where Lizzie had indicated her husband was hiding. Although Allie didn't say anything, she felt relieved to know that her father would be investigating C. J.'s latest project.

"What do you suppose C. J. is doing?" Meredith asked, leaning close so that Jane and Minerva couldn't hear.

"Who knows?" Allie said with a shrug. "It must be something pretty spectacular, if Lizzie wanted Pa to check up on him." She knew from the time Cupid was knee-high to a cricket, he always had some secret invention or another in the works. She also remembered how mad he got if anyone else found out about it before he was ready.

Allie could tell by the nervous way her mother chewed the end of her finger and stared at the icehouse that Lizzie was not the only one who was worried.

C. J.'s inventions were usually disasters, but a few times they had been downright dangerous. Like the time he'd used a shotgun to rig a coyote trap in the chicken pen. He'd darn near shot their grandma when she'd gone to gather the eggs.

Then there was the time he cut a hole in the barn loft and rigged a pulley to raise and lower the hay. It worked fine. The only trouble was C. J. forgot to tell anybody else. When it came Atlas's turn to feed the cows, he as usual had his nose buried in a book, and had stepped through the opening and broken his leg.

Remembering the scared look on Lizzie's face, Allie had the feeling that this invention would end up putting the rest of C. J.'s adventures to shame.

"Odie and Lee are on their way back," Minerva said. "Now maybe we can find out what's happened."

"Well?" Jane asked when he was close enough to hear her.

Odie shrugged. "He wasn't there. We looked around but didn't find a trace of him. Maybe we all were worried for nothing."

"Sure," Lee said smoothly. "He probably gave it up and is sleeping in the shade somewhere."

Allie didn't believe a word of it. She could tell by their expressions that nobody else did either. The truth was, C. J. had probably heard her pa and Lee coming; they weren't the quietest pair she had ever seen. A bunch of startled chickens made less noise, and that was when they were *trying* to be quiet. C. J. hadn't given up anything; he'd simply lit out until the coast was clear.

Well, since it looked like it was going to be left to her to find out what he was up to, she stretched and got to her feet. "I'm powerful thirsty. Anybody else want a drink of water?"

Her pa lifted a container. "Got a whole jugful of water right here—ugh!" Minerva had jabbed him in the ribs.

"You run along, Allie. Take your time," her grandma said.

"I intend to." She gave her grandmother a wink.

She left her family and set out in search of her brother. Bunches of people were gathered around one contraption or another. The way they guarded the things reminded her of a flock of buzzards all huddled around one worm. Ignoring the suspicious looks they gave her, she ascertained her brother wasn't among them, then went on her way.

When she did find C. J., she was amazed. C. J. wasn't building any invention. He was crawling on all fours, giving a piggyback ride to his two-year-old daughter, who chortled with glee as she tugged at his hair.

"Howdy, Allie," he said, falling on the ground. "Ready to take a turn? She's worn me to a frazzle."

Discovering that her horse had collapsed, Thalia let out a loud wail.

"No!" Allie said quickly. "I'm not about to ruin this dress. Not after all the trouble I went to to make it." Then eyeing the sobbing child, she felt a twinge of sympathy and knelt beside her. "Want a stick candy?"

Her lower lip stuck out in a pout like C. J.'s, Thalia nodded. "Caney." She couldn't pronounce it perfectly, but she knew what she wanted.

Allie held out her hand.

The child abandoned her father, who had rolled over, locked his hands behind his head, and already appeared to be sound asleep. Thalia grasped Allie's fingers. "Caney," she insisted.

"Okay. Let's go."

Halfway to the mercantile, Allie turned to wave at her brother, but the area beneath the tree was empty. She halted in her tracks and turned to scan the area.

C. J. was nowhere in sight.

He did that on purpose. He knew she was the only one who had ever been able to find him. She had stepped into his trap as easily as a bear would be lured to honey.

"Caney?" Thalia pleaded, tugging on her skirt.

She gazed down at the small child. "I wonder, did you have anything to do with this?"

Thalia gave her an angelic grin that was so much like C. J.'s that Allie began to laugh.

"Caney," she said, her blue eyes filling with tears.

"All right, baby. Candy it is. We'll let your father get away with it for now, but sooner or later I'll find him."

Thalia headed for the mercantile as fast as her short, chubby legs could carry her, which Allie thought was pretty fast indeed for a child her age. Well, at least she knew two things the child liked—candy and fireworks.

A while later, thoroughly eager to surrender her charge, Allie was grateful to discover Lizzie sitting with her parents. "This belong to somebody here?" she said, pointing to the sticky child.

Thalia had a peppermint stick in each hand and a running trail of syrup from her chin to her feet.

"Oh, my. What a mess," Lizzie said with a shudder. "I'm not sure I want her."

"You should have thought of that three years ago," Lee said, laughing.

Thalia's lower lip quivered, then stuck out in a pout.

"Danged if she isn't the spittin' image of Cupid," Odie said, dampening a rag to wipe her chin. "When are you going to have another one? With babies this pretty, it would be a shame to stop at just one. Besides, y'all are letting Lee and Meredith get way ahead of you."

"Odie!" Jane said, scandalized.

"C. J. and I plan to talk about that after we get back from San Francisco," she said, smiling at Allie.

"Did you notice Allie's new dress?" Jane said. "She made it especially for the dance tonight."

"Oh, that's right. I'd almost forgotten," Lizzie exclaimed, her dark eyes twinkling.

"It's lovely, Allie. And so many bows," Meredith said, examining the frock.

"Not too many, I hope." Allie frowned down at the dots of blue she'd sewn here and there. "I wouldn't want everybody to think I was trying to copy Miss Lavender." The elderly lady wore so many ruffles and bows she was a walking advertisement for her millinery establishment. "I stuck my finger so many times I had to figure out something to cover up the spots of blood. I finished so late last night, I didn't have time to wash it."

Allie heard her mother give a strangled sound, then Jane turned her back to examine the crowd, her hand shading her eyes.

"Actually I think it's quite—unique," Meredith said. "I think you did wonderfully well for your first effort."

"Probably be her last one, too," Lee teased. He glanced behind her and grinned.

"Howdy, Miss Allie," a strange voice rumbled. "You shore do look purty today."

Ignoring Lee's snicker, she turned and smiled up at Deputy Jones. "Hello, Dudley. Thank you for the compliment."

" 'Tain't no compliment. 'Tis the honest-to-God truth." He gave her an admiring glance. "Purty as a field of bluebonnets."

Lee gave a choked sound and Meredith shoved a glass of water at him.

Knowing her brother was about to embarrass her shamefully, Allie blushed crimson and got to her feet. "Dudley, I'm powerful thirsty. Do you suppose we could find some lemonade?"

"I think they have a barrel of it yonder beneath that tree."

The deputy straightened and she could have sworn he puffed out his chest when she slid her hand in the crook of his arm. *Men,* she thought. At least Dudley was one she could figure out. He was as transparent as glass. Not like others she knew. She scanned the crowd for three other familiar faces, but neither C. J., Hal, nor Clay was anywhere in sight.

Down the street, in the office of the *Gazette,* Clay eyed the man seated across from him. "I thought we were square. After all, I did buy her cake."

"We are square," Hal agreed. "I just thought you ought to know she came to this shindig, even made herself a new dress, all because she hoped you'd ask her to dance."

Clay didn't say anything. She wasn't his type, not his style at all. He liked his women tall, seductive, beautiful, and lusty. Allie Daltry was none of those. He'd been

bored out of his mind at the social. He thought if he
shocked her enough she'd leave him alone. But, hell,
she'd been so damned innocent, she hadn't even realized
what he'd done. She'd thought he had paid her a compliment. Anybody with any experience would have slapped
his face.

Venus would have—shortly before she fetched her pa
with his shotgun. Venus. Now there was a woman. Visions
of the buxom blond came into his mind. He imagined her
hot with passion, giving him that come-hither look with
those big blue eyes. A man could go places with a woman
like her on his arm. Too bad she'd married that blind
writer. He glanced up and realized Hal was still waiting
for an answer. "All right, damn it. But this time you owe
me."

Hal nodded and got to his feet. He got as far as the
door, then came back.

"Now what?"

"One more thing. You treat her like a lady."

"Or what?" Clay challenged.

Hal planted his palms on the desk, his green eyes hard
and angry. "Or, by God, you'll answer to me." He spun on
his heel and stalked out, slamming the door behind him.

"So that's the way the land lies." Clay rocked back in
his chair and stared at the ceiling. He had too many problems of his own to care about Hal Anderson's love life.
Far too many problems. He was broke. Didn't have
enough money to pay next month's rent. News traveled
faster from mouth to mouth than he could get it into
print. And nobody, except the Daltrys, had placed an ad
in months. And that had been for a rainmaker. He shook
his head, unable to imagine wasting all that money on
such foolishness. But it was their money and it kept him
from starving. Besides, they had plenty to spare.

His eyes narrowed. Plenty to spare. Right now Minerva

Daltry controlled the purse strings, but she was more than generous with those in her family. Besides, the old lady was getting on in years. And when she was gone . . . a slow smile widened his mouth.

Hal Anderson had just done him one helluva favor.

Eleven

WHEN ALLIE DID FIND HAL SHE WISHED SHE HADN'T, FOR ONCE again the dance hall girl was at his side. Allie remembered the kisses she and Hal had shared the night before, and a sharp pain stabbed her heart. Had he kissed that floozy the same way he'd kissed her?

She had been watching Hal so intently she didn't see the whirling dirt until it had captured her in its midst. It spun about her, lifting her skirts and peppering her with sharp bits of sand and dirt. Then, as quickly as it had appeared, it spun away. Choking and wiping her stinging eyes, Allie stumbled into a tall figure. "I'm sorry," she murmured and started to move away.

The man gripped her upper arms, and she peered up through her tears to see Clay Masterson.

"Allie, is anything wrong?" he asked in that deep, smooth voice.

Allie blinked, trying to clear her grit-filled eyes. "I got caught in a dust devil. I think I still have some dirt in my eyes." Flushing red with embarrassment, she wiped at the tears that flowed down her cheeks.

"Here, let me see." He drew an immaculate linen hand-kerchief from his pocket, then stepped close. His brown eyes peered into hers. "Open wide." He gently probed each eye several times. "Now, how does that feel?"

Actually her tears had washed her eyes clean and now her eyes felt fine, but noticing Hal and the gaudily dressed woman headed their way, Allie lied. "I think this one still has a speck in it."

One hand cupping her chin, the other holding the kerchief, Clay leaned toward her until she felt his warm breath on her cheek. His lips, classically molded and smoothly sensual, were so close that she would have only had to tilt her head a fraction more to press her own against them. He gently lifted her lashes, then touched the cloth to the corners of her eye, blotting away a tear. "There, I think we got the last of it." She expected him to step away, but he continued to hold her. Allie felt her heartbeat quicken.

"You have lovely eyes, Allie," he murmured. "Like quicksilver beneath a rippling stream." He drew a finger-tip gently down her cheek. He had bathed that morning, for she caught the scent of soap and the oil that controlled his sleek black hair. He smiled, his teeth white and even beneath a neat mustache. He was handsome, sophisti-cated, and polite, the vision of any woman's dreams.

Captured in his hypnotic gaze, a tremor skittered up her spine.

"Something wrong, Allie?" Hal demanded in a harsh tone.

"What?" She turned her head and saw him standing beside her.

"Is anything wrong?" he said, glaring at Clay. "You look kind of funny."

"Allie had some dirt in her eye," Clay said smoothly,

dropping his hand from her chin. "I was attempting to remove it."

"Seems like she gets a lot of that these days." Hal gave her a pointed look, then whipped out his handkerchief. "Let me take a peek."

"It's all right now," she said quickly, noticing the brassy redhead's smug smile. "*Clay* took care of it for me." She looped her arm through the newspaperman's and gave him a bright smile.

"I'll wait for you by the lemonade stand, honey," the woman whispered to Hal, just loud enough for Allie to hear.

"Yeah, sure," Hal agreed somewhat absently, his attention still on her and Clay.

The floozy gave him one last seductive look, then sashayed away.

"Run along and quench your thirst, Anderson," Clay said silkily. "Don't worry about Allie; I intend to take real good care of her." He slid a possessive arm around her waist.

Hal's eyes narrowed. "Yeah. I 'spect you will." Without another word, he turned on his heel and strode away.

Confused by Hal's behavior, Allie nodded toward the trees. "The lemonade's over there." Her gaze remained fixed on Hal's broad back.

"I have a feeling lemonade wouldn't near quench the thirst that's nagging him," Clay said with a chuckle. "But I think a glass or two might be just what we need." He gave her a little squeeze, then guided her toward the barrel.

The rest of the day passed without Allie catching a glimpse of Hal, which was all right with her—until she remembered she hadn't seen the dance hall girl either. The thought that the two of them might be closeted away together somewhere didn't bother her as much as it might have if she hadn't been so worried about C. J.

Nobody had seen her blond Adonis of a brother, even though the whole family had searched for him. When Clay excused himself, saying he had some business to tend to, she took that opportunity to try to ferret out Cupid's hiding place.

Since he'd last been spotted over by the icehouse, Allie decided that was the first place she would look. She headed in that direction, then changed her tactics. If he was in there, he probably had a peephole somewhere. He was sly as a fox when it came to hiding. Well, she just wouldn't give him the opportunity to see her coming.

She strolled down Main Street as if she were on her way to do some shopping in the mercantile, casually passing Miss Sallie's shop and the newspaper office, which to her surprise was locked up tight. Apparently Clay was conducting his business somewhere else.

When she reached the mercantile, she hurried on by. The last thing she wanted was for Hank to spot her. The owner of the mercantile, while likable, was just about the nosiest and most talkative person in town. If he saw her she could depend on being there until dark while he showed her every newfangled gadget in the store, which nobody ever bought because not a single soul but Hank knew what they were for or how to use them.

Letting out a sigh of relief when she reached the Horse Hotel, she ducked into the darkened stable and cautiously peered out the back door. Perfect. From here she had a clear view of the icehouse, which sat a short distance behind the mercantile. Now all she had to do was wait.

"Where's your boyfriend?" came a voice out of the gloom.

"Jehoshaphat! You scared me out of ten-years' growth," she said, whirling to confront Hal, who was stretched out on a stack of hay. "Where's your girlfriend?" she snapped back, oddly grateful that he was alone.

"She's around." He got to his feet and staggered toward her. "I'm supposed to meet her later," he said, closing one eye in a bleary-eyed wink. Wisps of hay clung to his tousled sandy hair. His shirt hung unbuttoned over his muscular chest, and his shadowed cheeks told her he needed a shave. He smelled of leather, horses, grass, and sweat.

"I see you've been at the *lemonade* again," she said with disgust.

"Lemonade, hell! I've been drinkin' whiskey." He raised a tanned hand to rub his stomach.

"I thought you didn't like whiskey."

"Maybe I acquired a taste for it," he said, stepping closer.

"I cannot abide a drunk." She took a step backward.

"No. You prefer a womanizer."

"Clay is a perfect gentleman."

"If you believe that, you are a perfect fool!"

"Why you—" She drew back her fist, and when it collided with his eye, she felt a jolt go clear up her arm.

Clutching his eye, he gazed at her in shocked disbelief.

Seeing the look of pure fury that came over his face, Allie raised trembling fingertips to cover her mouth. He stalked toward her.

She retreated until her back was pressed against the rough boards of the barn wall.

"Hal . . ." She put out a hand to stop him. In all the time she'd known him, she'd never seen him like this.

"Allie . . ." he mimicked in a deadly soft voice.

Beads of crimson oozed to the surface just below his eyebrow, and the flesh around it had already begun to puff.

Appalled that she had done such a thing, she reached out to touch him.

He grabbed her wrist. "Don't," he warned, his eyes like shards of glittering green glass.

"Dang it, Hal. Why'd you have to make me so mad?"

"Did he kiss you yet?" he asked coldly.

"No," she said, surprised by the question. Not that it was any of his business.

"Then maybe you'd like another lesson."

Before she could protest, he yanked her into his arms. His mouth ground down on hers, bruising her lips in a savage kiss.

She struggled, but his hand tangled in her hair, holding her captive. When she pounded him with her fists, his assault gentled but was no less insistent. He kissed her long and persuasively until she forgot about C. J., or Clay, or where she was. She was conscious of nothing but Hal and the sensations he was causing deep inside her.

He slid his hand up to knead her breast, and his thumb gently stroked the nipple until she cursed the layer of clothing that kept them apart.

His tongue dove deep, tasting, caressing, seducing. All reason gone, she wrapped her arms around his neck and pulled him even closer. He tasted like lemonade, honey, and mint.

Her eyes shot open. *He isn't drunk! He knows exactly what he's doing.* Anger tightened her muscles.

Bent on revenge, she kissed him back, her tongue copying every move his had made. She slipped her hand inside his shirt and felt him tremble when she stroked his bare skin. She tangled her fingers in the narrow band of hair on his chest, then ran her thumb over his nipple and felt it harden under her caress. Just like hers, she thought with amazement.

Was a fire also raging inside him, building until it was

blinding hot and tormenting? She pressed her body against his and noted the hard ridge of his arousal.

The knowledge that she could do this to him gave her a sense of power. Soon all thought of getting even vanished and she surrendered to the passion rising inside her. Her body pulsated, her own urgent rhythm matching the dance of his tongue. Lost in newly awakened desire, she moaned, urging him onward. Now she wanted nothing but blessed release and couldn't have stopped if the whole of Paradise Plains had suddenly stepped through the stable door.

Just when she had reached the brink of some great pinnacle, he put his hands on her shoulders and stepped away.

Bereft and dazed, she raised her lashes.

He stared down at her for a moment, then his lean, tanned face twisted in a mocking smile.

Why had he stopped? Didn't he realize she wanted it as much as he? Maybe if she showed him. She moistened her lips, closed her eyes, and leaned forward.

He closed his hands on her shoulders and held her at bay. "Now don't go gettin' all walleyed on me."

"Walleyed?" She blinked.

"Walleyed," he affirmed. "You get that way every time I kiss you."

"Then why do you bother?"

He ran a hand though his sun-streaked hair. "Hell, Allie, I was just trying to teach you a lesson."

"What kind of a lesson?" she hissed between gritted teeth.

"About what you can expect from gentlemen."

"You're no gentleman!"

He curled his lip. "Neither is Clay Masterson." He reached out a finger and ran it over her kiss-swollen lips. "But for that matter, you're no lady."

Desire turning to pure fury, Allie slammed her fist against his other eye.

The ground beneath their feet began to shake and a low rumble, like distant thunder, filled the air.

Hal, cupping his hand over his eye, stared at her as if she had done it.

Then Allie remembered why she had come there in the first place—C. J. Terrified of what she might find, she raced from the barn.

Wisps of smoke spurted from around the edges of the icehouse, and the building fairly quivered on its foundation.

"C. J.!" she screamed.

The door burst open and C. J. sprinted toward her.

"Get down, Al—" Lee yelled from somewhere behind her.

The rest of his words were drowned in the roar of the explosion, but Allie wouldn't have heard anyway because Hal caught her in a flying tackle and pinned her to the ground. Through one eye, she saw the little building shiver, then it began to rise into the air. As it sailed overhead, rocks and dirt, boards and nails, along with sawdust and shards of ice, peppered the ground beside her. A swirling cloud of dust followed. Finally the debris quit falling, but Hal still didn't move.

"You're squishing me!" she cried out of the side of her mouth not ground into the dirt.

"Hal, I think it's safe to let her up now," C. J. said.

Hal shifted his weight, then she was free. She stuck out her hand, expecting Hal to help her up, but he ignored the gesture. Eyes swollen almost shut, he gave her a piercing glance, then he turned on his heel and strode away.

"She does look a little squished, don't she?" she heard Lee say. She stared up at her big lummox of a brother.

Lee reached out and plucked her upright beside him,

then he began to pound on her back like she was a down pillow that needed fluffing.

"Jehoshaphat!" she yelled, slapping his hamlike hands away. "If you treat Meredith like that, I wouldn't blame her one bit if she shot you!" She whirled and stalked toward the black-faced C. J., who smiled so sweetly she wanted to slap him just for the hell of it. "And you—" she spluttered, vibrating with fury.

"Uh, I wouldn't let her get too close," Lee warned from behind her.

C. J. cautiously danced out of reach.

"From now on you can blow yourself up—see if I give a damn!" Allie spun on her heel and marched away.

"What did I do?" C. J. asked.

"Well, for starters, I'd say you broke every window for five miles."

"I did that?" C. J. asked in amazement.

"And look up there." Lee pointed overhead, where a column of dust was still rising. "I'd say you sent half of Hank's icehouse to Wyoming."

Shielding his eyes to peer at the huge dust cloud, C. J. grinned. "But do you think I'll make it rain?"

Lee rolled his eyes in a silent plea toward heaven. "I don't know, little brother, but if that don't make it rain, nothing will."

Lee eyed the angry group of shopkeepers that had gathered behind the mercantile and hoped Hank didn't have any tar and feathers handy. Deciding discretion was the better part of valor, he grabbed C. J. by the tattered remains of his shirt and pulled him to the alley by the livery. They watched until, one by one, the mob dispersed. "I guess we ought to go and tell Pa what happened before somebody sends for the militia. And you," he jabbed a finger at C. J., "had better start buttering Grandma up, because she's the one who will have to pay for the damages."

C. J. grimaced. "Five miles?"

"Maybe ten."

"Ten?" C. J. let a whistle of air slide between his teeth. "That will cost a fortune."

"You know those little candies Gram likes so well?"

"Yeah?"

"Couldn't hurt."

"She's gonna be mad." C. J. eyed him hopefully. "Could you—"

"Nope." Lee shook his head. "*You* did it. *You* tell her."

C. J. stared at the ground for a minute; then, glancing toward Main Street, he reached out and gripped Lee's arm. "Look. There by the water trough. You don't suppose *I* did that to him?"

"Nope. Allie," Lee said solemnly, glancing over at Hal.

"Our little Allie?" C. J. put his hands on his knees and peered toward the street.

"Why did you think I warned you not to get too close? I know how prideful you are of your looks."

"Why?"

"Why, what?" Lee asked impatiently.

"Why'd she do it?"

"He kissed her."

C. J.'s smoke-blackened face wrinkled in a frown. "Maybe we ought to have a talk with the boy."

"What for? She kissed him back."

"Well, I guess that does put a different light on it." C. J. thought for a moment. "That still doesn't explain why she hit him."

"He quit."

"What?" C. J. gave him a baffled look.

"You're the expert on love, Cupid. You figure it out."

"You call me that again where anybody can hear and I'll black *your* eyes."

"Well?" Lee said, enjoying his brother's dilemma.

C. J.'s brows wrinkled in concentration. "He kissed her. She kissed him. He quit. She hit him." He grinned. "She didn't want him to quit?"

"That's right."

"That's one for the books. I got hit when I kissed a girl before, but never when I stopped."

"Yeah, but that's Allie for you. She doesn't think like anybody else."

"A Daltry through and through," C. J. agreed.

"Women!"

Lee rubbed his chin and glanced toward Hal, who was holding a wet cloth over his discolored eyes. "Maybe we should have a talk with him, at that."

"Why?"

"I just thought maybe we ought to show him how to duck."

"Or run. Comes in handy."

Lee chuckled. "You, too?"

"My Lizzie's got a temper like a Comanche on the warpath."

"And my Red can dot your eye with a rock from fifty paces."

"On second thought, maybe we shouldn't talk to Hal," C. J. said. "We could get Allie mad at *us*. Maybe we ought to let well enough alone."

"Good thinking, little brother. Speaking of mad—what are you going to do about Lizzie?"

"Think she'll be upset?"

Lee let out a whoop. "That's putting it mildly."

"That bad, huh?"

Lee nodded. "You know, while you're seeing about that

candy, maybe you ought to pick up some doodad or another to smooth your wife's feathers."

"Think it will help?"

"Couldn't hurt." Lee thought a minute. "Maybe while you're shopping, I should pick up something for Meredith."

"She mad at you?"

"I don't think so, but with women you can never tell. Best to stay on their good side."

C. J. nodded, and they both hurried toward the mercantile.

Twelve

MAD ENOUGH TO SPIT, ALLIE STORMED AWAY FROM THE LIVERY stable, leaving a dust cloud trailing in her wake. Thanks to Hal and her half-witted brothers, she looked an absolute sight. Her new dress was dirty and spotted with soot. Bits of hay clung to her hair, and somewhere in the fracas she'd lost her blue ribbon. Her knuckles throbbed and she knew her mouth must look like she'd been sucking persimmons.

Her mood hadn't improved when she rejoined the female members of her family.

"Allie, what happened?" Her eyes wide with alarm, Allie's ma scrambled to her feet.

"Men," Allie said through clenched teeth.

"I'll bet C. J. was one of them," Lizzie said, her dark eyes angry. "You know that the icehouse passed right over our heads? Somebody else had to tell me the fool was alive—he didn't have the nerve to tell me himself." She got up and helped Jane and Minerva brush the dirt off Allie's skirt. "Have you seen him?"

"He's just dandy. The last time I saw him he was grinning like a black-faced opossum."

"He won't be for long," Lizzie promised.

"Was Lee with him?" Meredith asked.

"Would he be anywhere else?"

"How did you get hay in your hair?" Her ma held up a piece of straw. "Did the livery blow up, too?"

"No." Ignoring their curious glances, Allie bent and vigorously beat at her hem.

"Now if we can just get some of that dirt off your face and han—" Her ma stared at her. "What happened to your knuckles?"

"I'd rather not talk about it." Allie took the dampened cloth her mother held out and scrubbed her face and hands.

"As soon as Allie's halfway presentable, why don't we go see what the rest of the town is up to," Minerva suggested.

"While there's anything left," Lizzie added grimly.

They left the churchyard, and after stopping at the library to see how Mrs. Cooper was managing with the children, they walked toward a cleared area where the rest of the hopeful rainmakers had gathered.

All of their projects looked interesting, but Allie doubted if any of their efforts could top C. J.'s. As they passed by the various groups, she strained to hear excited snatches of conversations.

There was not a piece of glass in town that hadn't shattered in the mysterious explosion. Some people thought a meteor had hit, because of the big crater it had left in the ground. The blast scared the widow Bibble's cats so bad that half of them were still running toward Abilene. Somebody suggested they ought to try it again to get rid of the other half. . . .

While everyone speculated about what had happened,

Allie gathered that no one actually knew C. J. was responsible for the detonation that had rocked the town. Considering the decrease in the cat population, maybe if they did they'd vote to give C. J. a medal. Lizzie could use it when she pinned his hide to the barn door. She noted that both C. J. and Lee were making themselves scarce. And the way Hal looked, he wouldn't dare show his face.

When they found her pa and informed him of C. J.'s disaster, he told her ma it was a good thing they didn't have ten kids. Minerva couldn't afford it.

Now that her temper had cooled, Allie's curiosity got the best of her. As she followed the crowd from one group to another and watched each contestant in turn try to make it rain, she found it amazing what lengths some people would go to for a hundred dollars.

In the first entry, the folks from the Buccaneer Restaurant had cooked up a huge potful of chili peppers, garlic, and onions. Allie didn't know about making it rain, but it did make your eyes water from a block away. When the concoction was finished, everybody stared at the cloudless sky for the allotted length of time, then shook their heads and went on their way. Fritz, the restaurant owner, shrugged and said he'd just add some beef and turn the mess into a pot of chili.

The next entry, the town ladies, had painted their faces and used their rolling pins to vigorously beat on washtubs. While they looked frightful enough to scare babies and made a damnable racket, they didn't make it rain.

Another group who prayed and shouted and spoke in tongues did manage to convert a few sinners, but the sky remained unblemished.

A group of elderly, buckskin-clad men formed a circle and shot buffalo guns into the brilliant blue sky. Her ears ringing, Allie gazed up through the thick, acrid gunsmoke. Nary a drop rewarded their efforts.

After watching a half-dozen or so other unsuccessful attempts, the entourage formed a semicircle around the front of a canvas-covered tepee. "Hey, Will, who you got in there, Cochise?" a man jokingly called out.

Rancher Will Moore and Charlie Simmons, one of his hands, made a great show of lifting the tent flap. An ancient, buckskin-clad Indian stepped through the opening. Allie knew he must be the shaman they had taken from the reservation. Even though the old man was not as tall as Allie, he had a dignity and presence that made you forget his lack of height. A cluster of eagle feathers adorned one of his silver braids and also decorated the deerskin bag he clutched in his hand. His dark skin was wrinkled, but his eyes, like black coals, burned with an ageless inner fire.

A slim Indian youth, naked except for a breechcloth and a necklace of beads, carried a hide-covered drum from the tent. Taking a position off to one side, he sat cross-legged on the ground and softly began to tap a pagan beat.

The shaman solemnly surveyed the group, then he raised his hands toward the sky and began to chant. While Allie couldn't understand the words, she figured he was praying.

Every eye fixed on the ancient Indian, the noisy bunch of townspeople became as still as if they were in church.

The medicine man reached into his pouch and took out what appeared to be herbs or grasses and tossed them as an offering to the four winds. While he chanted and shuffled his feet to the beat of a hypnotic dance, his hands rose and fell in a fluttering motion as he cast white feathers into the air. Allie thought the feathers might represent clouds or rain.

The drumbeat became more frenzied and the shaman's incantation increased in volume, then something large and dark passed overhead, casting a mysterious shadow over the crowd. An audible gasp rose from the group, as if they feared the medicine man had called something other than rain down upon their heads, but it was only a very large black bird. As the dance continued, a dog began to howl and some people shifted uneasily, while others glanced over their shoulders from time to time.

Allie, too, was hard-pressed to calm her pounding heart and curb the shiver that ran up her spine in spite of the blistering heat. She caught Meredith's gaze and knew she, too, felt the unseen entity.

Finally the ceremony ended, and when the old man closed his bag and disappeared inside the tent, a sigh of relief rippled through the crowd. The faces around Allie were somber, some appeared frightened. Here and there a nervous giggle erupted as the group dispersed and hurried away. Even though the sky had grown a little hazy, it still showed no sign of rain.

Allie had the feeling that even if the wizened medicine man had caused a downpour, the town would think twice before trying something like that again.

After the Indian shaman, the rainmaker's machine almost seemed like an afterthought. Although the professor appeared a little perturbed that the old Indian had stolen his thunder, his dramatic gestures and elaborate spiel soon caught and held the crowd's attention. When he at last uncovered the machine that had caused so much curiosity, Allie fought to control a giggle.

Mounted on a wagon, the thing strongly resembled something C. J. had once contrived to keep the crows out of the garden. The machine had a mass of tubes connected to a kettle, and wires and wheels and spinning blades. She thought it looked like it would come nearer to flying than producing rain.

After a lofty and lengthy speech, Professor Ambrose lit a flame under a large copper container.

A man in the audience snickered. "Hell, that thing ain't nothing more than a glorified whiskey still connected to a windmill."

However, when the kettle boiled and tubes began to belch huge clouds of black smoke, everyone admitted the sight was pretty impressive. Then the professor aimed and fired something that resembled a Gatling gun toward the sky. Seconds later, white pellets fell and sprinkled the audience. When one landed on her shoulder, Allie put it to the tip of her tongue and found it was a crystal of salt.

When his first efforts failed, Professor Ambrose tried again—with the same results. No rain.

Finally the frustrated rainmaker conceded defeat. He angrily blamed all the unsuccessful tries before his, claiming all the commotion confused the elements. He collected his money and hitched his wagon. Twilight saw his wagon headed across the prairie.

After the professor left, the morose group of people slowly wandered back toward the church.

"Well, we didn't make it rain, but we shore gave it a darned good try," her father said softly. Everyone had to agree on that.

"All right, folks, gather around," Sheriff Sampson bellowed from the dance platform in the churchyard. "We're here to decide who did the best job of making it rain. Any nominations?"

"Fritz Tittle, from the Buccaneer," called one. "He might not have made rain, but that pot of onions and chilies he cooked sure cleared my sinuses."

"C. J. Daltry," called out another. "At least *he* made rain."

"Hell, that weren't rain. That was water from the ice," a

man scoffed. "Besides, it weren't enough to get anybody wet."

After a lengthy discussion, a vote was taken from among the contestants. Since not one of them had made it rain, they decided to divide the contest money between the shopkeepers to buy new windows.

"Now that that's settled," Sheriff Sampson said, "we'll give you an opportunity to do your own rain dance. If the fiddlers will tune their instruments, we'll get the rest of this shindig underway."

The female members of the Daltry family hurriedly gathered their belongings, then they laid claim to a spot close to the dance floor and spread their quilt.

The lanterns around the raised board area were lit and the air vibrated with the screech of fiddles and the twang of guitars, saws, and Jew's harps as everyone tried to start off in the same key.

"Yey hoo! Grab yore partner, boys," the sheriff bellowed.

The moment Allie had both anticipated and dreaded was at hand. She peered into the shadowy darkness. No sign of Clay, and if Hal did show up she doubted he would come anywhere near her. After everything she'd gone through in preparation for the occasion, what if no one asked her to dance?

Thirteen

ALLIE WAS READY TO FLEE INTO THE DARKNESS BEYOND THE lantern-lit square when someone tapped her on the shoulder. "May I have this dance, Miss Daltry?" a deep voice rumbled.

"I'd be delighted, sir," Allie said, beaming a grateful look at her brother.

Though freshly washed, Lee's face still bore traces of the black powder, which made the smile he gave her even brighter. He held out his brawny arms and hoisted her to her feet, then he led her to the dance floor.

Tense as a drawn bow, Allie attempted to follow Lee's footsteps, but it seemed that in spite of the practice sessions with Hal, her feet couldn't keep time with the beat. After she'd thoroughly removed the shine from the toes of her brother's boots, she sighed in dismay. "I just can't seem to get the hang of it."

"You're trying too hard. You can do it." He gave her an encouraging hug. "Relax, Allie, and concentrate on the music. And smile! Dancing is supposed to be fun, and you 'pear like you're going to your own execution."

She felt like it, too; but seeing that Lee didn't intend to give up, she forced herself to comply with his instructions.

"See. That wasn't so hard, was it?"

Amazed to find herself actually dancing, Allie smiled into her brother's twinkling blue eyes. "I was afraid I'd be a wallflower, too." She glanced at a group of unattached females who were seated on a bench at one side of the area.

"Now, you know we wouldn't let that happen, little sister. Besides, I'd be willing to bet that before the night's over, you'll be the belle of the ball."

While she knew that he was only trying to make her feel good, for a moment she actually allowed herself to believe it. When the fiddles screeched to a stop, Lee gave her a kiss on the cheek, then escorted her back to the rest of the family.

"Now it's my turn." C. J. stepped from the crowd and clasped her hand.

"I wondered what had happened to you," she said.

"I thought it wise to make myself scarce and give Lizzie a chance to cool off."

"Well, at least you ain't the dumbest bunny in the bunch," Allie said, returning his grin.

"Do you think it's safe yet?" He glanced at the pallet, where his wife sat watching.

"How should I know? You're the one who's married to her."

"She still looks pretty upset. I think I'll wait a while longer."

While Lee's dancing was more sedate, C. J.'s style was a mixture of swoops, dips, and twirls. Through a spinning haze, Allie noticed that Lee had chosen one of the homelier single girls for his partner, while her father danced with another of the unattached maidens. Allie's breast swelled with pride that the men in her family could be so considerate of the feelings of others.

After the dance ended, C. J. gave her an affectionate peck on the cheek, then he, too, ambled toward the bench of unmarried or widowed women.

Allie saw her pa heading in her direction, but before he could reach her, Clay stepped from the shadows and took her hand.

"I believe this must be my dance, sweet Allie."

Allie glanced up at her pa, who winked and nodded. Then Odie left the platform to join her mother and grandma.

The music was slow and dreamy, and clasped in the newspaperman's arms, Allie succumbed to its spell. While she might have wished it were Hal, she found Clay an accomplished dancer and had no trouble following his lead. Under his light but firm guidance, she felt as light as a butterfly that had just emerged from a cocoon.

When the dance ended, Clay showed no inclination to release her, but instead led her from the platform. "I think some liquid refreshments might be in order about now."

"Amen to that," Allie said, fanning herself with her hand. They walked to a table where a large chunk of ice floated in a washtub full of lemonade. She thought it was probably the only piece of ice left in town after her brother's mishap with the icehouse.

Clay filled a cup with the tin dipper and handed it to her.

"Thank you," Allie said gratefully. She took a large gulp, then remembering her manners followed it with a tiny sip. When her cup was empty, she eyed the tub wistfully. No. A lady didn't drink like an overheated horse. A lady probably didn't sweat like one either, she thought, embarrassed by the steady stream of moisture that trick-led between her breasts. "My, it is warm tonight."

"Would you like to walk a bit before we return to the dance floor?" Clay asked, setting his cup aside.

"I'd like that very much."

He took her hand and tucked it in the crook of his arm, then he led her away from the lights and the crowd. A while later, he stopped as they reached a small rise on the moonlit prairie.

Feeling a bit uncomfortable with the silence between them, Allie searched her mind for witty things to say. But the only thing that came out was, "Mighty warm, isn't it?" *I already said that,* she thought. "He'll think I'm a com-plete ninny." She didn't realize until the words were said that she'd spoken out loud.

Clay chuckled. "Not at all. I think you are enchanting." He cupped her chin with his hand. "You are a beautiful woman, Allie. Did you know that?"

"No. I'm not. My sister Venus is beautiful. Beside her I look plain as a mud-dabbed fence."

"I'll admit Venus is pleasing to the eyes, but your beauty is unique. It comes from the soul." He put his hands on her shoulders, then gently pressed his lips to the corner of her mouth.

Shocked, Allie stared at him.

"I hope I haven't offended you."

"No. Nothing like that," she said quickly. "You sur-prised me, that's all. It was very nice." While Clay's kiss was pleasant, it certainly hadn't affected her like Hal's. Maybe it was because she hadn't expected it.

"May I kiss you again?"

She nodded. But this time, instead of a peck on her mouth, he cupped the back of her head in his hands, then slowly bent and claimed her lips.

The mouth he pressed against hers was cool and tasted

of tangy lemonade—and something else. Something a bit more potent.

Allie kissed him back as Hal had taught her, but it still wasn't the same. She started to pull away.

Clay held on to her, kissing her eagerly, hungrily, until she feared he might actually take a bite out of her. He slid his arms around her waist and pulled her so close she felt like butter being pressed into a mold. While she found the experience exciting, she also discovered she couldn't breathe. She raised her hands and pushed against his chest.

He hesitated, then reluctantly let her go. "Forgive me," he said on a harsh breath.

"For what?"

"For frightening you. For forgetting that you are innocent."

"Oh, that," she said, catching her breath. She ducked her head, hoping he couldn't tell she was blushing. "I guess I am a mite innocent where men are concerned, but I do know it would take more than a kiss to scare me."

Clay looked at her in amazement, then he laughed.

"Did I do it right?"

"Do it right?"

"You know." She pointed to her mouth. "The kiss."

"My dear, if you had done it any better, I wouldn't want to be responsible for the consequences." He reached out and took her hand and brought it to his lips. "You are like a rare and precious jewel. I'm glad I didn't frighten you. But I think it might be better for both our sakes if we went back to the dance."

Consequences? Why did men always seem to be talking in riddles?

Clay escorted her back to the dance area, then to her dismay, he courteously bid her good night.

As she watched his dark figure walk away, she had a

hard time hiding her disappointment. She'd hoped he might kiss her again, to compare it to Hal's, if nothing else. Too bad they'd quit just when she'd thought she was beginning to get the hang of it. She released a wistful sigh. Maybe Hal was right—maybe she did need more practice.

From his place in the moon-dappled shadows, Hal clenched his fists as he watched Clay Masterson leave Allie and walk away. Dang it all! Clay was only supposed to dance with her. *I didn't say nothing about takin' her for a walk in the moonlight—or kissing her.* Hal had witnessed that kiss. That long, lingering kiss. Remembering the one he and Allie had shared in the stable, he grew warm.

For someone who didn't know a thing about kissing until last night, Allie sure was a fast learner. But Hal knew that was his own fault, since he was the one who'd put the idea in her head. *Did Clay kiss her like I did? And did she like it?*

Maybe she hadn't liked it, because she had pushed Clay away.

But she hadn't hit the newsman. Hal touched his injured eyes. *She might have poked me, but she sure didn't push me away.* In fact she'd driven him to the edge of his sanity. But then Allie never did anything halfway.

If she had stayed in Masterson's arms a minute longer, Hal didn't know what he would have done. He drew back his foot and viciously kicked at a rock. Yes, he did know what he would have done. He would have broken Clay Masterson's perfect nose and then taken Allie back to her pa.

A voice inside nagged at him. *Allie is not a child. Are you going to hit every man who kisses her? Every man she kisses? She must have wanted Clay to kiss her, otherwise she wouldn't have stood for it.* And what would he do when she decided kissing wasn't enough?

"You blamed fool," he muttered angrily. "You started it. You asked Clay to bid on her basket. To dance with her." But he danged sure had never mentioned anything else.

Ignoring the fact that he resembled a violet-eyed raccoon, Hal pushed away from the tree and strode toward the dance floor, where Allie began the next dance in the arms of Charlie Simmons, a cowboy from a nearby ranch. She smiled up at the cowpuncher and laughed at something he said.

When the music ended, Hal hesitated for a moment, then knowing Allie's temper usually cooled as quickly as it flared, he decided to ask her to dance. He stepped onto the platform, but before he had the chance to claim her, she was swept away in the arms of the deputy sheriff. It was then that Hal saw that other men had lined up, waiting their turn, their gazes never leaving her lithe figure.

Hal studied the couple. While the man's movements were stiff and deliberate, Allie swayed like a willow limb in an evening breeze. He reminded himself that he had taught her that, too.

Remembering the outrageous inclinations he'd had in the barn, he thought it was a good thing he hadn't taught her anything else.

Suddenly aware that she had caught him spying on her, Hal met her silvery gaze.

Allie flashed him a sweet smile, then her companion said something and recaptured her attention.

Since she already had so many admirers, she sure didn't need him, Hal thought, scowling. During the next several dances, he pretended to ignore her, but found he was never more aware of her presence. The way the dimples appeared and disappeared in her cheeks. The lantern light glazing her curly head with gold. The lushness of her strawberry-red mouth. The smallness of her waist, the upward thrust of her breasts, all reminding him of the way she felt when he'd held her in his arms.

Well, he wasn't holding her now, and the way things looked he wasn't going to get the chance to, either. Feeling like a cat that had been left out in the rain, he shot her one last resentful look, then strode down the platform steps and headed for his horse.

Out of the corner of her eye, Allie saw Hal leave. While she was hoping that he might ask her to dance, she had no shortage of partners.

Men who had never paid her any attention until the newspaperman had started hanging around her had sought her out as a dance partner. Allie thought she might drown if another one of several would-be dance partners appeared with yet another glass of tart lemonade. When she'd mentioned she was hot, another had fanned her so vigorously that she actually felt chilled in spite of the heat.

All in all, she'd had a grand time. Dipping and whirling across the floor in time to the music, Allie decided that she also liked dancing.

The lanterns dimmed for the last waltz and she saw her pa standing by her side. He held out his arms and she gave him a hug. "Did you see me?"

"The belle of the ball," he said, squeezing her back. "You know, daughter, I had half a dozen fellers ask if they could come calling."

"What did you tell them?"

He grinned. "I told them they would have to come out and ask you."

A half-dozen? That was almost as many suitors as Venus had had.

The music began and her father swept her onto the floor. Allie couldn't hold back the grin that spread across her face. A few months ago, no man except Hal had ever come to see her, and now she had not one but six who wanted to come a-calling.

And while she didn't quite know what to think of her sudden popularity, she was determined to enjoy it before it disappeared.

Fourteen

THE NEXT DAY, ALLIE WONDERED IF THE WHOLE THING HAD been a dream, but her sore feet and worn dancing slippers at the foot of her bed told her it hadn't. She pulled on a clean pair of jeans and a blue shirt, then because her feet were so tender, she bypassed her boots in favor of a pair of soft deerskin moccasins.

Since they had arrived home very late last night, she expected most of the household would still be asleep when she went down the stairs for breakfast, but to her surprise, both her ma and grandma sat at the table.

"Good morning, Allie," Minerva said brightly. "Did you have a good time at the celebration?"

"It was fun," she admitted, helping herself to a cup of coffee. She filled a plate from the platter of ham and eggs that sat on one side of the stove and buttered a couple of fluffy biscuits.

"I noticed Clay Masterson seemed quite smitten with you," her ma teased. "And he wasn't the only one."

"With the way my feet feel this morning, I think I must

have danced with pert near every man in the county, except Hal," she said, joining them at the table.

"That Anderson boy must have been brawling again by the looks of his eyes," her ma said in disgust.

Allie remained quiet and added cream and sugar to her cup.

Her ma sniffed. "I saw him leave—and head straight for the Lucky Chance."

So that's where he had gone. An ache tightened the middle of her chest, but she immediately dismissed it. If Hal wanted to run around with that hussy it didn't make no never mind to her. She attacked the slice of ham with a vengeance and shoved a piece into her mouth. When she thought of Hal and the woman together, kissing and no telling what else . . . suddenly she was glad she had kissed Clay Masterson in the moonlight. She only wished Hal had seen her do it.

"Allie, you're going to beat that cup plumb to death," Minerva said.

"Besides making a mess all over my tablecloth," her mother scolded. "That bowlful of sugar you dumped in there has got to be dissolved by now."

"I'm sorry, Ma." Allie took the spoon out of her cup and placed it on the table. She stared at the swirling coffee, waited for it to settle, then took a gulp. Grimacing, she swallowed the mouthful of syrupy mixture, then took the mug to the sink and dumped the rest. She refilled the cup from the large enamel pot that sat on one edge of the nickel-plated cookstove; then, her appetite gone, she abandoned her half-eaten breakfast and left the house and walked toward the corral.

It was midmorning when Hal finished splitting the rest of the wood he'd cut and carried it inside the small house he and his father shared on the outskirts of town.

His pa glanced up from the stack of pancakes he was eating and grinned. "Plenty more batter by the stove."

"I think I'll pass," Hal said, trying to repress a shudder. "Something I ate yesterday isn't sitting too good on my stomach." In reality, it had been something he'd drunk, but he didn't want to tell that to his pa, especially when his father had managed to stay sober through the celebration. Hal felt a bit ashamed that he'd been the one to succumb to spirits. Contrary to what folks thought, he rarely imbibed, but the times he did were memorable for several reasons: He usually ended up making a gol–derned fool of himself, and the aftereffects he suffered were horrendous.

"Did you see Allie last night?"

"Yeah, I saw her."

"I caught a glimpse of her on the dance floor. With her face all flushed and in that dress she looked pretty as a Texas rose." His pa stabbed another forkful of butter-drenched pancakes and shoved it into his mouth, then he pointed the empty fork at Hal. "Didn't see you dancin'. How come?"

"Wasn't in the mood." He had been in the mood until he'd seen Allie going off in the dark with Clay, then witnessed that kiss. Not any respectable peck on the cheek, but a long, passionate embrace. Just thinking about it made him mad all over. Didn't she care anything about her reputation? Of course he was the only one who had seen her, and he wasn't about to tell anybody. He sighed. He couldn't really put the blame on Allie. She was so innocent she didn't know any better. But Masterson did; he knew exactly what he was doing. If Odie had caught the newspaperman, he'd still be bleeding printers' ink. Hal would have fetched Odie himself, if it wouldn't have been so embarrassing for Allie. Might show a few people what kind of a scoundrel Clay Masterson really was.

"Hal, you deef or somethin'? I asked if you and Allie had a fight. She was the one who gave you those shiners, wasn't she?"

"I'm not deaf. And no, we didn't have a fight. We did have a disagreement. And she did punch me," he added reluctantly. Not anxious to answer any more questions, he shoved on his hat and went out the door. Then he glanced down the road toward Paradise Plains. He couldn't spend the whole day wandering about town—not the way he looked.

He ought to go out to the canyon and do some more work with the horses, but his head and stomach didn't feel up to the task.

He could go see Allie and try to make amends. He rejected the idea. The mood he was in, they'd be sure to get in another argument. The next time she might break his nose.

What, then? Masterson, he thought menacingly. That's where he'd go. He wanted a few words with that "perfect" bastard.

"Allie," Jane called, gazing up at her daughter's bedroom.

Putting aside the shirt she'd been attempting to mend, Allie stuck her head out of her bedroom window and spied her ma at the edge of her flower bed. "What is it?"

Shading her eyes with one hand, Jane raised the other and pointed toward the road, where a cloud of dust rose from the wheels of a wagon. "Company coming. Can you see who it is?"

Allie squinted. "Looks like Charlie Simmons in the wagon. The horseman is Deputy Dudley Jones. Wonder what they're doin' way out here?"

"Probably came to see Odie." Jane stuck a stray lock of hair back into place, then glanced down at her dust-streaked dress. "My, I am a mess. Could you fetch them some lemonade while I change? I'd ask Minerva to do it, but she's taking a nap."

Allie nodded, then ducked back inside the window. She stifled a yawn and glanced toward the bed. Suddenly a nap didn't sound like such a bad idea, although she'd never been one to sleep in the daytime. But then she'd never used up so much energy dancing, either. She drew the curtain together to shut out the sun, noticing as she did so that she'd also closed off the only hint of a breeze. Too hot to sleep anyway. As she went down the stairs, she thought of the river and how good it would feel on a hot day like this. The idea sounded inviting. She'd cool off and ease her sore muscles at the same time.

Detecting the clank of wheels and harness in the yard, she hurried toward the kitchen, where she quickly opened the top chamber of the International refrigerator and chipped some ice into a pair of tall glasses. She lifted the pitcher of lemonade and filled the containers to the brim, then she wiped her hands and went to meet their guests.

"Howdy, boys," she said, smiling up at the two men, who in the sweltering heat had faces as brilliant as the sunlit sky. "Ice-cold lemonade in the kitchen. Make yourselves comfortable and I'll go tell Pa you're here."

"Lemonade sounds good, Allie, but—but we didn't come to see Odie," the first of the callers stammered as he dismounted.

"We came to see you," the second finished. The short, stocky deputy reached into the back of the wagon and took out a bouquet of thoroughly wilted wildflowers and shoved them in her direction.

Then the tall, lanky cowboy reached into his pocket and handed her a sackful of licorice sticks. "These are for you, too."

Blushing as furiously as her beet-faced suitors, Allie

managed to murmur thank you to each; then, not knowing what else to say, she invited them into the house.

"Hello, Anderson. Looks like you ran into somebody's barn door," Clay said from behind his desk. "What brings you in today?"

"I think you've got a pretty good idea."

"Not really. Would you care to enlighten me?" Clay reached into a humidor and retrieved a cigar. After trimming the end, he lit it.

"Allie Daltry." Hal straddled one of the chairs across from the newsman.

"Allie? Quite a charming young lady." He blew a cloud of smoke into the air.

"That's just it. She is young. And innocent. And she is a lady."

"I agree, so what's the problem?"

"Just what are your intentions?" Hal asked, narrowing his puffed eyes.

"What business is it of yours? You're not her father."

"I saw you kiss her last night."

"So?"

"So—" He paused threateningly. "You'd better not do it again." Rising, Hal kicked the chair into the desk, then stalked out.

He mounted his horse and headed out of town. Now that he'd stated what was on his mind, he should have felt better, but instead he was more miserable than ever. Maybe because he knew nothing he'd said would make the slightest bit of difference. Clay would do what Clay wanted to do, and outside of punching the man in the nose, there was no way Hal could stop him.

Another worry now nagging at him was what Allie would say if she found out his part in this mess. He ran a hand over his injured eyes, knowing he'd rather stick his face in a nest of hornets than face Allie in a temper.

A faint puff of wind rustled the dry grass along the edge of the road and lifted a swirl of dirt into the air. Hal gazed at the parched rangeland around him. He'd never seen a summer so hot or so powdery dry. But then the previous winter of 1885 had been the worst on record.

He thought about the ranch his pa had lost. Even in the best of years the well had been pretty iffy. He had no doubt it would be dry. Others in the area and even farther north were having the same problem. No water, no rain, and ungodly heat. Feeling about as thirsty as a frog in the middle of the desert, he turned his horse and headed for the river. If he couldn't get cool, at least he could get wet.

From the front porch of the house, Allie waved the last of her visitors good-bye. Where she'd never had a gentleman caller before, today she'd had several, and it had been the most awkward day in her life. The only thing that made it bearable was the fact that most of them had been as ill at ease as she. They'd discussed the rainmaking contest and dance down to the last quiver of the fiddle, then exhausted the subject of the weather. Even the discussion of horses paled after a while, until finally they just sat, foundered themselves on lemonade and cookies, and smiled.

Allie rubbed her aching cheeks, wondering if her mouth had frozen in a pasted-on grin. Dancing was tiring, she decided, but entertaining was far worse. She eyed the stairs and considered retreating to her room, but afraid somebody else might arrive for a visit, she whirled and headed for the corral.

"Where are you going, Allie?" her ma called through the kitchen window. "It's almost time for supper."

"I'll grab a bite tonight when I get back. Right now I want to go swimming."

Allie quickly saddled her horse and raced out of the yard. Now if anyone else came at least she wouldn't be the one forced to amuse them.

When Allie reached the river she unsaddled Circe and gave her a playful swat on the rump.

The mare snorted, then trotted into the river, not stopping until the water lapped halfway up her belly.

"Blamed horse likes to swim almost as much as I do." Determined not to let the animal have all the fun, Allie took off her boots, shirt, and britches; then, after a moment's hesitation, she stripped down to her skin. She tossed her undergarments onto the pile with the rest of her things, then she, too, ran into the slow-flowing river. Even though the water was warm, she found it a good deal cooler than the air outside. Allie swam and floated and played with Circe until the mare finally waded from the stream. After a few slow and easy laps Allie left the water and stretched out to dry on a large rock in the sun-dappled shade of a sycamore tree. Lulled by the sounds of bees and cicadas and the hint of breeze on her bare skin, she yawned and closed her eyes.

Hal guided his horse down the steep, narrow path that led to the bank of the river and the hole where he and Allie had swum and fished ever since they were children. He thought of those carefree times when they'd pretended to be Indians. Or jungle men, like the ones they had seen in a traveling show, swinging from ropes high in the branches of a tall tree and dropping into the water. The fish they'd shared over an open fire. The secrets they had whispered.

He sighed, fearing those days were gone for good. Nowadays it seemed they couldn't get within shouting distance of each other without ending up in a fight. He didn't know what was different. He was the same as he always had been, and Allie was as contrary and bullheaded as ever. It was her, he decided. Something about her had changed.

It all started with that blamed birthday. Ever since then she had started primping, letting her hair grow and such. Now she even wore dresses.

Before she'd hated dresses.

Then she wanted to learn to waltz. Then that bit about kissing.

He had to admit he couldn't blame the kissing on Allie, since that part of it had been his notion. That bothered him. The idea that he would actually want to kiss her.

Before he'd thought of her as Al, his pard, his buddy, one of the boys.

Somehow she'd become Allie, all big eyes, warm and sweet, and curvy in places he'd never noticed before.

He let out an exasperated sigh. Hell, it *was* her fault. She had grown up and turned into a woman. A warm, desirable woman. And for that he could never forgive her.

He wasn't aware he had company until his horse nickered, then he saw Circe leaving a patch of chokecherry trees and trotting toward him.

Hal groaned and for a moment considered turning tail and running back to town. No! This was his place the same as it was hers. They were bound to run into each other sooner or later. May as well get it over with. He just wouldn't let her get within hitting distance. Glaring toward the water, he clenched his jaw and nudged his horse forward.

When he rounded the bend he pulled his mount to a sudden stop and suddenly wished he'd obeyed his first inclination. Dead ahead of him, Allie lay stretched out on her stomach on a rock, sound asleep and bare as the day she was born.

His horse pranced, wanting to go down to the water.

Hal tightened his grip on the reins. Now what the hell was he going to do? If he went any further, he'd wake her up. If he tried to go back, she'd likely waken then, too.

It wasn't like he had never seen her naked before. They always swam like that when they were kids. Even when they were older they'd only worn their underwear. He tried to look away, but her body drew his gaze like a magnet. Tanned where the sun had touched her face and arms, the rest of her was like pale cream. His eyes traced the curve of her long, slender legs, her pert little bottom, her small waist. She looked cool and comfortable, he thought resentfully.

His own mouth dry as cotton, he licked his lips. Trails of sweat ran down his back and chest.

But she wouldn't be comfortable long, because she was getting sunburned, he thought, noticing the pink tinge to her skin. Apparently the sun had shifted since she had stretched out. He was wondering how to alert her to that fact when she shifted position, then, to his shock, rolled over onto her back.

He'd seen naked females before, and most of them had been more amply endowed, but none of them could hold a candle to Allie. Her sun-streaked hair, curving softly around her face, gave her an innocent, childlike look. But the rest of her was anything but a child. He tried not to look at the small but perfect pink-crested breasts that jutted toward the sun. Or below a board-flat abdomen, the nest of curls that lay like a golden treasure at the junction of her long, shapely legs.

Imagining those hidden delights, a warmth that had nothing to do with the weather flooded him, leaving his britches uncomfortably tight. Ashamed of his body's reaction, he felt like an incestuous Peeping Tom. He wanted to turn the horse and run, but he couldn't leave her to get more sunburned.

And what if somebody else should happen along? Another man might not be content with just looking. Another man might . . . He shut his eyes to block out the image.

He edged the gelding away from the pool, to a spot further upstream, where he dismounted and left the animal to drink and graze. He pulled off his boots so he wouldn't make any noise, then he removed his shirt and quietly made his way back to where Allie lay sleeping.

Fifteen

WHEN HAL REACHED THE SPOT WHERE HE'D LAST SEEN ALLIE, the rock was empty. And so was the pool. He dropped the shirt he had intended to use to cover her and scanned the brush for her horse, but Circe no longer grazed in the patch of mesquite.

"Allie," he called after a few minutes, thinking she might be tending to personal needs, but she didn't answer. It was then he noticed that her clothes and saddle no longer lay in a pile on the ground. "Must have gone home," he muttered, disappointed but at the same time relieved. Now she would never know he had spied on her, because that was one piece of information he had no intention of revealing.

Well, since she's gone, that means I've got the swimming hole all to myself. He stripped off the rest of his clothes and plunged into the river. He cut through the water with vigorous strokes, savoring the coolness against his aching eyes and parched skin. He dove deep, then when his breath gave out, he shot back to the surface.

"Wondered if I was going to have to rescue you," a voice drawled from the shore.

Surprised, Hal turned, making the water swirl about him.

Allie stood, fully dressed, legs spread, arms crossed, watching him from the bank.

"I thought you'd gone home," he said, realizing his mistake too late.

Allie's eyes narrowed. "So you admit it."

"Admit what? I don't admit anything."

"You spied on me."

"No! I came down here to go swimming. I didn't know you'd be sprawled naked all over that rock." Watching the fury wash over her face, he wished he'd had the good sense to keep his mouth shut.

"So you did see me!"

"You knew it was me."

"I did not! I heard the horse leaving. I didn't see it—or who was riding it."

"Maybe you were hoping it was somebody else," he said, remembering the scene he'd witnessed between her and the newsman at the dance.

"What?"

"Clay Masterson, for instance."

"Why, you low-down sneaky son of a snake." She bent and just as quickly straightened.

"Allie, you put down that rock!"

"I intend to. Right on top of your head!" She drew back her arm and let fly.

Hal ducked beneath the water and saw the missile sink beside him. Her aim hadn't changed. She would have gotten him for sure. He bobbed back to the surface, only to have another stone hit his shoulder. "Oww! That hurt."

"Serves you right!"

"That's what I get for coming back to make sure you didn't get too sunburned. I should have let you fry."

"You didn't come back because I was getting sunburned. You came back for another look." She threw another stone.

"I did not," Hal grated, too mad to duck. The rock cut the air with a faint whoosh, then thunked off the side of his head. Pain exploded and he clutched his temple, then darkness engulfed him and he sank beneath the surface.

"Hal?" Horrified that she might have actually hurt him, Allie kicked off her moccasins and ran into the water. She swam to the spot where she'd last seen him and dived deep into the hole. She frantically groped the muddy depths until she found him, then wrapping her arms around his middle, she pulled him to the surface. Her lungs burning from lack of oxygen, she gulped the sultry air. She treaded water and tried to keep Hal, who was a dead weight in her arms, afloat. "Hal?" Had she killed him? No, he was still breathing. Bright beads of blood oozed from his forehead and stained the water. Terrified by the sight, she hooked an arm around his neck and swam for the shallows, then tugged him onto the shore.

She bent and cradled his head in her arms; then, her tears mixing with river water, she smothered his face with wet kisses. "Hal, I didn't mean it. I'm so sorry." No response. Why didn't he wake up? Maybe he'd swallowed too much water. She rolled him over and straddled his backside, then she pushed on his ribs. "Wake up, Hal. You've got to wake up," she cried, pushing harder.

He coughed, then spit up a stream of muddy water. "Ow!"

"Hal?" She stopped pushing and peered down at his face.

He twisted until he was on his back beneath her. His lashes wet with drops of water, he stared into her eyes.

So relieved that he seemed to be all right, she wrapped her arms around his neck and hugged him tight, then raised her head and gazed down into his face. "I didn't mean to hurt you."

"Allie, honey, I'm fine. Really." He shifted his weight. "Except for the rock under me." He reached beneath his spine and withdrew a sharp stone, then tossed it to one side.

"Your head is bleeding," she said, trying to examine the wound. "Maybe if I tie something around it—" She scanned the area, then saw the pile of clothes next to the bank. It was only then that she realized the man she strad-dled wasn't wearing a stitch. "Oh, my," she said, her color rising, not sure whether to jump off and run or remain where she was.

"What's the matter?"

"Your clothes."

"What about them?"

"You aren't wearing any."

"I don't usually go swimming in my clothes." He grinned. "But I see what you mean."

"I guess we're even."

"Even?" He rubbed his head. "Not quite. But consider-ing I don't have any intention of blacking your eyes or raising a knot on your head, we'll call it a draw."

"Does it hurt much?" She lifted a lock of sun-bleached hair out of his eyes. The spot on his head was raised like a goose egg and already turning the same purple as his eyes.

"You could kiss it again," he suggested roguishly.

Again? Allie frowned. How did he know she'd kissed him if he had been unconscious? Unless he hadn't been unconscious. "Do you think that would help?"

"Oh, I'm dang near positive," he said, his expression suspiciously innocent.

"Let's see, now how did I do that?"

He raised his hand and pointed to his face. "You kissed me here, and here, and here—and here," he said, stopping at his lips.

Allie scrambled to her feet. "I did no such thing, you faker. I did not kiss you on the mouth."

Hal raised himself on one elbow and grinned at her. "You did before. Once when we were practicing kissing. And another time in the barn. Remember?"

Remember? How could she forget?

She stared at the lean, lanky man stretched out at her feet. Hal, her chum, her pard, her childhood friend. But the feelings roiling within her were anything but friendlike. For the first time she became aware of Hal as a man. She took in the naked length of him. The muscular, hair-sprinkled chest, the narrow waist, the . . . She sucked in a breath. A very virile man.

"Even?" he said softly.

"Even," she whispered. Not daring to meet his eyes, she turned and ran for her horse.

After she was well away from the river, Allie guided Circe to a stand of elm trees; then, waiting to make sure that Hal hadn't followed, she dismounted. She pulled her still-wet shirt away from her skin. She couldn't go home. While her family would have no trouble believing she had gone swimming fully clothed, she couldn't tell them that without them sensing that something else had happened. Something she wouldn't—and couldn't—explain, because she didn't fully understand it herself. She stripped off the heavy denim pants and draped them over a tree limb to dry; then, wearing only her shirt and underwear, she sat down on a rock to think.

She'd been frightened when she'd heard the horse trotting away. With the rangeland dispute still going on between the ranchers and the farmers, and all sorts of undesirables coming in to take part in the fight, she was usually more careful. She'd actually been relieved to find out it was Hal. But the idea that he'd been ogling her for no telling how long—well, she wasn't sure how she felt about that. Her face burned remembering she'd done quite a bit of ogling on her own.

One thing she could say in Hal's favor was that he had left, but then come back to cover her because she was getting sunburned. She hugged herself and smiled, remembering how he'd blurted it out. Hal had never been able to keep a secret. But then she wasn't too good at that herself.

Why had he mentioned Clay Masterson? Heck, if she didn't know better, she'd think Hal was jealous. Now wouldn't that be something?

It was twilight when Allie rode back to the ranch. She tended to Circe and put her out to pasture, then hearing voices in the darkness, strolled toward the gazebo.

"Allie, where have you been?" her mother asked.

"Swimming."

"You missed supper," her pa said. "But I didn't eat it all, so you'll find some fried chicken and potato salad in the icebox."

"Thanks." She gazed at her parents, who sat arm in arm on a wicker bench, and wondered if she'd be half as happy when she married—if she married. She'd never given it much thought until now. "Where's Grandma?"

"She's up at the house, writing a letter to Atlas. You might want to add a line or two of your own when she's through."

"After I polish off the rest of that chicken, I might just do that." Bidding them good night, she strolled toward the house.

"I was hoping to have that chicken for a midnight snack," she overheard her pa say.

"If you eat any more snacks, you won't be able to fit into your pants," her ma teased.

"More of me to love. Give me a kiss, woman."

Allie smiled, but her stomach growled, reminding her of her own hunger, and she hurried toward the kitchen.

Hal stayed at the river until the stars twinkled brightly overhead, then he reluctantly dressed and headed back to town. He gingerly touched the sore spot on his head and was thankful she hadn't thrown harder. But remembering the tender kisses she'd planted on his face, he almost thought the discomfort worth it.

She'd sure gotten mad when he'd mentioned Clay Masterson. Maybe she didn't like Clay as much as he thought. That supposition made his heart beat faster, especially when he recalled how flustered she'd been when she'd remembered he was naked. She'd sure eyed him some, though.

She hadn't shown that much interest in his body since the time she was three and he was four and she'd discovered he had something she hadn't. After his ma had explained to the small girl that she and Hal had been born different and that she'd never be able to pee standing up, Allie had grudgingly accepted the fact.

They swam unclothed together until they had gotten big enough that he had suggested it might be better if they kept their underclothes on, in case anybody else should happen by and see them. Now that he thought back on it, he decided that even though Allie knew they were created different, she never seemed to realize that she was a girl.

He shook his head. Now she wasn't a girl, but a woman. He closed his eyes and remembered how she'd looked without a stitch. All soft and curvy and innocent sensuality. A very desirable woman. His groin tightened. Uncomfortable with the turn his thoughts were taking, he forced himself to recall how that very same curvaceous figure had knocked him cold with a rock. He touched the lump under the edge of his hat and grimaced. She might have turned into a woman, but she was still the hot-tempered, contrary Allie he'd always known.

Sixteen

WHEN THE CLOCK ON THE KITCHEN WALL CHIMED MIDNIGHT, Allie glanced up from the letter to her brother in surprise. Anytime any one of them wrote to another member of the family, the letter wasn't considered finished until everyone had added their own line or two; but unlike the others, she had added several pages. With Atlas's love for details, he would want to know everything that had been going on in his absence. Even with all that she'd told him, she knew Bub's return letter would be mostly pages and pages of questions. She read through what she had written, then because she was too tired to write any more, she signed her name and sealed the fat envelope, leaving it on the kitchen table to be mailed. Her mood pensive, she headed up the stairs.

She and Atlas had always been close, even though he was a year younger and far more bookish than she had ever been. She missed him. It seemed to her like he had been away at school forever, and she looked forward to the time when he would come home.

Walking softly to avoid waking her grandmother or her

parents, who had gone up earlier, Allie entered her room and got ready for bed. Sighing as her head touched the pillow, she thought about her own situation and wished she shared her brother's ability to get straight to the heart of the matter. As confused as she was, the more she thought about it, the more of a muddle it became.

For the first time in her life, men—not horses—occupied most of her thoughts.

Clay Masterson, sophisticated and handsome, a bachelor who attracted women in droves. She still found it amazing that such a man would bother to give her the time of day. She thought about the kiss they had shared, and while it had been pleasant, it wasn't anything to get all giddy about.

Then there was the deputy, Dudley Jones. Warm and friendly, he reminded her of an overeager pup. She felt comfortable with Dudley, and he made her laugh.

Charlie Simmons, who worked on the ranch next to them, tall and somber, but good-natured as the day was long. He was fairly new to the range, but everybody who knew him agreed that Charlie was a good man.

Then of course there was Hal Anderson. Hal, whom she'd known for most of her life, whom she now felt she didn't know at all. Tall and rawhide-lean, his quiet manner hid feelings that ran like a deep river—until you got him fighting mad. Even then that mood passed quickly. She smiled, remembering how furious he'd been with her; yet in spite of that he had attempted to save her from a painful sunburn. His kisses had ignited something deep inside her, something she didn't understand. And every time, when she'd reached the brink of discovery, he'd backed away.

Why?

Sighing, she closed her eyes. And the worst part was that Hal's kisses *did* make her go all giddy.

*   *   *

All the next week, Allie had no time to think, because it seemed that everything in the garden had ripened at once. With Persy gone, and Bo Jack out on the range cooking for the hands, it had been up to her to help her mother and grandma with the preserving of the fruits and vegetables.

It was late afternoon when Allie packed the last of the green Mason jars, then carried them into the pantry and put them away. While she appreciated the sight of the colorful vegetables in their gleaming pale green glass display, she also guiltily gave thanks they had no room for more.

Her back ached from long hours of snapping beans, scraping corn, and peeling tomatoes, not to mention the time she'd spent standing over the stove. In one corner of the kitchen the wall was lined with baskets of food they had packed for those less fortunate, and with the drought conditions so critical, she knew there would be more takers this year than ever before.

She poured herself a glass of lemonade and went to join her mother and grandmother, who had retired to the shade of the porch. "I thought it would be cooler out here."

"It is, but not much, I'm afraid," her ma said, handing Allie a fan.

"There will be heat lightning again tonight," Minerva said, glancing at the clouds in the sky.

"Lightning and no rain, a rancher's worst nightmare," murmured her mother. "How long do you think this will last?"

Minerva shook her head. "Only the good Lord knows that. I just hope he sees fit to send us some rain before the whole state of Texas either burns up or blows away." She raised her hand to shield her eyes from the ever-blowing dust. "Odie's home."

Allie saw her pa leave the wagon in the care of one of the hands at the barn, then knocking the dirt from his hat against the leg of his jeans, he strode toward them.

"Did you find C. J. some water?" her ma asked, rising from the chair to greet him.

"Had to dig plumb to China." He took a bandanna from his pocket and wiped his sweat-stained brow. "But we finally hit a good-sized trickle. Only hope it lasts until we get some rain."

"Have a seat and I'll fetch you some lemonade." Jane patted his shoulder, then disappeared into the house.

Pulling her perspiration-soaked dress away from her skin, Allie thought about the mustangs she and Hal had trapped in the canyon and wondered if they still had water, or if that spring had gone dry, too. After all their hard work, it would be a shame if the drought forced Hal to turn the horses loose before he had them ready to sell. She knew from the marking string they kept by the ranch well that the water level dropped every day.

Thinking of the mustangs made her wonder how Hal was faring without her. She hadn't seen him since the day they'd met at the swimming hole. She'd been too busy to go to the canyon and he hadn't come by the ranch, though they'd had plenty of other callers, both known and unknown. In fact, there had been so many unsavory-looking strangers around lately, for the first time in her life her pa had cautioned her about being out on the range alone.

She pressed the surface of the moisture-drenched glass of lemonade against her forehead, and wished she had enough of the icy drops to take a bath. She squinted against another blast of wind-swirled dirt and longed for the cool green lawn that had once covered the area in front of the house, an area where now only a few patches of sun-dried grass remained. If the weather didn't break soon, she thought, the range war would end, because there wouldn't be anything left to fight over.

Since the Daltrys farmed and raised cattle they could see the situation from both sides. But other ranchers, desperately fighting for their survival, had demanded that her pa quit straddling the fence. When he had remained neutral, mysterious fires had been set to the tinder-dry fields, demolishing some of their best cotton crop.

The farmers, angry because Odie wouldn't side with them, had blamed him and the other ranchers for some of their misfortunes, such as cattle straying into their cornfields and holes shot in their water tanks.

She hoped she'd never see the day when neighbor fought against neighbor, but in these days of unending heat and flaring tempers, she had the feeling the worst was yet to come.

"How about it, Allie?" Odie said, touching her arm.

Allie looked up in surprise. "What, Pa?"

"I said that you ladies look plumb wilted. I think it would be grand if we packed a picnic supper and took it to the river. We could all save well water by going swimming, we could fill barrels so that your ma could give her posies a drink, and after that we could eat."

"Best idea I've heard all day," her grandma said, smiling.

"It does sound good," Allie agreed.

"Now if I can only remember where I packed those bathing costumes," her mother said, frowning.

"Shoot, wear your bloomers. I won't peek." Her pa grinned.

Not like somebody else I know, Allie thought. She blushed, remembering when Hal had caught her without a stitch.

The supper basket was packed and they were getting

into the wagon when a man on horseback trotted into the yard—Clay Masterson.

"Hello, folks. Hello, Allie," he said, removing his black-crowned hat. Immaculately dressed, as usual, the only sign he bore of the sweltering heat was a faint band of perspiration on his forehead.

"Hello, Clay." Embarrassed to be caught in her sweat-stained dress and her hair every which way, Allie found it difficult to pretend she was glad to see him. But Clay didn't seem to mind. He apologized for arriving without any notice and said since they were ready for an outing he would postpone his visit till another day. He asked if Friday would be convenient.

"Nonsense," her pa said, shaking his head. "We've got plenty of fixings. Come along and swim with us, then we'll have some vittles."

"Odie," her ma whispered, tugging on his arm. "We have no bathing costumes."

"Oh, shucks. Forgot about that." He gave Clay an apologetic grin. "My ladies are afraid you might see them in the altogether, so I guess Friday will have to do."

"Odie! For heaven's sake," her ma said, blushing crimson.

"Friday will be fine. I'll be looking forward to it." He tilted his hat. "Good evening, Allie. Ladies."

Placing his hat back on his head, Clay turned his horse and rode away. The smile he had pasted on his face disappeared. A scowl took its place. What with one thing and another happening in town, he hadn't been able to get away until today.

Last week, he had arrived at the Circle D to find that damned deputy, Dudley Jones, seated on the veranda. When Allie had left them alone long enough to go into the house after some liquid refreshments, Clay told the lawman in no uncertain terms that his presence wasn't wanted, but the lovesick fool refused to leave. Not that Dudley could give him any competition, but the man had been a nuisance. He'd been forced to sit there the whole evening and grit his teeth and watch the inept deputy's attempt at courting. He'd tried to outstay Dudley, but when the rest of the household retired for the night and Odie appeared on the front porch, he'd decided his best course of action was to bid Allie a discreet good night. The lawman left, too, but then the oaf had the audacity to accompany him back to town.

Clay kicked the horse into a trot. He had to do something, and soon. His only chance was to get Allie to commit to him before he went bankrupt. After they were married, he didn't care what happened to the paper. It could blow away with the rest of the state as far as he was concerned. He'd always hated the smell and mess of ink and newsprint.

As for Allie? He shuddered, contemplating life with such an unsophisticated hick. He remembered the kiss he'd given her and laughed. Did she do it right? she'd asked. He thought he would choke. On the other hand, Allie would probably be entertaining in bed, as she seemed to have no inhibitions.

And when he tired of her? He knew women found him attractive, and the fact that he was married wouldn't make any difference to most of them. And he wouldn't have to worry about them pressing him for a commitment. He'd have to be discreet, of course. He wouldn't want to do anything to upset her family. Minerva Daltry was a tough old bird. She wouldn't stand for any shenanigans on his part, especially where her granddaughter was concerned. Yes, he would play it close to the vest, court the girl as well as her mother and grandmother.

With the Daltry name and money backing him, an educated man like himself could run for the legislature. After that, who knew how far he could go? He smiled. Governor Clay Masterson had a nice ring to it. He'd make it happen.

The key to everything was Allie.

Not caring that his horse was already lathered from the heat, he kicked the animal into a gallop.

Allie lay on the moonlit riverbank and stared at the star-studded sky. In the distance, heat lightning danced across the purple horizon, and the soft rumble of thunder seemed ominous in its promise of the storm to come. Night air, thick and heavy, wrapped around her, making it hard to breathe. For once, even the insects were silent, as if their song took too much effort, but an occasional frog croaked on the edge of the slow-moving water.

Beside Allie, her pa was finishing up the leftover chicken. He wiped his hands on a cloth. "Well, girls. Time for one more dip, then we'd better head for home."

"Minerva's asleep already," Jane whispered. "But I would love to get wet again."

"Allie?"

"I think I'll just lie here. I'm still waterlogged from the last time."

"Care to try it without clothes?" her pa suggested to her mother in a whisper.

"Why not?" her mother said somewhat breathlessly. Giggling like naughty children, they disappeared into the shadows.

Allie smiled, glad that no one had intruded to spoil her parents' special time. She thought about the last time she'd been here with Hal and wondered what would have happened if they had been alone in the moonlight. Would they have swum naked? Would they have kissed? The idea sent a fluttering sensation through her middle. She closed her eyes and envisioned Hal's smooth, hard flesh, still wet, a smile on his face, the devil dancing in his green eyes. She imagined him lying down beside her, his arms drawing her close, his warm breath upon her face as his lips molded to hers. She sucked in a ragged breath.

"Allie, you all right?" her grandmother asked.

"Uh, yes," Allie said quickly, jolted back to the present. "Why?" she asked, hoping she hadn't said anything out loud.

"You were breathing funny. I thought the heat might be affecting you."

"I'm fine, Grandma," she said, glad the moonlight couldn't reveal the flush she felt on her cheeks. The heat affecting her had nothing to do with the weather.

Laughter made her glance toward a stand of willows, and she saw her parents emerging from the darkness. Now fully clothed, they walked hand in hand.

"Last chance for a dip, you two," her pa called out.

"Can't pass that up, can we, Allie?" Minerva said, scrambling to her feet.

Yawning, Allie rose and stretched her arms over her head. "Race you to the water, Grandma," she cried, giving the older woman a good head start. Allowing Minerva to enter the river a second before she did, Allie made up for lost time by swimming to the opposite shore and back.

Minerva dove and floated, the motions reminding Allie of a plump, playful otter. Content to drift in the water, they remained silent, floated, then finally waded onto the shore.

"Wish I could ride home in my bloomers," Minerva grumbled as they approached the others. "Sure a sight cooler than that dress."

"Nobody around to see. Odie could stop and let you get dressed when we get near the house," Jane said.

"Sounds like a good deal to me. How about you, granddaughter?" Tilting her head, she gave Allie a hopeful look.

"Sounds good to me, too," Allie said, chuckling.

Minerva gathered up her clothes and shoes, then Odie helped her into the wagon. Dripping wet, her gray hair straggling about her face, her sun-weathered face split in a wide grin.

No matter how old Minerva got, her grandma never ceased to amaze her. While a lot of townsfolk labeled her eccentric, Allie thought she was wonderful. She only hoped she could pass that same sense of adventure on to her own grandchildren someday.

Grandchildren? Allie grew thoughtful. If she ever did have grandchildren, she hoped they'd be boys, then she could teach them how to ride, and rope. She frowned, wondering how their grandpa would feel about that.

Grandpa? Grandchildren meant children, and that meant getting married. Until recently, *that* was something she'd never considered.

"Allie, Clay's here," her ma called out from the porch, where she sat doing her mending.

"I see him." Allie quickly wiped the last of the dishes and put them into the cupboard; then, determined not to let him catch her looking like a mess again, she removed her apron and hung it on a peg. Earlier, she'd experimented with her hair, arranging the back in a cluster of curls, leaving several wispy coils free to curl about her face. Her blue dress, although simple of style, showed a hint of bosom and was heavy enough that she hadn't needed to bother with either corset or petticoats. On the way to the door, she stopped to gaze into the mirror and wondered if Hal would like her new appearance.

"Hello, Mrs. Daltry," Clay said, pausing on the front

porch. "Your flowers are lovely." He motioned to the boxes of blooms that lined the edge of the porch.

"Thank you, Clay. I'm afraid some folks think they are frivolous, what with the drought and all. I couldn't plant my usual display this year, but these brighten the place up a bit. How are things in town?"

"The same as usual," Clay said with a laugh. "Everyone grumbling about the weather. A few more wagons leaving than usual. Folks heading for greener pastures."

"I can't help but feel sorry for them. It must be hard to abandon everything you've worked so hard for and move on to start from scratch again."

"At least they have the sense to do it, not like some who stay on until they have nothing left," Clay said, wondering impatiently where Allie was. He'd seen Charlie Simmons in town, all duded up and headed for the mercantile. Clay assumed Charlie would soon be on his way out here. He glanced back at the road, hoping he wouldn't see any telltale dust.

"Hello, Clay."

"Allie, my dear. You look pretty as a picture." He held out the somewhat melted box of chocolates. "These are for you."

"Why, thank you," she said with a shy smile. "I'll get them on ice." She took the box and went back into the house.

Determined not to get stuck at the ranch all evening, Clay followed her inside. "Since it's a bit cooler out, I brought the buggy. I thought it would be nice to take a drive."

"What a wonderful idea," she said, her gray eyes sparkling in her heart-shaped face. The simple blue frock, while revealing an enticing swell of breasts, made her seem childlike and demure. The idea pleased him. It would make everything that much easier.

"Are you ready?" he asked, trying to hurry her without appearing to be pushy. When she nodded, he bid her mother good-bye and escorted Allie to the small, two-wheeled carriage and helped her inside. As he joined her on the seat, his keen gaze picked out a speck of dust on the horizon—the lovesick cowboy, no doubt. Flashing Allie a brilliant smile, he wheeled the rig at a spanking trot and headed in the opposite direction. When they were a good distance from the house, he turned onto a little-used trail and slowed the horse to a walk.

Bunches of knee-high gama grass crackled in the hot wind and the hum of insects filled the air. Spotting movement, he stopped the buggy and pointed out a doe and two fawns who were browsing at the edge of a grove of trees.

"Aren't they lovely? Oh, I'm afraid they've seen us," she said as they bounded away.

Clay guided the horse to a tree-covered knoll and pulled it to a stop. "I thought we might enjoy some refreshments while we watch the sunset."

"Refreshments?"

Clay smiled. "It's a surprise."

"I love surprises."

He helped her to the ground, then he picked up a blanket-topped basket from the back of the buggy and led the way to a grove of oak trees. He spread the quilt on the dry grass, then turned to Allie. "Would you like to walk or would you like to taste the surprise?"

"What is it?" she said, sinking to her knees on the blanket.

Clay removed a pristine white cloth and spread it beside her, then he withdrew two crystal glasses. "Champagne." He watched her face as he reached into an ice-filled keg and took out a frosty dark bottle.

"I've never had champagne," she admitted. "But I *am* awfully thirsty."

Then it shouldn't take much. "You'll love it," he assured her. He uncorked the bottle and poured the effervescent liquid into her glass. "Take a sip."

Allie did as he directed, then her eyes filled with delight. "Why, it tickles. And look, it's full of little bubbles."

"Do you like it?"

"It's very good—and so cold." She took another swallow.

"Slowly, my dear," he said, refilling hers and sipping from his own glass. While he wanted her to be inebriated enough to be agreeable, he certainly didn't want her to get drunk and pass out. "Let's take our glasses over to that rock. We can see the sun go down from there." He helped her to her feet, then took her hand. When they reached the large, flat, tree-shaded boulder, he lifted her up, took a seat beside her, then slid an arm around her waist.

She gave him an alarmed look, then moved a short distance away.

Slowly, damn it, he told himself. Allie wasn't like most of the women who fell into his arms, eager for a romantic encounter. She was inexperienced, gauche, but with the proper training she would make an acceptable—and rich —wife. He sipped his wine, and when she finished hers, a slow smile crept across his face.

The sun sank lower, enveloping the sky in luminous shades of purple, orange, and crimson. The swollen ball of fire hovered, caressing the thrusting peaks, then it shifted position, its golden shafts penetrating ever deeper into the heated hills. Like an ardent lover, it traced each mound, each crevice, then it impatiently ended the game of seduction. With one last possessive thrust, it saturated the valleys and filled them with quivering lavender shadows.

Finally sated, the sun withdrew the last of its clinging fingers and shuddered to rest behind the horizon.

"Oh, my," Allie said with a sigh; then with wide eyes, she smiled at him.

"I thought you might like that," Clay said, his own body throbbing. "May I get you some more?" He motioned to the glass.

"Yes, please."

Clay strolled back to the blanket and took his time about refilling their glasses. Twilight blanketed the land, giving it a hazy, almost ethereal, appearance. With the sun gone the air became cooler. Although darkness had not yet arrived, the first stars popped into sight. And a glow in the east told him a full moon would soon be rising. He carried the glasses back and handed one to Allie. "You are very lovely this evening, Allie, dear." He saw her duck her head, and a slow flush spread over her cheeks. " 'She walks in beauty, like the night . . .' " he began softly.

She raised her lashes and gave him an inquisitive look. "What?"

"Lord Byron. It's a poem. I think it describes you very well," he said smoothly. "Hasn't anybody ever quoted poetry to you before?"

"Not that I can remember." She took a drink from her glass. "I like this stuff, but it makes me a little dizzy."

"That's because you aren't used to it. Most people around here aren't familiar with it, but champagne is the accepted beverage in the more elite circles of society. That's where you belong, my sweet."

"Oh?" She took another sip, then set the glass on the rock. "My, I feel light-headed enough to float away."

"Then I had better hold on to keep you here." He stepped close and put his hands on her shoulders. "You belong where people could appreciate your intelligence, your beauty."

Her eyes wide and innocent, she gave him a dreamy smile.

This was going to be almost too easy, he thought. His eyes locked on hers, then he bent his head and claimed her mouth in a deceptively light but deliberately sensual kiss. When he released her she sighed and swayed toward him. He sat down beside her and pulled her into his arms. He breathed passionate words into her ear as he nuzzled her neck and lips. While she didn't object to his advances, he noted she also didn't seem overcome with desire.

Maybe a little more wine might help. He didn't want this to take all night. "Better finish your drink, my sweet." He lifted the glass she had placed on the boulder and held it to her lips. After she obediently swallowed the last of the liquid, he set her glass aside. "After all, this is a celebration."

"A celebration?"

"My friends in Austin have nominated me as a candidate in the coming election. And while I would like nothing better than to be a legislator, I find I also have strong ties to Paradise Plains."

"I can see how hard it would be to leave your paper."

He cupped her face between his hands and gazed into her eyes. "I wasn't referring to the newspaper. I was talking about you. My darling, I wanted to wait until we knew one another better, but I'm a man of little patience. Allie, when I leave for Austin, I want you by my side." He kissed one eyelid, then the other. "I think of you every moment. At night you haunt my dreams." He breathed soft kisses on her temples. "And I long to wake up beside you in the morning," he said softly. "For a lifetime." He captured her mouth, nibbling, teasing, then dipped lower to seductively nuzzle her throat and neck. He drew her against the hard ridge in his trousers. When she shifted away, he smiled and breathed light kisses upon her lips until she

relaxed in his arms. He covered her again, pressing her
back against the rock. "I want to make love to you, sweet
Allie." He slowly slid his hand up to massage her breast.
Feeling her tremble, he kissed her again, long and deep,
until she let out a quivering sigh. "Here. Now." He drew
back and stared into her dazed eyes. "Do you know what I
am saying?"

"Yes—no—I don't know. I'm so dizzy," she whispered,
raising a fluttering hand.

Capturing it, Clay smiled and brought it to his lips, biting and then suckling each small fingertip. She giggled,
but didn't pull away. He slowly trailed his other hand
down her skirt, then he began to gather the material into
his palm. His fingers had just touched the bare flesh of her
thigh when a noise made him glance up.

"I thought I'd never find y'all."

Cursing, Clay shifted, surreptitiously lowering the hem
of Allie's dress back into place.

Eyes narrowed, Hal Anderson watched for a moment,
then he dismounted and strode toward them.

"We don't want your company," Clay snapped, "so you
can turn around and leave."

"Now that ain't exactly sociable. Hello, Allie," Hal said
quietly, removing his hat. If the girl had been anybody
else but Allie Daltry, he might have taken the newsman's
suggestion. But he had no intention of leaving Allie to the
mercy of a snake like Clay Masterson. "Ridin' out here I
worked up a powerful thirst. Don't reckon y'all got any
more of that stuff anywhere," he said, eyeing the glasses.

"In the basket," Clay said, his tone sharp and un-
friendly. "Take a drink and go!"

Hal walked to the blanket and pulled the bottle out of
the ice-filled bucket. He pulled the cork with his teeth and
took a long swig, then he raised his eyebrows in appreciation. Expensive. He started to replace the bottle, then

shook his head. By the look of her, Allie had drunk more
than enough. And Masterson could die of thirst for all he
cared. He tipped the dark bottle again, letting the smooth
liquid flow down his parched throat.

When he caught Clay's eye, the man gestured for him
to get on his horse and leave. Hal pretended he didn't
understand. From the little he'd seen, Hal knew the oily
newsman was up to no good, and he had no intention of
leaving Allie alone with him. And while Hal wanted to
yank her up and pack her back home where she belonged,
he couldn't very well do that, either. But he could put a
crimp in Clay's evening.

The bottle still clutched in one hand, he ambled toward
the rock.

Masterson slid a possessive arm around the girl's waist.

"Uh-oh. I'm not feeling so good," she murmured. Suddenly, she pulled free of the man's grip, clamped her hand
over her mouth, and darted behind a tree.

"Hell!" Masterson let out an exasperated sigh and
shook his head.

"Here, honey." Striding forward, Hal dampened his
neckerchief with the champagne, then handed the cloth to
Allie. "You'll feel better now that you've got that stuff out
of your stomach."

He left her and stalked toward Clay. "You shouldn't
have given her spirits. Her daddy wouldn't like it. *I* don't
like it."

"For your information, I can handle Odie. Besides, Allie is a grown woman. What she does is none of your
business," the newsman said, his eyes like shards of black
glass. Clay walked toward the white-faced girl and put an
arm around her. "Isn't that right, darling?" he said, giving
Hal a daunting sneer.

Darling? Suspicious, Hal glanced from Clay to the girl
and saw her weave unsteadily on her feet. *Good thing I got*

here when I did. Hell, in her present condition, she might have agreed to anything.

Allie frowned and murmured something Hal couldn't quite catch. "Would you like to go home now, Allie?" he asked, his jaw clenched in determination.

Allie glanced up and nodded.

Determined not to leave her alone with the newsman, Hal took her other arm. "I'll just stay here with you while Mr. Masterson gathers up his things, then we can all ride back to the ranch together."

His figure tense with rage, Clay grabbed the empty glasses, apparently not caring when the slender stems snapped in his hand. Hal watched him shove the pieces and the cloth into the basket, then he wrapped the whole mess into the blanket and tossed it into the back of the buggy.

"I feel so awful," Allie said, laying her head against Hal's shoulder.

"Darlin', I expect you do." He put his arm around her waist to support her. A cold rage washed over him as he thought of the raw deal she'd been given. Knowing Masterson was watching, he deliberately raised the expensive champagne and finished the bottle.

His face set in anger, Clay hurried toward them. "I'll take over now."

"I don't think so," Hal said, not about to relinquish his claim. Before Clay could intervene, he lifted Allie into his arms and strode toward the buggy. He sat her on the seat, then climbed in beside her. "Since I'm a mite dizzy myself, I'll just ride up here beside you," he said, ignoring the furious look Clay shot at him.

"What about your horse?" Clay challenged.

Hal put two fingers between his teeth and whistled. The buckskin trotted forward. "He'll follow."

"The seat isn't big enough."

"I think we fit just fine." He looped one arm over the back of the seat, encasing Allie's slender shoulders in his sheltering fold.

Clay shot him a furious look, then despite the roughness of the road, he urged the horse into a trot.

On the ride back, Hal talked about one thing and another, more to irritate Clay than any desire he might have had to carry on a conversation.

Allie dozed, her head on his shoulder, until Clay pulled the buggy up in front of the hitching rail at the Daltry house.

"Allie, honey, you're home," Hal said, shaking her shoulder.

She blinked sleep-laden eyes and gazed up at him.

"I'll help you to the door." His face daring Hal to interfere, Clay took her arm and assisted her from the buggy, then escorted her to the door. There, he brushed a kiss against her lips. "You've made me a very happy man, Allie. You'll make a beautiful bride." Ignoring her somewhat bewildered look, he smiled. "I have to go to Austin for a week on business. We'll talk about when to have the wedding as soon as I get back." He kissed her again, then opened the door and waited until she was inside.

He stalked toward the buggy, but the cowboy was nowhere in sight. Figures. Clay unwrapped the reins and pointed the horse toward town. It wasn't the plan he'd had in mind, but it might be better this way. She hadn't actually said yes, but the nosy cowboy didn't know that.

He laughed, the sound triumphant on the prairie wind. Whether Allie Daltry knew it or not, she was about to become his wife.

Seventeen

A BRILLIANT SHAFT OF SUNLIGHT PENETRATED THE GLOOM. ALLIE stirred and opened her eyes. Nothing focused. She knew by the familiar feel of the bed that she was in her own room, but for the life of her she couldn't remember how she got there. She tried to sit up and immediately wished she hadn't, as the movement sent a viciously stabbing pain though the center of her head. Lifting one arm to block the glare, she groaned and collapsed back against her pillow. Even the effort of breathing made her head clang like the cookhouse triangle at high noon.

She must be sick, she decided. Or maybe she'd been injured. She gingerly probed her throbbing head. No bandage. No bumps. When something tickled her cheek, she squinted and found it was the lace on her dress sleeve. What was she doing with all her clothes on? Surely she didn't wear them to bed.

She tried to think, but the pain was too excruciating, so she squinted up at the ceiling instead. The room tilted and the bed began to whirl. She reached out and frantically grasped the edges of the mattress to keep from falling off.

She couldn't get up. Couldn't move. Couldn't do anything but lie there.

The knock on her door sounded like a bullet richocheting inside her brain. "Go 'way," she groaned.

The door opened a crack and Hal stuck his head inside. "I saw your ma and grandma headed for town. Bo Jack said you didn't come down for breakfast, so I thought I'd better check and see how you were feelin'."

Allie moaned and peered at him through bloodshot eyes. "I think I'm dyin'."

"Humph! I don't wonder."

"Whadya mean by that?" she whispered, her voice thick, the words slurred.

"How much did you drink last night?"

"You know I don't drink," she said through gritted teeth.

He walked to the window and pulled back the curtains.

"Aww!" She grabbed her head and pressed her palms against her eyes.

"For somebody who doesn't drink, you shore got one hell of a hangover," he said dryly.

With the impact of a mule's kick the events of the night before came rushing back. She and Clay had gone for a ride. It had been hot and she'd been thirsty. "Champagne!"

"So you do remember." Hal shook his head, then he ambled to the window and pulled the curtains shut. "That better?"

Allie let out a sigh of relief.

"We'd better get you into shape before your ma gets home. Can you sit up?"

Unable to shake her head, she rolled it from side to side.

"That's what I figured," he said with a chuckle. "I'll fetch some coffee while you reflect on how you got into such pitiful condition." When he strode out of the room, she thought the noise of his boot heels on the wooden floor sounded like a herd of stampeding cattle.

Champagne. How much of the bubbly stuff did she drink? A glass? Two? Three, four? More? She did recall being awfully thirsty. Who'd think anything that tasted so good could feel so terrible the morning after?

Whistling merrily, Hal arrived with a breakfast tray and a bucket that he carried by the bail.

"Qui–et!" she breathed softly, glaring at him.

"Did you remember?" he asked. His one eye fixing her with a penetrating look, he placed the coffee on a table beside her bed. He set the bucket on the floor.

"Some of it."

"Let's sit ya up, then you can tell me about it." Before she could protest, he slid an arm behind her, jerked her upright in the bed, and shoved the pillows behind her back.

"Ohhh!" Allie quivered from head to foot.

He shoved a cup of steaming coffee into her trembling hands.

She took one whiff, gasped, then turned away. "Sick."

"Thought so." He shoved the bucket under her chin. When she had finished, he brought a wet cloth and wiped her face. "Feel better?"

Feel better? She stared at him. She'd never felt worse in her life.

He reached into his hip pocket and took out an amber flask. "Take a swallow," he ordered.

"No!" She tried to shove his hand away. "You're loco. I'm dying from champagne, and you want me to drink whiskey?"

He pressed the container against her mouth with one large hand, the other held her nose. When she opened her mouth to breathe, he sloshed a measure inside. "Swallow," he growled.

She gasped and choked, but since she had no other choice, she swallowed. Her mouth, throat, and stomach felt like she'd just downed a hot branding iron.

"One more."

When he started to hold her nose again, she yanked the flask from his hand. Her eyes filling with tears, she gave him an accusing look and took a long swig. "Now. Satisfied?"

"You'll feel better in a minute," he said.

Surprisingly enough, she did. The room had settled to a gentle sway, the noise in her head to a dull roar. She even managed a feeble smile. "I think I can handle some of that coffee now."

"Okay." He handed her the cup he'd poured. Bo Jack's coffee tasted like it had been boiled for hours in a pot with ground acorns, chicory, and pecan hulls. Black as the devil's heart and bitter as gall, the cook boasted that it would put hair on your chest, as well as cure you of whatever ailed you.

Taking a sip, Allie hoped the latter part of his claim was right. After she'd drained the cup, Hal refilled it again. She gave him a lopsided grin. "Thanks, pard."

"You ready to tell me about it?" he said soberly.

"Nothing much to tell. Clay and I went for a ride. It was hot, and I was thirsty. He had some champagne and I drank it."

"You do anything else you shouldn't have?"

"Jehoshaphat!" Allie said indignantly. Then remembering the condition she'd been in, she lowered her voice. "Not that I know of." In the vague recesses of her mind, it seemed that something else had happened, something of momentous importance. But for the life of her she couldn't recollect what it was. She did recall getting sick and someone handing her a handkerchief. Hal. She lifted her head and met his green eyes. "You were there, weren't you?" she said, vaguely recalling the cowboy's appearance.

His face softened. "You remember that?"

"Yes," she said. She didn't tell him she'd been so fuzzy-headed at the time, she couldn't swear to anything. Reluctant to answer any more questions, she sipped her coffee.

"Feel up to having some breakfast?"

"Not just yet." The idea of greasy bacon and eggs made her stomach uneasy. "But I shore would like a bath."

"Bo Jack's got the water boiling. I'll tell him you're ready." He poured her one last cup of the bitter coffee, then picked up the tray.

"Hal."

"Yeah?"

"Thank you."

"That's what pards are for." He winked and picked up the bucket, then he left the room. A few minutes later, she heard his horse gallop away.

Allie eased over the side of the bed, took a few tottering steps, then leaned against the dresser to steady herself. Shocked, she stared into the mirror. "Jehoshaphat, if you ain't a sight!"

Her hair, matted and tangled, bore traces of grass and dried leaves. Her bloodshot eyes were ringed with dark shadows. The freckles not usually noticeable in her tanned complexion now stood out like small islands on skin a sickly yellow-green. Her pretty muslin dress had ugly stains down the front and a large rip near the ground where she'd apparently stepped on the hem. In all her born days she'd never seen anything that looked quite as bad as she did at that moment. No wonder Hal asked if anything had happened. She couldn't blame him for thinking the worst. Humiliation and shame flooded her.

And Clay—being so sophisticated and all—what had he thought about her? She didn't know, but she could imagine his reaction. How could she ever face him again?

She struggled to recall the events of the night before. She vaguely remembered being held in Clay's arms and that he'd kissed her. Had she kissed him back? she wondered.

Probably.

And if she had, remembering the way she had responded to Hal that day in the barn, what else might she have done?

That was a sobering thought. She wished she could recall just when Hal happened onto the scene and what was taking place between her and Clay at the time. Had Hal caught them kissing? She plucked a dried piece of grass from her hair. Or worse? Surely he would have said something. Or would he? He did keep asking her what she remembered.

She rubbed her throbbing temples. Outside of a gawdawful headache, she didn't feel any different. But how could she be sure? She didn't know how a woman was supposed to feel after something like that, and she sure couldn't ask her ma.

Even if she hadn't done anything she shouldn't, she had kissed Clay and she had gotten drunk. Hal wasn't inclined to gossip, but she wasn't so sure about the newspaperman. For all she knew, her disgrace could be common knowledge all over the county. She could just imagine what her pa would say. And her grandma. She had been taught from childhood that drinking was a sin, and she knew very well what the Good Book said about the wages of sin. . . . She closed her eyes.

Now that she was certain she would survive, and realizing the scandal that threatened to come down on her head, death seemed almost preferable.

Eighteen

BORED OF HER SELF-IMPOSED CONFINEMENT, ALLIE ROSE FROM her bed and hurriedly dressed. Then, after packing a hefty lunch, she headed for the corral and saddled her horse.

It had been three days since the buggy ride with Clay Masterson, and in that interim she had neither seen nor heard from the newsman. Not that she blamed him. He had probably been so disgusted he'd dumped her on her doorstep and run.

Thanks to Hal's and Bo Jack's intervention, her folks hadn't found out about her outrageous condition. And if anybody else had heard anything about the outing, they hadn't said anything to her or her family.

After waving good-bye to her mother, who carried the bucket she'd filled from the barrels to water her precious flowers, Allie nudged Circe into a trot. Anxious to see Hal, she pointed the mare toward the canyon where the mustangs were being held.

Orange, yellow, and gold streaked the eastern horizon, while to the west an almost imperceptible moon hovered low in the western sky. She inhaled the early morning coolness, dreading the heat that would bake the land later in the day.

A white-tailed deer leaped from beside a clump of mesquite where it had been sleeping and bounded away on springlike legs. Numerous rabbits scurried here and there, pausing to browse on sagebrush and whatever other vegetation they could find.

Ordinarily at this time of year grass, thick and waving, would nudge the mare's belly. Now what little there was of it crunched under Circe's hooves. All the creatures she'd spotted seemed thinner than usual. Apparently cattle and sheep weren't the only critters suffering because of the drought.

She gazed at the cloudless sky and wondered just how long the dry spell would last. At supper last night after her pa had ridden back from Paradise Plains, he'd told of passing several farmers with barrel-laden wagons, all headed toward the river. Many ranchers he knew had been forced to cut their herds severely and had driven the cattle to Abilene only to find the pens there already full of animals waiting to be shipped to eastern markets. Those lucky enough to sell their herds received a few dollars a head. The unlucky ones had abandoned their cows rather than go to the trouble of driving them back to die of thirst on their home range. Bad times that would only get worse before it was over, he'd said. And she had no doubt it was true.

Allie thought about Hal and his pa, whose ranch had been marginal even in the best of times. Only the section that his grandpa had willed to Hal had any water, and that ran for a short distance along the west bank of the river.

She'd felt remorse after drinking a few glasses of champagne. She wondered how Hal's father could live with the guilt of knowing his own father had fought Indians, Mexicans, and comancheros to keep land that he, in a moment of weakness, had gambled away in a game of chance.

She gave thanks that her own father, while he did take a glass or two at social functions, had neither the inclination nor the desire to get drunk or gamble at cards.

When she reached the red-walled canyon, Allie entered the enclosure, then tied the gate shut behind her; then, to keep her food sack cool and safe from any hungry animals, she removed it from her pommel and tied it to the limb of a shade tree. She found the breaking corral empty. There was no sign of either Hal or the mustangs. Filled with disappointment, she rode deep into the canyon to investigate the state of the spring.

It was there, ringed by a circle of curious horses, that she found Hal.

Shovel in hand, hip deep in muck, he glanced up. "Howdy, pard."

"Hi, yourself, cowboy. You going in for mud baths these days?" she teased.

"I'm thankful there is mud. Maybe if I get this overflow basin cleaned out, these cayuses will have something to drink."

"Could you use some help?" she asked, swinging to the ground.

"I'd never turn down an extra pair of hands." His handsome, mud-splattered face crinkled into a smile. "You could dump these buckets over there out of the way, while I fill the others."

After turning Circe loose to graze, Allie strode forward and lifted the wire handle. The blamed bucket wouldn't move. She tried again, then straightened and looked at Hal. "I've got a better idea. *You* dump the buckets and *I'll* fill them."

"You'll get dirty."

"It won't be the first time," she pointed out as she

pulled off her boots. "Besides, Venus told me that mud baths are all the rage in Europe. Supposed to do wondas foah yuah complexshun," she drawled, imitating her sister's voice.

Hal chuckled and hoisted himself out of the hole, then stood beside her. The only places not coated with mud were his eyeballs and a spot on top of his head that had been covered by his hat. "If what your sister says is true, we both ought to be plumb beautiful by this evening."

Unable to imagine either of them beautiful, Allie grinned.

Hours later, his arms and back aching, his body layered with dried mud, Hal took Allie's hand and pulled her out of the hole. He ran a fingertip down her forehead, her nose, and stopped on her chin.

"Did it work?" she asked, her gray eyes dancing. "Am I beautiful yet?"

"Can't tell," he answered, eyeing her thoughtfully. "You're too much of a mess."

She brushed a hand down her arm, removing a layer of slime which she slung toward him. "You're not too clean yourself," she said, laughing.

"Why you little—" He lunged for her. Losing his footing in the slick mud, he skidded straight into the muddy water hole.

"Decided to take a bath?" she teased, bending over him.

"At least now it's more water than mud. Help me out?" He held out his arm. When she took his hand, he leaned backward, pulling her in on top of him. "Decided to join me, I see."

"Hal Anderson, that was a dirty trick!"

"Dirty is right." He lifted a strand of her mud-caked hair. "Hold still and I'll see if I can clean you up a bit."

He scooped up a double handful of water and dumped it on her head. Ignoring her spluttering protest, he rubbed it around, then pushed her under. "That's better," he said when she popped up. "Now for your clothes."

He vigorously massaged her arms between his hands, then while she squirmed and giggled, he did the same with her back. He tossed a scoop against her neck, then followed it with another. Intent on what he was doing, he ran his hands down her front.

When she gasped, he glanced up—right into her startled gray eyes. It was then he realized his hands were on her breasts. Her nipples, hard and swollen, thrust against his palm. His own body hardened in immediate response.

The water-soaked shirt molded to her slender figure like a second skin, defining every rise and curve. He stared, his vision flooding with the memory of how she'd looked that time at the river when she'd worn nothing at all. Every fiber of his being quivering with awareness, he strove to extinguish the fire that threatened his senses. This is Allie, not some dance hall whore, his conscience shouted. Fighting his desire, he yanked his hands away; then, in an attempt to hide his rampaging emotions, he quickly began to scrub his own body.

Her face crimson, Allie did the same.

"I guess things are hard."

"What?" He jerked his head up. With the waist-deep water, she couldn't know his condition. Could she?

"Living in town and all," she said softly. "I know you must hate it."

"Oh," he said, letting out a sigh of relief. Meeting her gaze, he wondered if what Venus had said was true. Even with her hair plastered to her head, and muddy trails streaking her face, Allie's eyes gleamed like quicksilver. She was beautiful. The troubled but sweet smile she gave him sent his heart drumming in his chest.

"Do you?"

Did he what? He tried to think what it was she had asked him. Something about not liking town. "I'd rather be here," he said huskily, half-submerged in muddy water with a sprite whose smile had the effect of a lightning bolt on his sanity.

"I guess we had better let them have it before they decide to jump in with us," she said, motioning to the ever-closing circle of wild horses.

"You might be right," he said, eyeing the thirsty mustangs. Grateful that his body had returned to normal, he picked the least muddy edge and hoisted himself to the bank. Then he grasped Allie's outstretched hands and lifted her out. The too-big shirt clung to her skin, leaving no detail to his imagination. Tempted beyond endurance, he gritted his teeth and fought the urge to pull her into his arms. He was losing the battle when she laughed and pointed, diverting his attention.

The horses stood shoulder to shoulder, legs spread apart, necks extended, each with its muzzle buried in the water.

"I hope they don't founder," she said.

"Naw. Wild horses have better sense than to drink too much." He looked around and retrieved his empty canteen. "I wish I'd thought to fill it before the horses gunked up the water. At least it would have been wet." He licked his parched lips. "I'm so dry I can't talk straight."

"What would you give for a drink of cool lemonade?" Allie asked, arching a brow.

"Depends on what you're asking for it."

She stared up at him, her eyes like silvered diamonds, her pulse beating like the wings of a captured bird at the base of her throat. She swayed forward, and for a moment he thought she might be going to kiss him, then she sucked in a breath and abruptly turned away. "It wouldn't be fair to ask for anything, considering how hard you've worked all day."

He stepped close behind her and put his hands on her shoulders. "I'd gladly give you anything you want, Allie, but then you already know that, don't you?"

"I'll remind you of that later," she said somewhat breathlessly. "Right now, my own thirst seems to be affecting my brain." She put two fingers in her mouth and gave a shrill whistle.

From the opposite side of the canyon, Circe trotted toward her.

Allie grasped the saddle pommel and swung herself astride.

"Where are you going?" Hal asked.

"After the water—and the food," she said, flashing him a smile before she galloped away.

"Food?" He hadn't eaten since yesterday. "Wait for me." Since his own horse was nowhere to be seen, he grabbed the mane of the nearest mustang and flung himself astride. "Hi-yii!" he yelled.

The startled animal rolled his eyes, then bolted after Circe, which luckily was exactly where Hal wanted to go. When the mare stopped, the mustang slid up beside her. Feeling the wild horse arch his back, Hal vaulted from his perch. "That one's half-broke now," he said to Allie, who stood in wide-eyed amazement.

"You're crazy! You know that, don't you?" she said, shaking her head when the horse sunfished a couple of times, then raced away.

"I know I'm thirsty—and hungry!" he said, rubbing his rumbling middle. "Whatcha got to eat?"

"Nothing much." She peered inside the gunnysack. "Sliced beef on bread, couple of tomatoes, boiled eggs, cake, and some peaches I picked yesterday."

"Nothing much? It sounds like a banquet to me."

"Spread my bedroll under that tree yonder and we'll eat."

He removed the blanket from behind her saddle. A moment later he sat cross-legged on one end of it, while Allie, on the other end, divided the fare.

"Tell Bo Jack if he was a female I'd marry him," he said, attempting to talk and chew at the same time.

"Bo Jack didn't fix it—I did," she said, her gray eyes peeping at him over a thick sandwich.

"I didn't know you could cook." He bit off another mouthful.

"Well, I can. Bo Jack's been giving me lessons. Besides, sandwiches aren't exactly cooking, and Ma made the cake."

"Bet she didn't know you'd be sharing it with me." He raised his gaze from the devil's food confection and saw an expression of sadness flit across her face. He cursed himself for ever bringing it up.

Since the time he'd yelled out to Jane Daltry from the second-story balcony of the Lucky Chance, she had barely given him the time of day. After he'd done it he'd realized she'd thought he was visiting one of the upstairs ladies, but he wasn't. He'd been doing some repairs on the stairway for Lucky Chandler. But since he didn't feel he owed Allie's mother any explanations one way or another, he hadn't bothered to correct her impression. Not that it would have done any good even if she had believed him.

He had the idea that her dislike for him wasn't anything personal and that anyone in his circumstances would have met with the same thing. Even if he had the inclination, which he didn't, what could someone like him offer a girl like Allie? A girl who had not only the respectability but all the advantages the Daltry wealth could give her, even though Allie herself had never seemed conscious of that fact.

He took in the scuffed, worn boots encasing her small feet, much like those any working cowhand might have owned. She could have new boots, hand-tooled of the finest leather, a different pair for every day of the week, if she'd desired them. But Allie had always preferred the plain and simple.

None of the Daltrys had ever put on airs—except for Venus, who would have been right at home on a southern plantation with a dozen personal slaves to tend to her every whim. He tried to imagine Venus mud-splattered from head to foot and sitting cross-legged on a blanket. He chuckled.

"What's so funny?"

"I was trying to imagine Venus doing what you did today."

Allie grinned. "As crazy as it sounds, she might have— if Buck had needed it done. She is purely wild about that man. She'd rather die than let any of us see it, but she has changed."

"Are we talking about your sister? The one who wouldn't leave the house as long as the sun was up?"

"Yep. Buck said that when they were doing research for one of his books, they had to camp outdoors. She cooked over an open fire, carted water, slept on the ground or in the bed of the wagon for weeks at a time. And—this is the most amazing part—she did it without once complaining."

"Well, I'll be."

"That's what Ma said. Grandma just grinned like an opossum and said she knew all the time that Venus had it in her."

"Your grandma's quite a woman."

"That she is. But some of her la—her notions, are a bit hard to live with."

Hal glanced overhead at the crimson and purple sunset

sky. "Be dark in a bit. We'd probably better head for home."

"Guess so," she agreed, stiffly getting to her feet. She gathered up the things she'd brought while he saddled his horse.

They exited the canyon, and Hal slid the gate poles back into place. "The horses seem content to stay put now that they have water," he said, observing the quietly grazing band.

"That seems kind of sad, considering how wild and free they once were."

"Sooner or later, most things have to give up their freedom."

"I would like to see somebody try to put hobbles on me," she said wryly.

"You don't want to get married? Have children?"

"Never thought that much about it. But if it means being tied to a cookstove and washpot all day, no, I wouldn't. As for children—" She shrugged. "While I do love her dearly, if Thalia is any example of what to expect, I'd say I could wait a long time before desiring any of them."

"So you'd be content to spend your days riding the range, digging out mud holes, and breaking wild horses?"

"Why not? Sounds like a good life to me." She lifted her reins. "See you tomorrow?"

"I'll be here."

She nodded, then nudged her mare into a gallop.

"Adios, pard," Hal said softly.

Riding toward town, he recalled what Allie had said about Venus and the way she'd changed. He also thought about Allie's declaration concerning marriage and children. Yessir, he feared it would take a powerful kind of love to make Allie want to put on the shackles.

Nineteen

HAL SPUN ON HIS HEEL AND LEFT THE SALOON. WHY HADN'T SHE told him? Why had she let him find out this way? He wouldn't have believed Allie could be so callous, so uncaring about his feelings. He stalked down the street, a bitter ache settling in the region of his heart.

He sucked in the cool night air in an effort to clear his mind of the muddling effects of the alcohol. His thoughts returned to the conversation they'd had in the canyon. If she was engaged to Clay Masterson, why hadn't she said so? And why had she said she didn't want to get married? It made no sense.

Determincd to get to the truth of the matter, he strode toward the newspaper office, only to find it closed and dark. He went to the boardinghouse and discovered that Clay wasn't there, either.

Since he hadn't seen Clay at the Lucky Chance and he wasn't in his room, that left only one logical place for him to be. The Circle D.

As he thought of Clay and Allie together, betrayal, like bitter gall, assaulted his emotions. Exhaustion and despondency settled like a heavy mantle on Hal's shoulders as he headed for home.

Hours later, he tossed in bed, tormented, unable to sleep.

Clay and Allie engaged.

Hal thought about the life they'd have together. She wouldn't have to cook or clean. After tasting her cake, Clay would probably insist on a housekeeper. That ought to make her happy, he thought resentfully.

On the other hand, Clay hated horses. Called them smelly, bad-tempered beasts.

Allie loved them. Would she give them up for Clay? The thought that she might have to made him angry.

And what if they had children?

Hal thought of them sharing a bed, then because it was too painful he drove his fist into his pillow and forced the picture out of his mind.

Clay wouldn't want children.

Allie claimed she didn't either.

But what if she changed her mind? Whether she realized it or not, Allie would make a wonderful mother. She was too good with baby animals not to be.

He closed his eyes, envisioning her with half a dozen. Girls with curly brown hair and big gray eyes. Sandy-haired, green-eyed boys.

Startled, he blinked. Green-eyed boys? Clay had brown eyes. *Those were my kids!*

Like a thunderbolt, realization hit him.

He should have been happy for Allie, but he wasn't. He wanted to shake her. Or turn her over his knee.

When he thought of Clay Masterson, he wanted to pound the man into a bloody pulp.

Hal sat up and buried his face in his hands. Whether he

wanted to admit it or not, he was passionately, indisputably, irrevocably in love with Allie Daltry.

"He said what?" Allie demanded, her feet spread in a wide stance, her hands on her hips.

A mutinous look on his face, Hal glared back at her. "Charlie Simmons told me that Clay said you two were getting married. Now, I didn't hear Clay say it personally. I just thought it was funny *you* hadn't mentioned it, especially since we're pards and all."

"Why, I haven't even seen the man in a week. Not since the night I . . ." Avoiding Hal's clear-eyed gaze, she thought back to that day at the grove when she'd gotten so sick on champagne. Now that she focused on it, she did vaguely recall some talk of getting married. Her head had been spinning so wildly at the time, she'd been more intent on keeping herself from passing out than paying any attention to the conversation.

Had she told Clay she'd marry him? Her mouth drew into a scowl. Not unless she'd swallowed a whole lot more of those little bubbles than she'd thought.

But she must have given Clay that impression, otherwise why would he say they were engaged?

"Why didn't you tell me?" Hal demanded.

"Because I—" She bit her lip. "It must have slipped my mind."

"Now I sure don't believe that!"

Allie heaved a sigh. Jehoshaphat! She could tell by the look on his face he wasn't about to give up. "I guess I forgot," she grudgingly admitted.

"Forgot you were getting married? Or forgot to tell me?"

He was worse than a dog with a bone. Wouldn't quit chewing till he was down to the marrow. "All right. Until you brought it up just now, I didn't remember. I was drunk!"

He shook his head. "Are you going to marry him?"

"According to you, he says I am. I haven't had time to think on it one way or another." Uneasy under his scrutiny, she turned toward the corral. "Are we gonna stand here jawing all day or are we gonna break some horses?"

Not knowing whether to be mad or glad, Hal watched her walk away. Somehow she'd managed to get herself engaged, but he could tell by her manner that she was as surprised by the news as he had been.

Hal bucked out the first two horses while Allie sat on the corral fence and stared at the ground. He rode the second horse around the circular enclosure, then stopped in front of her. "You shore don't appear to be the happiest bunny in the burrow," he said, borrowing her favorite childhood expression. "Want to talk about it?"

She gazed up at him, her eyes dark with confusion. She hesitated, then slowly shook her head. "Talked enough. It's thinking I've got to do. Right now I just want to break horses." She glanced toward the three left in the pen. "You already did two?"

He nodded.

"Then the next two are mine." She jumped down from the fence. Shaking out a rope, she tossed a loop over the nearest mustang.

Hal led the one he'd broke out of the corral and hobbled it next to the first one, then he went back to help Allie.

He was relieved to see the one she'd chosen was the same horse he'd ridden for a short time the day before. She allowed it to buck itself out, then rode it around the corral, teaching it to respond to her reins and knees. After a bit, she hobbled it near the others.

"Let's take a break," Hal said, handing her the canteen.

She drank long and deep, then gave the canteen back to him. "You ever get drunk on champagne?"

"Once. Some celebration or another."

"Who'd ever think all them tiny bubbles could be so potent?"

"Sure addled my senses," he admitted.

"It did?" She peered at him from under long sable lashes.

"I probably did something plumb silly, but I don't remember. I do recall having a dilly of a headache the next day," he said, lifting a sun-streaked curl out of her eyes.

"That I do remember," she said, grinning.

"I like your hair like this," he said softly, threading his fingers through her silky curls.

"All I did was comb it."

"It's grown some." He straightened out one of the satiny coils. "Looks real pretty."

"I haven't been whacking it off like I used to." Instinctively, she pressed her cheek against his palm.

Hal drew a thumbtip across her lips; then, afraid he would give in to the impulses that stampeded through his body, he withdrew his hand and shoved it into his hip pocket.

"Are you hungry?" she asked.

"No." The hunger he felt had nothing to do with food.

"Me neither. Could use some more water, though."

He held out the canteen. When she handed it back and walked away, he took a drink from the same place, making believe the rim was her lips.

Sunlight danced among her wind-tousled curls. The hot blast molded the oversized shirt to her soft curves, sending desire leaping to life in his middle.

How could he allow her to marry another, loving her the way he did?

How could he not?

Even if she did agree to marry him, he had nothing to offer her. Even the section of land his grandpa had left him was virtually worthless because of the black goo that constantly seeped out of the ground. He couldn't—wouldn't—allow her to do the providing. That was the man's job.

Clay, on the other hand, had a prosperous business and held a position of respect in the community. Clay was also taller, a classy dresser, and better-looking, Hal thought resentfully.

Knowing it was useless to fret over something that could never be, he jabbed the toe of his boot into the dirt. Whoever she chose, he only wanted Allie to be happy.

He watched her saddle the mustang she'd snubbed to the corral post, then quick as lightning she vaulted into the saddle. A flick of her wrist released the snubbing rope.

The cayuse stood stiff-legged and still for a moment, then he exploded into action. Deceptively calm while in the corral, the horse now showed his true nature. A natural outlaw. One that any bronc buster dreaded to come across.

"Allie!" Hal cried. "Look out! He's gonna roll!" Hal raced forward and saw her kick her feet loose from the stirrups.

Instead of rolling, as Hal had thought, the horse slammed hard against the side of the fence, then put his head between his legs. His back end rose high into the air. He twisted, then landed with a bone-jarring jolt.

Half out of the saddle already, Allie flew over his head and landed in a crumpled heap in the thick dust.

Hal jumped the fence, afraid she would be trampled.

But the horse, free of his rider, stood off to one side, head down, sides heaving.

Hal knelt beside her as she lay white-faced and limp. A small trickle of blood ran from one corner of her mouth.

"Allie? Allie, darlin?"

She didn't answer.

Frantic, he ran his hands over her body, checking for any broken bones. He didn't find any. Still afraid to move her, but not daring to leave her there, he lifted her as carefully as if she were made of glass. He carried her from the corral to a shaded spot and lay her on a patch of grass. He uncorked the canteen with his teeth and dampened his neckerchief with the tepid water. His hands shaking, he tenderly bathed her white face.

She moaned.

"Allie. Can you hear me, sweetheart?"

"Ohh. What happened?" she groaned, opening her eyes. She raised her head.

He pushed her back. "Don't move. Do you hurt anywhere?"

"I'm not sure. I just feel numb."

"Numb?" *Could she be paralyzed?* He pulled off her boot and sock and ran a finger from her toes to her heel, a motion that ordinarily would have sent her into spasms of laughter.

She didn't move.

"How about your legs? Can you feel this?" He grasped her calf, her knee, her thigh.

She shook her head. "Maybe I can't feel it because of the jeans."

He slid his hand under her shirt and pressed his palm to her midriff. "Feel that?"

"I'm not sure. Do it again."

The bare flesh under his palm was warm and smooth as satin. In a motion both gentle and caressing, he massaged his way from one side to the other. When she shivered, he jerked his head up and met her eyes. "Does it hurt?"

"No. It makes me feel all warm inside."

"You felt it then?"

She nodded. "I can feel my legs now, too."

Sagging in relief, Hal closed his eyes and breathed a silent prayer of thanks.

"Hal?" She sat up. Her eyes full of concern, she placed her hand against his cheek. "I'm fine. Really I am. I guess it just knocked the breath out of me."

He took her hand and brought it to his mouth. He gazed deep into her eyes, as if to reassure himself she told the truth. "That damned horse could have killed you and it would have been my fault."

"Don't say things like that," she scolded. "Besides, if I was hurt, could I do this?" She raised her hands and began to tickle his sides.

Hal gasped, then fell to one side, laughing. He grasped her wrists, bringing her over him. "So you feel like playing, do you?" He tumbled her onto her back and straddled her, then he reached tickling fingers toward her ribs.

She sucked in a breath, her eyes bright as quicksilver; then, giggling, she locked her fingers behind his head and pulled him over on top of her. "I've got you now," she said gleefully, wrapping her legs around his back.

"That you have," he admitted. "Now that you've got me, what do you intend to do with me?"

The smile left her face and she stared into his eyes. Her hair bore traces of dirt and leaves. A smudge covered the end of her nose, and a purplish bruise marred one tanned cheek where she'd hit the ground.

She was absolutely breathtaking.

"Allie. Sweet, sweet, Allie." Unable to help himself, he pressed his lips against the mark. From there, he kissed each eyelid, her nose, and then her mouth. The lips beneath his were warm, full, and welcoming.

When he raised his head, she gave a quivering sigh and pulled him back. Her eyes were half-closed and dreamy. The lips she molded to his were moist and slightly parted.

On fire with want, he slid his hands beneath her shirt. The soft mounds of her breasts filled his palms. His thumbs reached and found the tender tips, already taut and thrusting against the thin fabric of her chemise. The discovery fed the fire already burning deep and hot inside him.

Allie's hands fumbled with buttons. First his shirt and then her own, until only her creamy, lace-edged camisole kept them apart. Her trembling fingers untied the satin ribbons, and then flesh pressed against flesh. She took his hand and kissed the palm, then laid it against the breast she'd bared.

He cradled the blue-veined globe in his hand, feeling it swell and the bud surge to a point between his fingertips. He bent his head and stroked the pink tip with his tongue, then gently teased it with his teeth.

Allie moaned and arched against him, pressing the other breast toward him in silent offering.

Unable to deny her, he left the one, then hungrily closed his mouth over the other.

Crying out, she cupped his head and tightened the grip her legs had around him, urging him still nearer.

His body pulsating with a primitive rhythm, he ground his swollen passion against the feminine softness between her thighs. All the while he suckled first one breast, then the other, like a greedy, hungry babe.

When he finally lifted his head, the eyes that met his were storm-cloud dark and glazed with passion. The idea that she could want him sent his heart thundering against his chest.

His hunger raw and savage, he claimed her lips, her neck, her mouth, taunting and teasing until she writhed under him.

"Allie. My Allie." He wanted—needed—to make her his.

Then it hit him. She wasn't his. She was betrothed to another.

She could never belong to him.

It took everything he had to push her away. To rise, trembling, to his feet. His breath ragged, he stared down at her.

Her lips swollen from his kisses and her hair tumbling wildly around her face gave her a wanton, untamed beauty. Her bosom proud and thrusting beckoned him to return.

Fighting the blinding-hot need, he forced his gaze away. He ran an unsteady hand through his hair.

"Hal?" she asked, her voice unhappy and bewildered. "What's wrong?"

He didn't look at her. He didn't dare. "Get dressed and go home," he said, his voice gruff with emotion.

He heard a soft rustle of cloth and in a few moments she stood by his side. "Hal?" She reached out to touch him.

He flinched away. "Go home, Allie. Don't come back."

"Why?"

He whirled to face her: "Because it was wrong. Because you are engaged."

Her eyes like those of a wounded doe, she gazed up at him. "You wanted me," she argued softly.

He gave a harsh laugh. "I wanted *you?* I wanted a woman! It was *lust,* pure and simple," he lied. "It would have been the same with anybody."

"I don't believe you."

He gripped her arms and forced her to look at him. "Don't you understand? *It didn't mean a thing.*"

She brought her hand to her mouth to muffle her anguished cry. Her eyes, tear-filled and accusing, lashed him like a bullwhacker's whip. Then she twisted away and ran for Circe. Within minutes she was out of sight.

Bleakly Hal stared after her, a gnawing emptiness growing in his middle. He'd hurt her. Badly. But he knew it was for the best.

Still, when he thought of never seeing, never being with her again, he wondered if he could survive the pain.

Twenty

HER GAZE UNSEEING, ALLIE RODE THE FOAM-FLECKED MARE through the approaching night. It was only when Circe stumbled from weariness that Allie realized that she would kill the horse if she didn't stop. Slowing her to a walk, she guided the heaving animal to a secluded spot by the river where she dismounted, then removed the saddle and used the blanket to wipe down her pet's sweat-drenched sides. "I'm sorry, Circe," she whispered against the satiny neck, realizing the mare would have run until her heart broke just because Allie asked it of her.

Her own heart aching, she thought of Hal and knew that without a moment's hesitation she would have done the same thing. She would have given herself to him—her heart, her body, her life, if necessary—without any thought of commitment or the consequences.

But he had refused her. Rejected her. Turned her away. Told her not to come back.

He'd said he wanted a woman.

She was a woman. Couldn't he see that? *Maybe she wasn't woman enough,* a voice whispered. She would be the first to admit, she hadn't had much practice. She still wasn't much of a cook. Barely knew how to thread a needle. There were a lot of other female things she didn't know much about. Like what went on between a man and a woman.

She bit her lip. That wasn't really true—she'd seen animals mating often enough to guess. Was it just instinct with a man, the same as it was with a stallion or a bull? Somehow she'd hoped for something more. Something warm, sheltering, tender. She'd seen that between her own father and mother. Was it something so rare?

She'd witnessed the other side, too, where men treated their women like cattle, something to be owned, used, and then neglected while they sought other arms, other pleasures in town.

The memory of the dance hall girl flashed into Allie's mind. The way the woman had clung to Hal's arm and gazed into his eyes. The way he'd laughed when she'd whispered in his ear. Allie would have bet her last dollar he wouldn't have sent the redhead packing.

Hot tears welled and spilled down her cheeks. One, then another, until finally they came in a flood of resentment and despair. When they ended, a sorrow deeper than anything she had ever known left her weak and empty, as if some vital part of her had been cut away, leaving a gaping, bleeding void.

She remembered Hal's angry accusation that she was engaged to Clay. Was she? There was so much about that night she couldn't remember. And the parts she did recall were so dreamlike she couldn't even be certain they were real.

What if it were true? Would that be so bad?

Clay was handsome and mannerly enough to make any woman's heart beat faster. She would be the envy of every woman in the territory. She had grown very fond of Clay and felt flattered by his attentiveness, but did she care enough to spend a lifetime with the man? And if she loved Clay, why had she carried on the way she had with Hal? Shame heated her cheeks. She had never behaved so wantonly in her life. No wonder Hal had been so disgusted with her. And Clay? If he knew he would be furious.

Maybe she was fretting for nothing. Maybe it was all a mistake. Clay was the only person who could tell her the truth of the matter, and he had gone to Austin on business.

She shook out the blanket and laid it to one side, then sat cross-legged on a rock and stared at the water until the moon rose high overhead. Hours later, realizing her family would be worried if she didn't return soon, she knelt by the river and washed her tear-streaked face. Beneath the star-studded sky, she saddled Circe and slowly headed for the ranch.

The next day and the day after, Allie kept to the house, mostly staying in her room. When she tired of everyone asking if she was sick, she told them it was her time of the month, which it was; but unlike Venus, who had taken to her bed for days, Allie had never let it keep her from doing anything she'd wanted to before. Melancholia had reduced her to such a miserable state that she was almost glad when her mother announced that she had a visitor. She went down the stairs and saw Clay standing in the dining room doorway.

He greeted her with a glad smile, then came forward and kissed her cheek. "Allie, my dear. You look so pale. Are you feeling all right?"

"I'm fine," she told him, attempting a smile. "Just a little tired. It's probably the heat."

"Why don't you two have a seat outside, while I make some lemonade," her mother suggested.

"That's a good idea." His brown eyes dark with concern, he guided Allie from the house and onto the veranda, where he seated her on a wicker bench, then took a place by her side.

"If you think it's hot here, you should have been with me in Austin. It was unbearable. I couldn't wait to get home. Besides, I missed you," he whispered, squeezing her hand. "I just broke the news to your parents. I hope you don't mind. I couldn't wait."

"News?" Her heart pounding, she stared at him.

"Our marriage, silly," he teased. "You haven't changed your mind, I hope. I've told everyone in the state what a happy man you've made me."

So it was true. The most important event in her life, yet she couldn't remember much of anything about it.

He drew her into his arms and gave her a lingering kiss. After a moment he released her, and his brow wrinkled in a frown. "Allie, is something wrong?"

"No. Of course not. Why do you ask?"

"You seem so quiet."

"I've had a lot to think about."

"I guess that's true," he said with a chuckle. "After all, it isn't every day a girl decides to get married."

"It isn't every day Allie can keep a secret, either," her mother said from behind them.

Allie turned and saw both of her parents and her grandmother. All were smiling.

Her mother came forward and clasped Allie in her arms. "Naughty child. Such wonderful news. Why didn't you tell us?"

"I guess she wanted to wait until I got back," Clay said, a pleased expression on his face.

"Well, Clay, let me be the first to welcome you to the family," her pa said, holding out his hand.

"Thank you." Clay shook his hand, then turned to Minerva. "I hope you are as happy about this as we are."

Her grandma gazed at Allie, her gray eyes thoughtful. "If it is what Atalanta wants, then I want it for her. My granddaughter's happiness means everything to me."

Allie gave her a tender smile. "Thank you, Grandma."

The rest of the night went by in a whirl, and by the time it ended Allie thought her face would crack if she smiled one more smile. As she dressed for bed, she thought about the events of the evening. All the well-wishing and the plans everyone was making. For her future, her happiness. But as she slid beneath the covers, Allie didn't feel happy at all.

The news spread through Paradise Plains like a wildfire on a windblown praire. In the next few weeks, Allie thought the town talked more about her forthcoming nuptials than they did about the Fourth of July celebration or even the drought. She was so tired of hearing about it that she thought if one more person offered their congratulations she would scream.

She had ridden to town in the wagon with her father and had just finished having lunch with Clay at the Buccaneer. He walked her back as far as the newspaper office.

"I wish I could take the rest of the day off and go shopping with you," he said in a warm tone.

"I know you must be busy, and I've kept you too long already. It wouldn't do for the newspaper to be late. Besides, I don't need to go shopping," she assured him.

"You need a new dress for the engagement party. Something fashionable." He studied her. "With your eyes, maybe silver-blue satin?"

"I wouldn't be comfortable in anything very fancy," she

said uneasily. Then seeing the determined look on his face, she sighed. "I'll see what Maybelle has at the mercantile, or maybe Ma can help me make something."

"Nonsense. Paradise Plains doesn't have much to offer. I'll find something for you in Austin."

"What if it doesn't fit, or I don't like it?" she protested.

"If it doesn't fit, your mother can alter it. Besides, I know exactly what I want you to wear."

Gripping her hands, he tilted his head and gazed at her. "Now, about the wedding itself. I know you wanted to get married at the ranch, but Austin has so much more to offer. That way your family could meet all of my business associates. Who knows, the governor himself might arrange to be there." Catching his reflection in the window, he released her hands and straightened his tie. "I've already spoken to him about it."

"We'll talk about it later," she said, her spirits plummeting.

He took her in his arms, and ignoring the fact that they were standing in front of the *Gazette* window in plain view of anybody passing by, he pulled her close in a passionate kiss. "Allie, waiting is unbearable. I wish we could be married now, today." He ran a possessive hand over her breast and gave it a squeeze.

"Clay, someone might see," she said, a crimson rush of heat flooding her body. "And you do have a paper to get out."

"All right." He released her with obvious reluctance. "Don't make me wait too long, Allie. I'm not a patient man." He brushed another kiss against her cheek, then escorted her to the door.

"About the dress—" she began, hoping she could change his mind.

"Allie, don't worry. I'll take care of everything."

He always took care of everything. She forced a smile

as she left the office. Spying a particularly gossipy trio of townswomen headed her way, she ducked into an alley and made her way to the library. She found her sister-in-law Meredith seated behind a desk.

"Allie," Meredith said, rising to give her a hug. "What brings you in here? I never knew you to be overly fond of books," she teased.

"Actually, I'm hiding." She gave Meredith a wry smile.

"Hiding? From what, or should I say, from whom?" she asked, peering over her wire-rimmed spectacles.

"From everybody." Allie glanced at the patrons, who watched her curiously. "Can we go somewhere private? Somewhere where we can talk?"

"Of course. Wait here. I'll be right back." Meredith disappeared behind a long rack of books. A moment later, she returned with a small, mousy-looking woman by her side. "I won't be back today, Martha, so I would like for you to lock up."

"Yes, Mrs. Daltry," the woman said.

After she and Meredith exited the library, Allie left a note for her father at the livery stable, telling him that she had gone home with Meredith. When they were in the buggy and safely out of town, Allie heaved a sigh and turned to the redheaded woman seated beside her. "Thank you."

Meredith gave her a speculative look. "I take it this has something to do with your engagement to Clay?"

"You take it right." She looked at the small woman who had captured her brother's heart. Even though Lee and Meredith had fought like cats and dogs when they'd first met, Allie thought she had never seen a happier couple. She fiddled with the engagement ring on her hand, turning the glittering blue stone to her palm. "When did you know?"

"Know what?"

"That you were really in love?"

Meredith smiled. "The first time I saw Lee, I felt the attraction; then when I found out *who* he was, everything about him infuriated me. I guess you heard I threw things at him."

"Yeah, he told us."

"No matter what I did, he *smiled*. You know what I mean. He did it on purpose."

"Lee's famous for that smile," Allie said with a grin. "Not many people can resist it." While her oldest brother wasn't the brightest one in the family, he certainly had more than his share of the Daltry charm.

"All teeth and dimples. It always got him his way. It made me furious that I, too, could fall under his spell, especially since your grandmother had given him the job that I worked so hard to get. I tried to ignore him, but that only made him more persistent. Then when we took custody of Jimmy, I began to see a different side to him, a tender, compassionate side. It was then I knew I was fighting a losing battle. Finally I just gave up." Meredith gave her a dreamy smile. "I'm sure glad I did." She clucked to the horses. "You did know I was the one who asked him to marry me?"

"It 'pears to me that saying yes was the smartest thing Lee ever did."

"He never did anything by the book. That was one of the things that upset me so."

Allie thought about her older brother. "He was certainly the most entertaining teacher we ever had. I'll never forget the look on his face when Grandma told him that was his labor. He sure didn't smile that day, or for a good time after." Lee, a schoolteacher. The idea still amazed her, and she shook her head. "I guess I can be happy my own labor wasn't any worse."

"How's it coming?"

"The first two parts are done," Allie said with relief. "I've made the cake, such as it was. And I made a dress for the dance. But I still have to take care of Thalia while Grandma, C. J., and Lizzie go to San Francisco. That's one reason I haven't set a date for the wedding."

"One reason?"

Allie looked at her sister-in-law. "Everything happened so fast. I don't feel that I know Clay that well, and yet I'm planning to spend the rest of my life with him."

"How do you feel about that?"

"I'm scared," Allie confessed. "I don't want to disappoint everyone, but I don't want to leave Paradise Plains."

"Why would you have to?"

"Clay wants to go into politics. He plans to sell the newspaper and move to Austin as soon as we are married."

Meredith pulled the buggy over into a shady spot by the river. "This is Lee's thinking spot. He always comes here to think things through when he is troubled. I don't imagine he would mind if you borrowed it."

Meredith took her hand and squeezed it. "Allie, it is your life. Good or bad. Think long and hard about what you want, and the devil take anybody who tries to tell you different. I'll be over at the house when you're ready for some company."

Allie nodded and climbed down from the buggy. She watched Meredith cross the bridge to the white house that sat on the other side of the river. Her pa and Lee had built it as a wedding surprise. Meredith, who'd been an orphan, said it was the only home she had ever had. And Allie knew it was the only home the woman would ever want.

Now that her sister-in-law had gone, Allie found a grassy place next to the water where she could sit and think about her own situation.

She tossed a twig into the river and watched it bob and weave as the current drew it downstream. She likened the stick to herself, the river to Clay. No matter what she said or did, it had no effect. She'd barely gotten used to the idea of being engaged, and now Clay seemed determined to hurry her into marriage. She thought about the vows she would take. So solemn. So final. She felt like a skittish colt being dragged toward a hot branding iron.

He knew how badly she wanted to be married at the ranch, but now he seemed set on having the ceremony in Austin. Just in case the governor might decided to favor them with his presence. What about her friends? The townsfolk, ranch owners, cowhands? They couldn't leave their responsibilities to travel to Austin.

And that dress. Blue satin? Just the idea of anything so lavish made her uncomfortable. She wished she had the nerve to tell him that if he liked blue satin so well, he could wear it. But he wouldn't understand her attitude. How could he, when she didn't understand it herself? Most any other woman would be thrilled to have such a fine garment.

It wasn't the dress as much as the idea that she hadn't been allowed to choose it. Clay's overbearing attitude made her have serious doubts about their relationship. She thought about the future they would have together. He, off on some political campaign or another. She . . . ? What would she do? What would he expect her to do? Once again doubts assailed her, as she wondered if she even loved Clay.

She was fond of him, and his kisses were pleasant enough—even if he did have the tendency to be a bit outrageous at times. Was that love?

The memory of other kisses, stolen by a dusty corral, assaulted her memory. Kisses that made her quiver with desire. *It was lust. It didn't mean a thing.* She closed her eyes against the pain. Was she marrying Clay because Hal didn't want her? She stared at the water. She didn't know. That was the problem.

Hours later she got to her feet and crossed the bridge to the house. She decided that the thinking spot must work only for Lee. It hadn't done her a bit of good.

She still wasn't sure about anything.

After supper, Lee and Meredith left Jupiter, Diana, and the baby in Lucy Cooper's capable hands and drove Allie back to the ranch.

"Seen Hal lately?" her brother asked.

"No," she said, feeling a familiar ache stab her heart.

"Thought you two were close."

"We were." She stared at the floor of the buggy. "We kind of had a fight." Glancing up, she wet her lips. "Have you seen him?"

"A time or two."

Allie waited, hoping he would say more, but he seemed content to remain silent. "Well?"

"Well, what?"

"You said you saw Hal."

"Yeah, I did."

Allie gritted her teeth. Sometimes her brother could be plumb exasperating. "What did he say?"

"Nothing much."

"Lee." Meredith put her hand on his arm. "Quit teasing your sister. Tell her about Hal."

"All right, Red. I'm getting to it."

Allie silently gave thanks for Meredith.

As if knowing he dare not procrastinate any longer, Lee flashed a toothy smile. "Like I said, Allie, he didn't say anything much. He did ask how you were. He said he hoped you and Clay would be happy. But he sure didn't look happy. He looked like he'd lost his best friend." Lee took his wife's hand. "Remember, honey, I told you about it."

Allie felt like a coiled spring had burst loose inside her. "You sure Hal asked about me?"

"Sure as shootin'." Lee's blue eyes gazed at her intently. "Maybe you should see about mending some fences."

"Mending fences?"

"With Hal, silly," he said, ruffling her hair. "You two have been like each other's shadow as long as I can remember. Seems a shame to let something spoil it at this late date."

"But I'm getting married."

"So? Meredith's married. She still is a person in her own right. I hope she can have friends if she wants to."

"I'll remember you said that the next time that handsome book salesman comes to call," her sister-in-law teased.

"Long as you remember you're married to me."

Meredith put her head on Lee's muscular arm. "As if I could ever forget that, Hercules."

Although Lee and his wife continued to chat, Allie remained quiet the rest of the trip. Her mind occupied by what Lee had said, she thought about her brothers and their wives. . . .

Meredith, a deep-running river, quiet and serene, providing a safe harbor for Lee and their children.

C. J. and Lizzie, whose household never ran smoothly, but whose happy turmoil provided its own rewards. Thalia, their two-year-old daughter and the light of their lives, proved that.

Venus and Buck. Opposites, with flaws that would have rendered them helpless alone. Venus, delicate and flighty as a bird. Buck, strong of character yet dependent because of his blindness. Together they forged a bond of tempered steel.

Shy Persy and Jake, the roguish saloon owner. Persy had gained confidence enough to tackle anything. Jake had learned compassion and how to love.

She and Clay. When they first became engaged, it seemed comforting to have Clay make all the decisions, but now the idea that he would decide her life without even asking her opinion troubled and annoyed her. He told her how to dress, how to wear her hair. Today at lunch he had chosen what she would eat. He even tried to tell her what to think.

It wasn't comforting. It was suffocating. She didn't even feel like Allie Daltry anymore. It was as if her old self were being vanquished and a new one molded to take its place. And that new one was Clay Masterson's fiancée.

When Lee pulled the buggy into the yard, the three of them joined the family, relaxing and enjoying the evening in the gazebo. Even though the hour was still early, after a few moments Allie said she was tired and bade them all good night.

Because she had seen Clay earlier in the day, she knew he would be busy getting the paper ready for tomorrow's edition. The knowledge that he wouldn't be visiting the ranch that evening filled her with a guilty sense of relief. At least tonight she wouldn't have to hear his plans for their future.

She needed time to get her thoughts in order. Time to contemplate just what a future with Clay would mean. Ever since they had become engaged her world had spun out of control.

What would happen to her when she became his wife?

Twenty-One

"YOU'RE SURE DOWN IN THE MOUTH. WHAT'S THE MATTER, SON, somebody steal your girl?" Jack Anderson said, leaving his bedroom to stride into the small kitchen, where Hal sat hunched over the table.

Hal stared into his coffee cup, wondering if his father knew how close he'd come to hitting the target. "Naw. I'm just tired."

"I heard you finished breaking the last of the horses." The silver-haired man poured himself a cup of coffee from the battered enamel pot and sat down in the ladder-back chair across from him. "Hal, I never told you how sorry I am for what happened. If I could change things and get the ranch back, I would. After your ma passed on, I felt like I had died, too."

"I know. I'm not blaming you. I miss her, too." Hal took a deep breath, then catching a whiff of bay rum, he raised his head, his eyes widening in surprise. "You shore are duded up," he said, noting that his father wore his Sunday best—the somewhat worn but newly pressed black suit, a white shirt, and freshly shined boots.

His father ran his fingertips over his smooth-shaven cheek and touched his slicked-down hair. "I've got a date."

"A date? Who is it?"

A flush stealing over his face, Jack said, "Melissa Greene."

"Isn't she the widow woman who works at Miss Lavender's millinery shop?"

"The same. We've been seeing each other for a couple of months now."

"I noticed you hadn't been around much lately," Hal said, thinking his pa reminded him of a kid on his first date. "She seems like a nice lady."

"She's very special." His pa's face grew somber. "Hal, there's something I've been meaning to ask you."

"Sure. Fire away."

"How would you feel about Melissa and me getting married?"

"Married?" He hadn't even realized his father had been seeing anybody before today, let alone that he might be considering marriage. He remained silent for a moment, letting the news soak in. "I'd say that's about the best news I've had in a long time. When is the big day?"

A look of relief washed over his father's face. "I don't rightly know. You see, she hasn't actually said yes yet. She wanted to see how you would take it first." He reached across the table and touched Hal's hand. "You know I'm not forgetting about your ma. She was a wonderful woman and no one will ever be able to take her place. It's just that I've been so damned lonely. And then there was the drinking and all."

"You've been on the wagon a good while now. Melissa have anything to do with that?"

Jack nodded. "Her first husband was a drunkard. After he died she swore she'd not have anything to do with a man that imbibed." He shrugged. "It was Melissa or the bottle, so I gave up the bottle."

Hal smiled, feeling like a large load had been lifted from his shoulders. "Have you made any plans? Where you're going to live and all?"

"Well, since Melissa only has a room at Miss Lavender's, I kind of thought we might live here. The place is small but the rent is reasonable. We could have a little garden in that patch of dirt out back. Melissa wants to keep her job, and as for me—well, the town could use a good carpenter and rock mason. Hank's hired me to build him a new icehouse." He grinned. "Of course, Miz Minerva is footin' the bill."

Hal chuckled. "She'll probably take it out of C. J.'s hide."

"She's a tough woman, but she's fair. We owe her a lot, and I don't mean just money."

"Well, the money part will be taken care of," Hal said with a measure of pride. "I collect on the horses today. By tomorrow she will be paid in full, so we can both start with a clean slate."

"Son, have you made any plans? You know you will always be welcome here, but I doubt you'd want to live with me and Melissa all your life." He rubbed his chin. "I always thought you and little Allie would end up hitched. And for the life of me I can't figure her falling for that Masterson feller."

"Well, she must love him or she wouldn't be marrying him," Hal said, trying to hide the pain.

"I can't help thinking there's something about that deal that just don't figure. I can see why Allie might be dazzled by a feller like that, but she just isn't his type."

"What do you mean by that? Any man should be proud to have a girl like Allie. She's pretty, sweet, and smart.

Why, that gal knows everything there is to know about horses."

"Now, Hal, don't get your dander up. I'm not saying anything bad about Allie. God knows I love that girl like she was my own." He rubbed his palm across the surface of the table. "It's something else that keeps nagging at me."

"What?"

"What kind of women have you seen Clay Masterson take an interest in?"

Hal glanced at the ceiling. "Well, there was Maybelle's cousin. You remember, that tall blond from Georgia. The one that looked and talked like Venus. A real southern belle."

"Uh-huh. And?"

"That tall brunet. Some senator's daughter. I heard she married a lawyer. Then, let's see—"

"Any of them remind you of Allie?"

"No. But that don't mean—"

"Clay's ambitious. He spends a lot of time in Austin."

"Yeah, I know," Hal said, impatiently. "He wants to get into politics."

"Politickin' takes money."

"Yeah. So?"

"Clay doesn't have any money."

He stared at his father. "But Allie does."

The older man nodded. "I think we've found the answer."

"That bastard!" Hal shot to his feet, sending his chair screeching backward to crash onto the floor. "He's marrying Allie because she's rich."

The next day, the money from the sale of the horses tucked in his jeans pocket, Hal headed for the Circle D to pay off the debt he owed Minerva Daltry.

All night he'd thought about the discovery he and his pa had made, but he still had no idea what to do about it. After what had happened that day in the canyon when he'd come so near to making love to Allie, the two of them weren't exactly on the best of terms. How could he tell her what he had learned about Clay without her thinking it was sour grapes on his part? No girl wanted to hear that a man was only interested in her because of her money. And besides, while he had a strong suspicion that was the case, he had no proof.

He considered confronting Clay, but knew the man would just deny it. And what if he was wrong? What if Clay really did love Allie?

That idea didn't make him too happy, either, considering his own feelings for her.

It was a case of damned if you do and damned if you don't, and he was caught smack dab in the middle.

He reined his horse in at the river, then dismounted, dampened his neckerchief in the water, and used it to wipe the dust and perspiration from his face.

Then there was Allie herself. Remembering what had almost happened between them in the canyon, he thought she didn't appear too clear on things, either. A girl that was crazy in love with one man didn't turn right around and make love to another. And that was exactly what would have happened if he hadn't stopped it when he did.

It made him angry that she had been so willing, not because of her fiancé's feelings—he didn't give a damn about the man—but because he wondered if she had behaved the same way with Clay. Considering that possibility, he clenched his jaw so hard a muscle jumped.

Allie had never been one to worry about propriety. But dang it, she had always been decent.

You can't go blaming it all on Allie, either, his conscience whispered, *especially when you can't seem to keep your own hands off her.* Just thinking about her made desire rise fierce and hot, and just for a minute he wished he *had* made love to her. He thought about what might have happened. . . .

Clay'd still be after her, because if the newsman was truly after her money, he would have married her anyway.

Odie would probably be peering at him over the barrel of his shotgun. A father wouldn't take that sort of thing kindly.

Her ma would be outraged. She didn't like him anyhow.

Miz Minerva? He didn't know how she would feel.

And Allie? He grinned. She would have demanded he marry her and shot him if he refused. And he would have refused. He loved her too much to subject her to the kind of life he could afford to give her.

He let out a heavy breath. He'd done the right thing, even if Allie would never understand the reason.

A while later, he rode under the arched entrance to the Daltry ranch. Keeping a wary eye out for Allie, he left his horse tied by the barn. After removing a package he'd picked up at the mercantile from behind his saddle, he strode toward the house.

Allie's mother sat on the porch, her mending in her lap. She looked up and made an attempt at a smile. "Hello, Hal. If you're looking for Allie, she isn't here. She and her fiancé are having dinner in town."

"I heard about the engagement," he said quietly, respectfully removing his hat. "I came to see Miz Minerva."

"I see," Jane said, getting to her feet. "I'll tell her you are here."

"Ma'am?"

She turned. "Yes?"

"Mrs. Daltry, I owe you an apology."

"Whatever for?"

"That day in town, when I yelled at you from the saloon."

"Oh," she said, her face turning crimson.

"Ma'am, it wasn't what you thought. I'd been fixing the outside stairs and railing for Lucky. It was hot and he brought me a couple of beers. I never thought about how it looked, and I'm real sorry if I caused you any embarrassment."

"You were fixing the stairs and railings. You weren't—?"

"No, ma'am!"

"Hal, it appears that I'm the one who owes you an apology." She held out her hand. "I am truly sorry."

Hal awkwardly enclosed her hand in his. "Miss Jane, you don't need to—"

"Oh, but I do." Retaining her hold, she tugged him up the steps. "Now come inside and have some lemonade. I'll tell Minerva you are here."

Hal allowed her to lead him into the kitchen, where he saw Bo Jack busily making apple pies.

Jane poured some lemonade and motioned for him to sit down at the long table, then she left to find Allie's grandma.

His hamlike hands covered with flour, the grizzled cook peered over at him. "Ain't seen you around in a spell. You and Allie have a fallin' out or somethin'?"

"Howdy to you, too," Hal said wryly. The large man puttering about the Daltry kitchen never failed to bring a smile to his face. But Bo Jack's cooking was anything but funny. The man could have cooked for kings.

"Well?" the old man repeated.

"Not a falling out, exactly. Well . . . sort of."

"Humph! Figures. She's shore been wearing a long face."

Hal glanced up in surprise. "You'd think she'd be happy. Getting engaged and all."

Hal had no chance to hear Bo Jack's comment, because Jane took that moment to come back into the room.

"Minerva's in the library. She said to tell you to go on in."

"Thank you, ma'am. See you later, Bo Jack." He drained the last of the tart beverage, picked up his package, and strode down the hall. He found Allie's grandma seated behind a big oak desk.

"Come in, boy. Close the door and have a seat."

Hal dug into his hip pocket and removed a wad of bills. He leaned forward and spread them out on the desk. "I think this makes us square." He lowered himself into the leather-covered chair across from her.

The gray-haired woman thumbed through the money and smiled. "So it does." She tucked the payment into a drawer and wrote out a receipt. "How's your pa?"

"Well, it's not official yet, but I think he and Melissa Greene might be getting hitched."

"Good for them." Then the smile left her face as she added, "Must be contagious. What have you got in the box?"

He laid the package on the desk. "These are the boots Allie wanted. I ordered them some time ago, and they came in yesterday." He placed a smaller stack of money on the table beside them. "This is for her, too. Since she helped with the horses, she earned it. Besides, she might need it, her getting married and all." He rose from the chair.

"Are you really going to let her do it?"

"What?"

"Don't you love her?"

He shifted uneasily. Minerva had never been one to

mince words. "Course I do. Allie and I have been friends for a long time."

"Friends?" she said scornfully. "Humph!"

He paused, his hand resting on the back of the chair. "I thought you'd be pleased about the wedding."

"I want her to be happy."

"Well, it was her choice," he said, more sharply than he'd intended.

"Was it? I'm not so sure." She squinted up at him. "You could stop her."

"I have nothing to offer her."

"Nothing except your love."

"That isn't enough," he said, striding toward the door.

"It's more than Clay is offering her."

"What do you mean?"

"You think I don't know he's after the Daltry money?"

"Then why are you letting her do it?"

"Right now she thinks that's what she wants. It's not up to me to tell her different."

It wasn't up to him, either. "I'd better be going," he said abruptly.

"Suit yourself. And tell your pa and Melissa I wish them my best."

"I'll do that," he said. "You'll give Allie the money and the boots?"

"I'll see that she gets them, though I don't expect she'll have much need for them in Austin."

Determined not to lose his temper again, Hal clenched his teeth. "Thank you for helping us out, Miz Minerva."

"Glad I was able to do it." She held out her hand.

He grasped it firmly. "Guess I'd better go now."

Her gray eyes bored into his. "You'll think on what I said about Allie, won't you?"

"Yeah." *But it wouldn't do any good.* He left the house and mounted his horse. A hot gust of wind threatened to lift his hat. As he gazed at the parched landscape, for the first time in his life he thought about leaving Texas. With his pa settled and Allie getting married, there was nothing to keep him in Paradise Plains.

You'll think on what I said about Allie, won't you? The words echoed inside his head.

All the way back to town, he could think of nothing else.

Twenty-Two

THE NIGHT OF HER ENGAGEMENT PARTY HAD ARRIVED AND ALLIE felt as jittery as an overweight hog on thin ice.

She fastened on the blue topaz earrings, then ran her hand down the front of the matching satin gown to remove a tiny crease from across her middle. If only she could loosen that danged corset! Her ma and Meredith had her trussed up so tight she felt like she was being lynched. She could scarcely take a breath, and besides that, the way the thing made her bulge above and below hardly seemed decent.

Eyeing herself in the mirror, she frowned and nervously fingered the square-cut neckline that dipped so low it barely covered the tips of her breasts. This might be what the ladies wore in society circles, but it made her feel half-naked. She hardly recognized herself. The creams Clay had brought her from Austin had successfully faded her tan. The makeup he'd insisted she wear took care of the sprinkling of freckles across her nose. A faint touch of kohl around her eyes made them appear like large gray saucers. She'd never been so gussied up in her life. Before, dressing up meant a simple skirt and blouse or a calico dress. Now every time she went to town she had to wear a hat, gloves, and carry a parasol. Clay insisted on it. She clenched her fists.

A soft tap sounded at her door. "Allie," Clay called from the hall.

"Come in," she said, turning toward the door. "I'm almost ready," she added when he entered the room. "I only need to put on my shoes."

"You look lovely." He took her hands.

Clay wore a suit of dove-gray that set off his dark good looks to perfection. His pristine white shirt was of the finest fabric, and his shoes were new and gleamed with wax. Altogether, he presented a picture so stunningly handsome he would have taken any girl's breath away. Reflecting on their upcoming marriage, she should have been giddy with anticipation, but when he pulled her toward him and gave her a chaste kiss, she felt a sense of dread.

Telling herself it was only nervousness because of the party, she forced a smile. "Well, tonight's the big night."

"Our guests are arriving. Most of them look hungry enough to devour both of those cows your pa cooked for the barbecue."

"They usually are," she said, thinking of other large gatherings that had taken place on the ranch. As she bent to put on her high-heeled slippers, her gaze touched on the box containing the boots Hal had given her. Whether Clay approved or not, she would take the boots to Austin, even if she never got the opportunity to wear them. But the money she intended to return to Hal.

She straightened. "I'm ready."

"Shall we go, then?" He gave her a dazzling smile, which quickly turned into a scowl. "Where's your engagement ring?"

"Oh. It's a good thing you reminded me. I think I put it in my jewelry box for safekeeping." She lifted the lid of the carved wooden chest Hal had made for her sixteenth birthday and sorted through her treasures. A bracelet woven from locks of hers and Hal's hair. A polished river rock he gave her when he was six. An envelope containing a four-leaf clover. A tiny, fragile blue egg they'd found in an abandoned nest.

Clay impatiently grabbed the box from her hands and dumped it out on the bed. "Nothing in here but junk." He angrily swept the contents off onto the floor.

"It's not junk!" she cried in protest. Dropping to her knees, she began to gather the treasured items.

"Get up! You're soiling your dress." He grasped her elbow and forced her to her feet. When he turned to search her dresser top, she immediately knelt again.

Spotting the ring on the floor, she scooped it up and placed it on the bed, but did not slip it on her finger.

"Put it on," he ordered, striding toward the door.

"Stop!" she cried, but it was too late. The tiny egg crunched under his feet. Her eyes blurring, she bent and touched a fingertip to the tiny shards of eggshell. "You broke it."

"Whatever it is, I'll buy you another. Now, let's go!"

"Some things can't be bought," she said bitterly, but Clay had already left the room.

A smile fixed upon his face, Clay clenched his fists and eyed Allie from across the room. If one more person told him how lucky he was to be marrying Allie Daltry, he thought he'd throw up.

Lucky? he thought bitterly. She'd spent the whole night sulking over that damned bird's egg. As far as he was concerned, the whole engagement party was a social disaster.

It galled him that she'd carelessly lost on the bedroom floor the ring he still owed for. And if that wasn't enough, the satin dress that he'd sold his diamond stickpin to buy now bore smudges of dirt as well as a large punch stain.

Everything about the girl irritated him. She was too short. She talked like a bumpkin. She ate like a cowhand. And the way she danced—he shivered. She hadn't a graceful bone in her body. *If it wasn't for the money . . . .* Watching her gallop about the floor, he wondered if even that would be enough.

Later that evening, after he'd considered his options, he'd decided that the money, along with the accompanying power, would be enough. Even though it irked him to have to do so, he'd hovered by her side, intent on soothing her ruffled feathers. When he saw her eyes light up and her face crinkle in a brilliant smile, he thought he had accomplished his purpose—until he discovered she wasn't even looking at him. He turned toward the doorway and saw a sandy-haired man enter the room. Hal Anderson.

Inside, Clay was a mass of fury, but he'd learned long ago to mask his emotions. His face twisted in a brittle smile, he tightened his arm around Allie's waist and led her in the opposite direction toward another group of guests.

Allie twisted to peer back over his shoulder.

A blind beggar could tell she still had feelings for the cowboy. He clenched his jaw and fought the urge to shake her until her teeth rattled. Instead he breathed a soft kiss upon her temple. He'd put up with too much to have Anderson come along and put a crimp in his plans. He raised a hand to smooth his hair, disturbed when he noticed that it trembled. He needed a drink. Badly!

He spotted Bo Jack in the crowd and motioned for the cook to join them. When the cook had come within speaking distance, Clay smiled. "Bo Jack, my good man, would you fetch me a brandy?"

Bo Jack squinted his one good eye. "I ain't your *good man.* And if you want a drink, go *fetch* it yourself. Me and Allie will be dancin'." When the brawny man held out his arms, Allie twisted from Clay's grasp and stepped forward.

Fury boiling within him, Clay watched them shuffle toward the dance floor. A gargoyle and a bumbling adolescent. Of all the Daltry females, how did he have the misfortune to get stuck with this one? He headed for the table at the end of the room where C. J. was tending bar. "Brandy. A double."

Allie's brother eyed him disapprovingly, then handed him a glass half-full of amber spirits.

He downed it in one gulp and held it out for a refill.

"Allie drivin' you to drink already?" C. J. asked, his blue eyes bright with amusement.

Clay straightened his suit coat. "No, of course not. I feel like celebrating a little, that's all."

C. J. peered past him, toward the dance floor. "If I was you, I'd do a little less celebrating until the horse was inside the barn and I had a padlock on the gate."

Clay whirled, following his gaze. He uttered a muffled curse.

"Will you dance with me, Allie?" Hal asked after tapping Bo Jack on the shoulder.

"You youngsters go ahead. My bum leg is acting up, anyhow," the cook growled. He hobbled away, leaving them alone on the dance floor.

Her heart fluttering wildly, Allie gazed into his green eyes as she moved into his arms.

"I didn't know if you would want to see me again after what happened," he said hesitantly.

Reminded of that day in the canyon, Allie fought the raw hurt that welled up inside. "Why? You only told the truth. I can't fault you none for that."

"What if it wasn't the truth?" he said softly. "What if I lied?" He pulled her closer and she felt him tremble. "What if I told you—?"

"Friends and neighbors," her father called out. "It gives me great pleasure to tell you that our little Allie and Clay Masterson are getting married." He smiled and waved his hand. "Get on up here, you two. Have the bottles ready, boys, I want to propose a toast."

"Anderson," Clay cut in, putting a possessive hand on her shoulder. "Thank you for entertaining *my fiancée*. But I'll take over now."

Hal dropped his arms. He gave her one last look, then he walked away.

"Hal?" She turned to follow, but Clay pulled her into his arms.

"Allie, my sweet, I've behaved like a brute all evening. Please say you'll forgive me?" He brought her hand to his lips.

"Clay, I need to see—"

"Come on, darling." Clay hooked his arm around her waist and ushered her to the front of the room. He took a glass of bubbling liquid from one of three on a tray and thrust it into her hand. He took one of the others, and her father took the one that was left.

"To Allie and Clay. May their life together be filled with happiness—and many children," her pa added with a grin. "Drink up, y'all."

Over the rim of the delicate crystal glass, Allie saw the fleeting look of distaste that washed over Clay's face. *Children.* He hated children. *Even if they were his own?* Looking at the expression on his taut face, she knew she would never be allowed to have a child.

"Drink up, dearest. Everyone is watching," he said, his silky tone edged with steel.

Meeting his gaze, she turned the glass up and drank it down. Tiny bubbles touched her lips and tickled their way down her throat. She forced herself to swallow, then set the empty glass back on the tray, vowing as she did so that no one would ever make her drink champagne again.

A cheer rose up from the crowd. Everyone surged forward to give her a hug and shake Clay's hand. Everyone except Hal. When the congratulations were finished, Clay bent his head, intending to claim her lips. But at the last moment, she turned her head to one side.

From where he stood in the doorway, Hal gave her a sweet, sad smile, then took his hat from the antler rack and left the house.

Don't go, she silently pleaded. What was it Hal was about to tell her before Clay intervened? She pushed at the arms that held her, wanting to rush outside and ask him before it was too late.

Sensing her intention, Clay tightened his grip. Then his other arm came around her, pulling her back against him, trapping her in his embrace.

Unable to free herself without making a scene, she forced herself to smile and listen to this one and that one, without having the vaguest idea of what any of them said.

When the party finally ended and she waved good-bye to the last wagonload of guests, Allie let out a long sigh of relief. "Well, that's over."

"One might think you'd gone through an ordeal, rather than just announced your engagement," Clay said plaintively.

"I suppose I'm just tired." She gathered her skirts and headed up the steps to the house.

Clay caught her by the hand. "Now that everyone has gone, let's walk to the gazebo. It's nice out, and some fresh air might do you some good. Besides, I've had to share you all night."

What she really wanted was to retreat to her room, take off the hated dress, and go to sleep. But since she didn't know how to tell Clay that without hurting his feelings, she smiled and squeezed his hand. "All right."

He hurried her into the ivy-draped gazebo, then when they were seated took her into his arms. "Alone at last, except for them." He hooked his thumb toward the trio of busty maidens that poured water in a neverending stream.

In honor of the celebration her father had ordered the fountain filled, and the tiny paddle wheels churned and splashed as they lifted the gurgling water to be circulated again. It was a comforting, familiar sound, and she closed her eyes and allowed the fountain's melodious song to drain the tension from her body.

"Allie," Clay breathed against her temple before he bent and pressed his mouth to hers. Despite the heat of the night, his lips were cold. When she didn't respond, the kiss, at first innocuous, became ruthless, bruising.

Frightened by the change, she raised her hands and pushed against his chest, but his arms held her like a steel vise.

He forced her back onto the stone seat, pinning her there with the weight of his body.

"Cl—"

He swallowed her protest, taking advantage of her parted lips to thrust his tongue deep into her mouth. His hand cupped her satin-covered breast, then she felt the fabric rip and he was kneading her bare flesh. To her horror, her breast swelled, the nipple hardened. When he left her mouth to suckle her, she gasped and tried to push him away. Raised with three brothers, she could usually hold her own in a rough-and-tumble, but Clay's crushing weight, coupled with the voluminous satin dress folds and the constricting corset, robbed her of breath. Spots swam before her eyes.

"Don't!"

"What difference does a month or two and a few mumbled words make? Now that everyone knows we're engaged, we don't have to wait."

"No!" Her protest had no effect. Stunned, she knew he intended to have his way whether she agreed to it or not. She tried to twist away. "I can't marry you. I don't love you," she managed to gasp, knowing it to be the truth.

"You think I didn't know you'd changed your mind. I saw you watching Anderson."

"Hal!" She did love Hal. Why hadn't she realized it before? She had to tell him before it was too late.

She opened her mouth to scream, but Clay's hand muffled her cry. His other hand tugged at her hip. The skirt tore, then the night air touched her legs. His own hard need pressed against her.

"It doesn't matter. After tonight he won't want you."

Hot tears of rage and helplessness filled her eyes and spilled down her cheeks. How could she have ever thought she loved Clay? Let alone convinced herself she wanted to marry him?

"Stop it," he hissed. "Conscious or unconscious, it doesn't matter to me."

When he grasped the waist of her pantalets, fear and desperation gave her the strength she needed. She forced herself to be calm, and when he raised himself to undo his pants, she drove her knee upward and into his groin.

Clutching himself, he rolled off her and onto the ground. "You bitch!"

Allie jumped to her feet. "You toad-eating son of Satan!"

"Allie?" Hal pushed his way through the maze of vines. "What's goin' on here?"

Allie whirled and shoved a lock of hair out of her eyes. "I just broke my engagement." She twisted the ring off her finger and threw it at the writhing man. "Mr. Masterson didn't like the news."

His eyes hard and narrow, Hal looked her up and down. "You all right, Allie?" he said, removing his shirt and handing it to her.

She nodded. Suddenly conscious of her half-naked state, she gratefully took the large garment and slipped her arms inside.

"You through with him?" Hal asked, his tone menacingly soft.

"I just want him to leave."

Hal rubbed his hands together. "Maybe you'd better go on up to the house. I've got a farewell present or two of my own I'd like to deliver."

"You can give him another lick or two from me," a feminine voice said from the shadows. Her grandma hurried into the clearing and took Allie into her arms. "Come on, honey. They don't need us here. Your pa and Hal can make sure that scalawag gets on his way." The elder woman hooked an arm around Allie's waist and led her toward the house.

"Pa?" Allie gasped, flushing with shame, noticing the large figure striding toward them. "How did you know?"

"I heard you from the porch. Don't fret, honey," Minerva said grimly. "It wasn't your fault, and that man isn't worth it. In the old days, we'd have strung Clay Masterson up in the nearest tree. Now, we'll just make him wish we had."

Her pa touched her cheek, and even in the moonlight, she could see his fury blaze. "She all right?"

"She's fine. We'll be going to bed now," Minerva said.

Her pa patted Allie's shoulder, then he stalked toward the muffled groans and curses. "Damn it Hal, save some of him for me."

Twenty-Three

"WHAT ON EARTH WILL WE TELL PEOPLE? ESPECIALLY AFTER WE announced your engagement only last night?" Allie's mother said, staring across the breakfast table at her.

"If anybody has nerve enough to ask, we'll tell them Allie finally came to her senses," her grandmother said firmly.

Allie flashed her grandmother a grateful smile. They had decided last night they wouldn't tell her mother any more than necessary about what had happened in the gazebo. That was the reason that, in spite of the heat, she'd worn a long-sleeved blouse that covered her bruised arms. Now that it was over and Clay was no longer a threat, Allie wanted to forget the shameful incident, to put it behind her and get on with her life.

After a moment, her mother asked, "Does Clay know you don't intend to marry him?"

"I told him last night, after the party," Allie said, using her fork to rearrange the untasted steak and eggs on her plate.

"I'll bet he wasn't too happy."

"No, he wasn't," she said quietly, praying she wouldn't keep asking questions.

Although her mother was generally good-natured, Jane Daltry could be a tigress when anything threatened her children. If her ma had any inkling of what had happened at the gazebo, she wouldn't rest until she had personally nailed Clay Masterson's hide to the barn door.

"What did the poor man say?" Jane persisted.

"Poor man, my foot!" Minerva said, setting her cup down with such force it rattled the saucer. "That no-account varmint was after the Daltry money and he thought he could bamboozle Allie into marriage. But she was too smart for him. Isn't that right, girl?" She peered over her spectacles at Allie.

"How did you know?" Allie asked. She'd only found out when Clay let it slip last night.

Her grandma's silver eyes gleamed. "He tried the same thing with Venus, but she had his number before he'd gotten warmed up. He never had the opportunity with Persy because I sent her to New York."

"If you knew the man was such a scoundrel, why didn't you say something before now?" Jane demanded.

"Didn't see any need to," the older lady muttered.

"What if she'd married him?"

"I was hoping it wouldn't go that far."

"And if it had?"

Minerva smiled. "Then I would have had the bastard arrested for attempted bigamy."

"Bigamy?" Allie and her mother echoed.

"Claybourne Masters—his real name—deserted his wife and two children shortly before he came to Paradise Plains. They live with her parents in New Orleans."

"How could you know all of this and not tell Allie?" Jane said in disbelief.

Allie wondered the same thing.

"Because I didn't know it either until Odie brought the mail this morning," Minerva said defensively. "I never did like that feller. He seemed a little too slick for my tastes. After I learned Allie was planning to marry him, I hired a detective. Masters covered his tracks well, but Herman Branson, the investigator, finally followed his trail back to Louisiana.

"Herman said Clay's wife wasn't too happy to find out her no-good husband was planning to get married again, especially since he was still married to her."

"Why that—! And I thought him to be such a fine gentleman!" Jane pushed back her chair and got up from the table. "Have one of the hands harness the wagon. I am going to tell Mr. Masterson just what I think of him."

"You're too late," Allie said quietly. "Pa and Hal put him on an eastbound train last night. I doubt if we'll be seeing him again." She didn't bother to add that her pa had promised to shoot the man if he ever showed his face in Texas again.

Jane eyed Allie and then Minerva. "So that's how Odie skinned his knuckles. I think your pa has some explaining to do. If you'll excuse me." A determined glint in her eye, she left the room.

"Pa won't tell her?"

"About last night? Of course not. Hal and I won't either. Nobody need ever know unless you decide to tell them."

"I sure wouldn't want anybody to know I was that big a fool," Allie said bitterly.

"It was a hard lesson, child. The man was so smooth, even I didn't know how much of a bounder he really was, and I have been around a good many more years than you." Minerva refilled their coffee cups from the tall pot at the end of the table, then she sat down and gazed thoughtfully at Allie. "Tell me one thing. If you didn't know he was after the money, why did you tell Clay you wouldn't marry him?"

"Because I didn't love him."

"You found your feelings lay in another direction?"

Allie nodded. "But now I don't know what to do about it."

"How does this other person feel about you?"

"I'm not sure. Sometimes I think he cares and other times . . ."

"It might behoove you to find out," her grandma said, giving her a wink. "By the way, I've been thinking it might be a good time for me to take that trip to San Francisco. You know, while the weather's still nice and all.

Allie's spirits plummeted. With all that had been going on, she'd almost forgotten she still had one labor to go, and in her opinion, it was the worst of the lot. The task of taking care of Thalia made the other two tasks seem like Sunday school picnics. Allie sighed. "When would you be leaving?"

"The first of next week." Minerva slid her an impish glance.

"That soon?" Allie had never spent more than a few minutes alone with her niece, and at the end of those minutes, she'd been almost desperate to give the child back. *A week.* How on earth would she ever cope?

"Too bad Hal won't be around to help you with the livestock. All of our hands, including Lee, are busy getting ready for the fall roundup. Yes—too bad that boy is set on leaving Texas."

Allie jerked her head up. "Hal's leaving?" Was that what he'd been trying to tell her at the engagement party? "How do you know?"

"Your pa told me. Said Hal's dead set on leaving Texas. Why, for all I know, he might be gone already."

Clay's departure had filled Allie with a sense of relief,

but the news that Hal might be gone left her with a loss so keen it was as though someone she loved had died. "Excuse me." She rose abruptly. Leaving the table, she raced out the door. She glanced down at the skirt she wore. Totally unsuitable for riding, especially astride. Should she return to the house and change? No. She couldn't—wouldn't—take the time. She lifted her skirts so they wouldn't impede her progress and hurried to the corral. A few minutes later, her dress hoisted up above her knees, she kicked Circe into a gallop and headed for town.

Ignoring the fact that she was covered with dust and her hair stuck out every which way, Allie raised a trembling hand and knocked on the door of the small house where Hal and his father had been staying. No answer. Maybe they didn't hear her. She knocked again, louder. Where were they?

"Allie?" Jack Anderson said from behind her. "Can I help you?"

She whirled, then ran to grip Jack's forearms. "I need to see Hal. Has he left yet?"

The gray-haired man gave her a puzzled smile. "I think he might be over at the Lucky Chance. He should be back in a bit."

She hurried to her horse.

Lucky Chance! Was he taking the dance hall woman with him? If he was . . . That possibility left her shaken. Whether he was or not, she had to see him one more time, if only to say good-bye.

She crossed the tracks and dismounted in front of the two-story clapboard building. Leaving Circe at the hitching rail, she pushed through the swinging doors and entered the saloon. She blinked, adjusting her eyes to the gloom.

The saloon was pretty much what she had expected. The main room was square and sparsely furnished, with a bar across one end, a few tables and chairs at the other. A piano sat at an angle in one corner and a few brass spittoons sat here and there in strategic places. Behind the bar, mirrors hung on either side of a painting of a somewhat plump naked lady, whose ample charms and seductive smile were apparently intended to lure cowboys in for a closer look.

The only occupants were two men perched on stools in front of the counter. Both met Allie's gaze with wide-eyed amazement.

If Hal was here, he must be upstairs. She lifted her skirts and started forward.

A long corridor ran parallel to the foot of the staircase. At the end of the hall, a door to the outside opened, and Lucky Chandler, his arms loaded with a heavy keg, staggered inside. He kicked the door shut, then turned to scowl at her. "You can't come in here. Your pa would have my hide."

"Then don't tell him," she said, heading up the stairway.

He set the keg down. "Allie Daltry, come back here," he said, his boots thumping across the board floor as he hurried after her.

On the upper level, she stared down the narrow hallway. Two doors. One open. She peered inside. Empty. She closed her hand on the knob of the one that was shut.

"Don't!" Lucky called out.

Afraid he might stop her, she closed her eyes and shoved the door open. "Hal?" she asked.

"Hal isn't here," a feminine voice said.

Allie opened her eyes. He wasn't here. The redhead was alone.

At that moment, Lucky grabbed her arm. "Downstairs. Now."

"Could I talk to you for a minute?" she called to the woman. "Please?"

"It's all right, Lucky." The redhead put down the book she was reading and rose from the chair. She walked forward and smiled. "Hello, Miss Daltry. What can I do for you?"

Allie glanced at Lucky and hesitated.

He swore and slammed out.

"I need to talk to you about Hal."

The woman raised an eyebrow. "Sure. Have a seat." She motioned toward the chair. Without her makeup and with her hair done up in a neat bun, the dance hall girl might have been any woman in town. She smoothed the skirt of her simple calico dress, then sat down on the edge of the neatly made but sagging bed. "You seem surprised."

"I'm sorry for staring," Allie said, flushing red. "You look so different."

"I wasn't born a whore, you know. And I don't intend to stay one any longer than I have to. With Hal's help, I intend to leave this place and never look back."

It was true. He was taking her with him. Her question answered before she'd asked it, Allie rose. "I hope you both will be very happy," she said in a choked voice.

"Both? I have an idea what you're thinking, and I feel I owe it to Hal to set you straight."

"I think I already know. You and Hal are leaving Texas together."

The girl laughed, a silvery tinkling sound that reminded Allie of a chorus of little bells. "We are both leaving Texas but not together. Not in a million years. Hal is a good friend, and we have had supper together a few times, but that's all."

"If that's all, then why is he here all the time?" Allie asked doubtfully.

"He has been teaching me to read."

"Read?" The tight band around her heart snapped, allowing a ray of hope to creep inside.

"I don't exactly enjoy living in a place like this." The redhead pointed toward the garish red paint and peeling, water-stained wallpaper. "I thought if I knew how to read, I could go someplace far away, someplace where nobody knows me, and start over. Get a decent job and make some money. Maybe even get married and have some kids."

Allie saw a wistful look come into the girl's eyes. A wave of compassion washed over her as she realized that, despite her profession, the woman was no different from any other. While circumstances might have forced her into a different sort of life, the girl only wanted a home and family. And Hal had made that dream possible. Her eyes blurring, Allie held out her hand. "I would like to wish you luck."

"Thanks. I think Hal might be at the livery," she confided. "If you hurry, you might be able to catch him."

Allie impulsively leaned forward and gave the girl a hug. "Good-bye and thank you." She dashed out the door and mounted Circe, then, her skirts flying, Allie raced toward the livery. There, she slid the horse to a stop. Afraid she might be too late, she hurried through an entrance flanked by open double doors. The stench of manure, hay, and horseflesh scented the air, a smell Allie found both familiar and comforting. Slender rays of sunlight slanted through gaps in the weathered board walls. Dust motes danced in the murky air.

Her heart drumming, she scanned the gloom and let out a faint sigh of relief when she spied Hal in front of one of the stalls. His horse was saddled; a packhorse stood next to it. He was ready, but he hadn't left yet. Her heart filled with love as she watched him.

Tan and whipcord lean, he wore a blue work shirt tucked into snug-fitting denim jeans. The tan leather vest covering his shirt was old and stained by years of hard work; his boots were worn and run down at the heel. He looked much like any other cowhand, neither tall, nor handsome, nor prosperous. Some folks might say he'd never have more than a nickel to his name, but he was a man of integrity and compassion and Allie knew he was all she would ever want.

Sensing a presence, he turned and looked at her. "Allie? What are you doing here?"

She wanted to fly into his arms and beg him to stay, but the set look to his jaw told her that might not be enough. "Looks like you're going somewhere," she said, running a trembling hand over the bedroll and canvas pouch he'd tied on the packhorse.

"Yeah." He glanced away and checked his cinch.

"Will you be gone long?"

"A spell."

"Without saying good-bye?"

Why didn't he say something? Allie bit her lip. In a minute, he would mount up and ride out—if she didn't stop him.

"Some pard you are," she said scornfully. "You owe me a favor, remember? Or were you planning on sneaking out of town so you wouldn't have to pay up?"

"What favor?" He whirled and his green eyes blazed into hers. "You don't want me to fetch Masterson back?"

"No! I'm glad he's gone." At least she'd managed to get his attention.

"If it ain't that, then what?"

She scanned her memory, trying to recall any promises he might have made. Then she smiled. "That day at the canyon. Remember when I brought you the food and lemonade? You said you would give me anything I asked for."

"Yeah. So?"

"I'm asking."

"Now? I was fixing to leave." He glanced toward his horse. "Will this favor take long?"

"What if it did? You didn't say anything about a time limit." She crossed her fingers behind her back.

"How long?"

"A week," she said hesitantly.

"Why a week?"

"Because that's how long C. J. and Lizzie will be gone. I have to stay at C. J.'s ranch and take care of Thalia, and I need you there to help with the stock."

"Can't Lee or your pa do it?"

"They're busy at our own place with the roundup. And Thalia is such a handful, if you won't help me, I don't know what I'll do."

"What's your pa going to say about me staying out there with you?"

"It isn't like we haven't been alone before. Besides, you'd be sleeping in the barn." When they were gathering the horses, they'd spent a whole week out on the range. But that was before she knew she loved him.

"Even then, your ma would never stand for it."

"If it'd make you feel better, I'll ask her. But after what you did last night, I doubt if she'll object."

"A week." He moved a dirt clod with the toe of his boot.

"Please."

"All right," he said with obvious reluctance. "I guess I can wait that long."

"Actually, it will be a little longer than that. Grandma is planning their departure for the first of next week. Tuesday, to be exact." She waited.

"Tuesday." Finally he nodded. "But you make sure it's all right with your ma."

"Thanks, pard," she whispered, raising herself on tiptoe to touch her lips to his cheek. "I'll meet you at C. J.'s." Afraid he might change his mind if she tarried any longer, she whirled and ran from the barn.

Her heart singing, she mounted Circe and rode out of town. She hadn't accomplished her purpose. He was still determined to leave. But he wouldn't be going today. She had ten days.

Ten days when she'd have her hands full with Thalia.

She wondered if ten days would be long enough to make Hal admit he loved her.

Perplexed, Hal watched the horse and rider disappear in a cloud of dust. Allie sure seemed upset. In fact, for a minute he thought she might break down and cry. He took off his hat and wiped his forehead, then he began to unsaddle his horse.

"Hal?"

"Over here, Pa."

Hal's father left the sunlit barn doorway and strode toward him. "Did Allie find you?"

"Yeah. And it sure was strange. The way she acted, you'd think I was leaving and never coming back."

"Minerva told her you were leaving Texas."

"So that's it." He had been going to—before Clay Masterson left town.

"Did you tell Allie you'd changed your mind?"

"No." Hal studied on it a minute, then he gazed at his father. "And don't you tell her, either. I want to make sure I know which way the land lays before I tell her about my plans."

"I wouldn't wait too long," his pa said with a grin. "Allie Daltry ain't exactly known for her patience." He took his watch from his pocket and checked the time. "Speaking of patience, I hope Melissa's got some. I was supposed to take her to the Buc for lunch, and I'm already late. See you later, son."

"Bye, Pa. Tell Melissa howdy."

Jack nodded and hurried from the livery.

Ten days. Hal rubbed his chin thoughtfully. Well, it wouldn't matter that much, one way or another. The old home place would still be there.

He wondered what Allie would say if she knew he had no intention of leaving Texas. That he was only moving out to the land his grandpa had left him. Now that his pa and Melissa were getting married, Hal had decided to tend to his own future. He had it all figured out. First he aimed to develop the land—repair the old stone house, build a barn, get a few head of cows, and, of course, horses. Then maybe someday, after he had everything set —a few years down the road—he kind of thought he might ask Allie to marry him.

In the meantime, the week at C. J.'s would give him a chance to see how things stood with Allie. And as for not telling her? He'd been worried sick when she'd been trailing after Clay Masterson. He figured it wouldn't hurt her to stew a bit.

Twenty-Four

TUESDAY ARRIVED AND ALLIE AND HER VACATION-BOUND grandmother arrived at C. J.'s ranch just after sunup. A little while later, the wagon carrying C. J., Lizzie, and Minerva left the ranchyard and rumbled down the road. Standing on her brother's front porch, Allie raised her arm in a farewell wave. The other arm she kept tightly wrapped around the squirming child. "Wave bye-bye," she said.

"No!" Thalia's lip came out in a mutinous pout. "Want Mama! Now!"

"How would you like a cookie?" Allie asked, hoping to sidetrack her niece before Thalia burst into tears.

The two-year-old eyed her suspiciously, then nodded. "Cookie. Now!"

Almost everything Thalia said was punctuated with that one word. Now! Allie hadn't been at C. J.'s twenty minutes and she already felt worn to a frazzle. The week with the obstinate tyke stretched out before her like an eternity.

As she took Thalia's chubby hand and led her into the

house, Allie cast one last look at the road. She had risen before dawn, bathed and washed her hair, then pulled the curls back from her face and fastened them with a blue satin ribbon. She'd also worn her new sky-blue calico dress. But Hal hadn't come. He'd either forgotten or had never had any intention of keeping his promise.

"Now!" Thalia wailed, her blue eyes filling with tears.

Allie felt like crying, too. Instead, she bit her lip, then managed a feeble smile. "All right, honey, Aunt Allie will get you a cookie. How about some milk to go with it?"

"Milk? Now?"

"Right now," she agreed, lifting the tot into the high chair Grandpa Odie had made. She handed Thalia one of the ginger cookies she'd baked the night before, then went to the icebox and removed the tall jar of cream-topped milk. She shook it, then poured two frothy glasses and carried them to the table. "Here we go. One for Thalia. One for Allie."

"Awie." The baby took a large swallow, then gave her a white-rimmed, toothy grin.

Allie dipped her cookie into the milk, then took a bite. "Mmm, good."

The fascinated child watched for a moment, then attempted to do the same. She popped the milk-soaked morsel into her mouth. "Good. Now!" She waited for Allie to repeat the process so she could copy her.

"Hope you saved enough for mc."

"Hal!" Overcome with joy, Allie whirled. Her hand struck the glass and sent it flying from the table. It hit the floor and shattered, sending a shower of milk over everything in the room.

"How!" Chortling gleefully, Thalia sent her glass flying after Allie's with much the same results.

"Whoa!" Hal backed through the doorway. "I know I'm

late, but I didn't know you'd start throwing things the minute I came in."

"What a mess! I'll grab the broom. You keep track of Thalia." Not giving him a chance to protest, she rushed to the porch. He hadn't forgotten. He still didn't appear too happy, but at least he was here. A silly grin on her face, she swept the glass into a dustpan and emptied it into the trash. Then she mopped up the milk and put the mop and bucket back on the porch.

She returned to the kitchen and eyed the sandy-haired man bouncing the laughing child on his knee. Both seemed oblivious to everything but each other. He would make a wonderful father, she thought. She imagined Hal with his own children. Their children, if she had anything to say about it. That idea amazed her, as she had never considered children with anything but apprehension before. She never knew what to do with the unruly little rascals. Now the thought of conceiving, giving birth, and nurturing Hal's child filled her with an almost desperate longing. He couldn't leave. She had to find a way to make him stay.

"What do you think of my niece?" she asked softly.

Hal glanced up and raised a brow. "Actually, she's kind of cute."

Thalia, only knowing that someone else had gained Hal's attention, frowned.

"Now that I have the floor cleaned up, are you ready for some milk and cookies?"

"Only if you don't throw them at me," he said, looking like he still might like to bolt through the door.

She filled two glasses and one tin cup, in case Thalia decided to repeat the incident on her own. But to her surprise, the child was on her best behavior, an occurrence Allie credited to Hal's presence.

Thalia ate one cookie and part of another, then played

in a spot of milk she'd dumped on the table. Allie finished her own treat and watched Hal devour the rest of his.

The tenseness so apparent earlier had left his face, due no doubt to the engaging little girl and the cookies. Gazing sorrowfully at the empty platter, he licked the last crumb from his finger. "Mighty good." Using his sleeve to wipe a stray drop of milk from his chin, he smiled. "Ginger cookies are my favorite."

"I know. That's why I made them." She removed the glasses and wiped the crumbs from the table.

"You made them?"

"Bo Jack has been teaching me how to cook."

"Well, I'll be." He crossed his arms on the table and leaned forward. "What else can you make?"

"Lots of things," she said proudly. "You'll be sampling a few of them this week."

"Did you ever get that cake figured out?"

"The last time I made it was for the social. The next time I try anything as complicated as that will be for the man I intend to marry." She gave him a pointed look, which he either didn't see or chose to ignore.

"Sorry it didn't work out with Clay," he said somberly.

"I'm not. Calling off that wedding was the smartest thing I ever did."

"Why did you call it off?"

"I realized I didn't love him."

He stared at her, his eyes becoming warm as a late spring meadow; then, just when she thought he might comment on what she had said, he pushed back from the table and got to his feet. "I'd best tend to the stock."

"How!" Thalia cried, holding up her arms to Hal.

"Want to go feed the horsies?" he asked, scooping the baby up and letting her straddle the back of his neck. "Hold on tight!"

The delighted child on his shoulders, he galloped toward the barn.

With the two of them gone, the house seemed lonely, and almost too quiet. Humming to herself to break the silence and feeling a bit at loose ends, Allie wandered into the large main room. Her eyes widened. She had managed to straighten the kitchen and dining room, but this would take forever to put to rights.

At one end of the room a large window, its lower half dotted with small handprints, looked out over the valley. A rock fireplace took up most of the other end, and she noticed with dismay that the hearth was the only place that wasn't stacked high with clutter. *Where in the world do they sit?* she wondered, as both the couch and two leather chairs, as well as most of the floor, were covered with this, that, and the other. Her brother and sister-in-law might be able to live like this, but she couldn't—not even for a week.

She rolled up her sleeves and tied an apron over her dress. Then after gathering up an array of saddle blankets, bridles, and two saddles she lugged them out and dumped them on the porch for Hal to put in the tack room in the barn. Then she picked up an armload of her brother's clothes and put them aside to wash. The toys were boxed and placed in the corner next to the window. A bucketful of stray apple cores she set aside for the hogs. After tugging a pair of braided rag rugs outside to be stretched over a limb and beaten, she returned to see what else needed to be done. With the odd assortment of litter removed, the room looked almost habitable. Now all it needed was a good cleaning.

Two hours later, exhausted and as grimy as the water she was dumping into the flower bed, she glanced up to see Hal and Thalia amble into the yard.

"What's for dinner?" Hal said, rubbing his flat stomach.

"Me and Thalia are hungry enough to eat a whole cow, horns and all."

"Eat?" She'd been so busy she'd forgotten all about the noon meal.

After using three tubful of precious well water for much-needed baths, Allie, Hal, and Thalia sat on the porch swing and watched a golden moon come up over the horizon.

"You've certainly made a hit with my niece," Allie said softly, so as not to awaken the sleeping child he held on his lap.

"I kind of like her, too. I never had any brothers or sisters, so I know what it's like to be little and alone."

Allie gazed at him in amazement. She'd always taken her siblings for granted, and there were times when she would gladly have been an only child. Hearing Hal's words gave her pause for reflection, and she tried to imagine the Daltry household without the noise and confusion, the laughter and the tears, and the childhood squabbles. She couldn't. Her family was as much a part of her as her own skin.

The times she'd visited Hal's home when she was a child, she'd envied him the peace and quiet; but now she realized how much he'd hungered for the very things she'd taken for granted.

He ran a callused hand through the baby's curls and smiled. "Guess you'd better put her to bed. She can't be too comfortable all crumpled up like this."

Although the child looked perfectly comfortable snuggled against Hal, Allie nodded in agreement. "You want to sit a spell after I tuck her in?" she asked hopefully.

"Naw. I'm plumb tuckered myself, and I want to get some of that fence fixed tomorrow, so I'll be saying goodnight, too." He slowly raised himself to his feet, the child carefully cradled in his arms. "You want me to carry her inside?"

"I can manage."

He passed Thalia over to her, then whispered good night.

She watched him shove his battered hat onto his head, then he went down the steps and crossed the yard, every line of his lanky body telling of his weariness. He was here because she'd asked him to help care for the stock, but he hadn't stopped at that. He'd not only helped her with Thalia, but he'd also repaired gates, cleaned the tack room, and mucked out the barn, probably accomplishing more in this one day than C. J. had in months.

Thinking about the kind of life she and Hal could have together, her heart swelled with a love she dared not reveal. Not yet. He still seemed a mite too skittish for anything like that. She needed time—time she didn't have. One day already gone. Six days left.

She waited until he'd entered the barn, then she reluctantly turned and carried Thalia into the house.

She tucked the baby into her own little pine bed, another gift from her doting grandfather, and kissed her. Carrying the oil lamp into C. J. and Lizzie's room, she glanced around and gave a sigh of relief. Outside of a few stray garments, discarded when they were packing, the room was neat and clean.

Allie smiled, remembering that most of the items in the living room had belonged to her brother. Even as a child, C. J. had been messy. Her ma had scolded him, but it usually hadn't done any good. Apparently Lizzie had given up on him as well.

She opened the small leather trunk C. J. had carried in for her earlier that morning and took out a lace-trimmed nightie to sleep in. Running a brush through her hair, she studied herself in the full-length mirror, C. J.'s prize from their grandma after he had completed his labor.

Gazing at the image reflected in the shining surface, Allie thought about her own twentieth birthday and how much she had changed since that time. Her hair, once cropped near her scalp, now curled around her shoulders, softly framing her heart-shaped face. Her figure, too, had lost the angular planes it once had, rounding to more shapely, womanly curves. Thanks to Venus's—and Clay's —creams her skin no longer had a leathery look and had paled to a becoming golden tan. She leaned closer and touched the tiny amber spots sprinkled across the bridge of her nose. She still had her freckles, but she didn't mind them so much. She would never be as beautiful as Venus, or as talented in the kitchen as Persy, but if the mirror told the truth, she wasn't homely, either. Had Hal noticed the changes? And did he like what he saw?

She blew out the light and crawled into the large oak bed her father had made as a wedding present for C. J. and his wife. He was always making something. She traced the initials carved in entwined hearts on the golden oak headboard, imagining they belonged to herself and Hal. Her thoughts on the man who lay alone in the barn on a bed of straw, she sighed, pulled the sheet up to her chin, and closed her eyes.

"Mama. Ma—ma."

Allie opened one eye and squinted toward the window. Daylight. Already? She brushed a hand across her face and pushed a stray lock of hair out of her eyes.

"Ma—ma," a child's voice wailed.

Thalia! She jumped out of bed and ran across the hall. She lifted the crying child into her arms. "What's the matter, honey?"

"Awie?" Thalia said between hiccuping sobs.

"Yes, baby. It's Allie."

"How?"

"Hal's sleeping in the barn. He'll be up to have breakfast with you."

"How barn?" The idea brought a tearful smile to the child's face. "Barn. Now!"

Allie groaned. At least she had quit crying. "We have to get dressed first, then we can go find Hal. Okay?" Before the child could protest, Allie had her changed out of her nightgown and into her clothes. She was buckling Thalia's shoes when she heard Hal whistling in the kitchen. "Hold on." She finished the last buckle. "Now!"

Thalia hit the floor at a run and headed for the stairway. Afraid the child might take a tumble, Allie raced to head her off.

"How! How!" the child cried, her chubby legs running in place when Allie grabbed the back of her dress.

"Whoa! Take my hand. Let's walk down slowly."

"What's all the commotion?" Hal said from the dining room doorway.

Seeing him, Thalia let out a delighted squeal. "How! Now!" She held out her one free arm.

"She heard you. After that it was impossible to hold her."

"Then let her go."

"What if she falls?"

"She lives here. It won't be the first time she's gone down those stairs." He grinned up at her. "Besides, I'll catch her if she takes a tumble."

"Slowly!" Against her better judgment, Allie released the baby's hand and watched her headlong dash down the stairs. When the little girl reached the bottom, she darted into Hal's waiting arms. Safe in his embrace, Thalia turned. Both he and the child gave her a triumphant grin. Pleased as punch, both of them.

"All right, you win," she said with a laugh.

"You sure look pretty this morning," he said, gazing up at her.

Suddenly aware that she was barefoot and wearing nothing more than a thin nightgown, an unaccustomed shyness brought a rush of heat to her cheeks. "I'd better get dressed."

"Shucks, just when I was enjoying the view," he teased, his hungry gaze locking on hers.

"Eat! Now!" Thalia demanded, patting her hand against Hal's cheek.

Allie turned and raced toward the bedroom.

After a breakfast of thick-sliced ham, potatoes, eggs, and hot biscuits and gravy, Hal pushed back from the table. "I can't believe you cooked that, but I saw it with my own eyes." He rubbed a hand across his middle and groaned. "Good thing I'm leaving in a week, or my horse wouldn't be able to carry me."

His words sent fear stabbing through her heart. This morning the desire she'd seen in his eyes when he'd caught her in her nightgown had given her false hope. What if she couldn't convince him to stay? She forced the thought from her mind. She had to. And that was that. "What are your plans for today?" she said brightly.

"Well, I thought I'd fix that corral gate and mend some fence. What about you?"

"I need to wash a load of clothes or two. That and entertaining Thalia will probably be all I can manage."

"Whew! I know what you mean. She's sure a bundle of energy." He finished the last of his coffee, then left the table and strode to the door. He waved good-bye to Thalia, who, both hands full of biscuits and gravy, waved back. Then he put on his hat and went out the door.

"How!" she whimpered.

"We'll see him later. Right now let's get you cleaned up." She lifted the tot from the chair and carried her to the sink. After wiping the remains of Thalia's breakfast from her chubby cheeks, Allie carried her into the living room and sat her in front of the box of toys. "Now, you play while I do the dishes." She waited to make certain the child was safely occupied, then she returned to clean up the kitchen and put water on for the wash.

When it had heated, she carried the hot kettles from the house and filled the boxlike contraption on the open back porch with water, then she added soap chips. She put in the clothes, then turned the hand crank on the side, setting the revolving paddles in motion. When that batch was clean enough to suit her, she removed it and added the other load. The washing part finished, she dumped the water, then repeated the process, this time with no soap. After the clothes were rinsed, she wrung the garments out and carried them to the line.

She interrupted her chores from time to time to check on the little girl. After a while, when Thalia tired of her toys, Allie brought her out into the yard and gave her a spoon and a battered pan. Leaving the energetic toddler to stir up a mud cake, Allie hung up the last load of wash.

She couldn't believe the child had been so well behaved, especially since every time she'd been around her before, Thalia had been a little hellion. Smiling, Allie turned to point out a bird that had landed on a nearby bush.

The dirt pile was empty. Her niece was nowhere in sight. "Thalia? Honey?"

No answer.

Allie dropped the wet shirt back into the basket, then went into the house, thinking the child might have returned to the box of toys. She found the house empty and ominously quiet. "Thalia?" she called, running back out to search the yard. She peered behind the wood box and under the porch. *Where is she?*

Forcing her pounding heart to calm, she made herself stand still and listen.

A faint clunk, clunk came from an area beside the barn.

The pan! Her knees weak with relief, she hurried around the side of the weathered building and saw the child bent over, her attention on a large, dark mound a short distance away in the dirt. "Did you make a big mud pie, baby?" Allie stepped forward to admire the creation.

Thalia grinned and pointed. "B–ssst!" she said to the ground, shaking her blond curls.

The mound moved, uncoiling to stretch like a fat diamond-patterned rope in the thick dust. A sinister buzzing filled the air.

The child looked from the spot to Allie and laughed.

Allie felt the fine hairs on her neck rise. Dear God. That wasn't a mud pie! The toddler was playing with a rattlesnake!

Allie looked around for a weapon and saw nothing but one small rock. She picked it up.

Bigger around than her upper arm and more than six feet long, the snake raised its spade-shaped head. Knowing any sudden move on her part would make it strike, Allie moved slowly, carefully, seeking to put herself between the child and the angry reptile.

"Buffly," Thalia said, lifting her spoon to point to a monarch butterfly that flitted overhead.

Catching the child's movement, the snake rattled again.

"Bad. No!" Thalia raised the pan, taking a step closer.

The snake raised its head and drew back.

"No!" Throwing the rock to divert the snake's attention, Allie snatched the child up into her arms. Trembling, her eyes closed, she held the warm little body close.

The ominous buzzing continued.

Desperately aware of the danger they were in, Allie scanned the barnyard, hoping to catch a glimpse of Hal. Then she noticed his horse was missing from the corral and remembered Hal had ridden out to mend the fence.

Thalia squirmed, pushing against Allie's arm. "Down. Now!" she whined.

"Shh!" Allie whispered, to no avail. The snake was becoming more agitated by the second. If Thalia decided to pitch a fit, it would surely strike.

"Down. Buffly," the toddler demanded.

If only she could get Thalia to safety, she was willing to take her own chances with the snake. "Pretty?" Allie pointed back toward the house. "Catch butterfly for Hal?"

Thalia grinned and nodded. "How."

Leaning as far away from the serpent as possible, Allie lowered the tyke to the ground.

Thalia, a gleeful smile on her face, raced off in pursuit of the yellow-and-black insect.

Now that her niece was out of harm's way, Allie decided she might be better off to remain where she was. If she stayed motionless, maybe the snake would go away.

But instead of leaving, the snake slithered closer, then coiled in the shade at Allie's moccasin-clad feet.

Allie froze, terror robbing her of the ability to think, to act, to speak. Her heart threatened to pound its way right through her skin. Fear-born sweat drenched her body and made a tickling trail down her spine.

Something cold and slick slid along her ankle.

Her breath coming in short, airless pants, she gave an involuntary shudder.

"Allie, don't move," Hal said, approaching the barnyard from the other side.

She closed her eyes and swallowed. He didn't have to worry. She couldn't move if she tried.

"Easy," he breathed softly. His approaching footsteps were muffled by the soft dirt.

The snake's buzz grew more insistent, and just when Allie was certain it would strike, she heard the thud of Hal's shovel. Something wet—blood—splattered against her legs and feet. She swayed, her legs no longer strong enough to hold her.

Hal hooked an arm around her waist and lifted her to safety. "It's all right, honey. He can't hurt you now."

Allie stared at the spot where she'd stood just seconds before. The same spot where the huge, headless reptile writhed and thrashed, its lifeblood staining the dust. Shaking so badly that her teeth chattered, she thought about the baby and what might have happened if Hal hadn't gotten there in time. She raised her lashes and saw his face still chalky white with fear.

"Allie, did he get you?"

She shook her head.

"Awie! How!" Her fat cheeks streaked with tears, Thalia toddled toward them.

It was then that Allie saw the crimson splotch on the little girl's dress, the blood running from an area just above her knee.

"Oh, God! No!" she screamed.

Then the earth tilted and she sank into darkness.

Twenty-Five

AL SQUEEZED THE EXCESS WATER FROM THE CLOTH AND GENT-
wiped Allie's cheeks.

She moaned and opened her eyes.

" 'Bout time you woke up," he said, his voice hoarse
ith emotion. "How do you feel?"

"What happened?" she asked, then she clutched his
and. "Thalia?"

"She wasn't bit."

"But the blood—"

"She scratched herself on the rosebush. Said something
out a—a 'buffly'? Whatever that is. I fixed her up just
e."

"Oh, thank God." She fingered the cover of the bed
here she lay and frowned. "How did I—?"

"Don't you remember? You fainted."

"That's ridiculous," she said, struggling upright. "I've
ver fainted in my life."

"Maybe you've never been so scared before," he said,
aking an attempt to smile. "I know I haven't."

She stared at him, then the color drained from her face.

"Allie, you ain't gonna faint on me again, are you?" h‹ said, cupping her head with his hand.

"I hope not." She took a deep breath, then gazed a Thalia. He felt a quiver go through her body, then sh‹ began to shake.

"Honey? What is it?"

She reached out and Hal drew her into his arms.

"She was playing with it," Allie cried, tears streamin down her face. "I was hanging clothes. When I turned, sh‹ was gone. I can't believe I let it happen. What if she ha‹ gotten bit? It would have been my fault."

"It wasn't your fault. It's a bad year for snakes becaus‹ of the drought. They're everywhere. I killed one in th‹ tack room yesterday. I didn't tell you because I didn' want you to be scared."

Holding her close, he ran a trembling hand through he hair and thanked God for making him so thirsty he had t‹ return to get a drink of water. If he hadn't come bac ... He couldn't stand to think about that.

"I still should have watched her better. What kind c mother would I be? I let a child p–play with a s–snake, she said with a sob.

"Allie, she's so quick, it would be impossible to watc her every minute." He put his fingers under her chin an‹ forced her to meet his eyes. "And as for that other part, can't think of anyone who would be a better mother." H would have said more, but a tug on his sleeve made hir look down to see Thalia's face crumple and her eyes we with tears.

"Awie?"

"Allie's fine, honey." He opened his arms to include th baby, and when she squirmed inside he gathered both th‹ child and Allie tight against his chest.

They sat there for a time, silent, hugging one anothe

giving thanks that they were safe. Finally the little girl's eyes drooped and she sagged against his arm.

Allie's eyes were shut, too, but he could tell by the pounding of her heart that she wasn't asleep. Reluctant to let her go, he continued to hold her, savoring her softness, the scent of her hair, the feel of her body pressed against his. He closed his eyes and began to dream dreams.

The next day, the remembrance of the rattler too keen in their minds, neither Allie nor Hal let the child out of their sight. After the baby had exhausted Allie in the house, Hal took her out into the yard. And while Thalia seemed pleased by all the attention, she grew whiny and restive as she sensed the worry and anxiety in the air. The fact that Hal had killed another snake only increased the tension.

"What are we going to do?" Allie asked, staring across the supper table at Hal.

"They're coming in after water. Everybody probably has the same problem."

"How?" the baby whimpered, holding out her arms.

Hal took her out of the high chair and set her on his lap. "Hi, sweetie. Want some of my potatoes?" He offered her some on a spoon.

"No, no, no!" The child frowned and turned away.

"I haven't been able to get anything down her all day. I hope she isn't getting sick," she said, smoothing the hair out of the little girl's eyes.

"She doesn't feel hot. I think she's getting bored with us."

"Probably so," Allie agreed, smothering a yawn. "Come on, niece. Let's get you into bed."

"No!" A mutinous gleam in her eyes, Thalia wrapped her arms around Hal's neck.

"I think we have a problem."

"Let me try," Hal said, getting to his feet. "Want Uncle Hal to tuck you in?"

Thalia grinned. "How. Now?"

"Now," he said, giving Allie a wink. "Show me where the stuff is and I'll get her ready."

"Middle drawer in the bureau."

While Hal readied Thalia for bed, Allie finished the last of the dishes and hung the cloth on the porch to dry. He joined her there a few minutes later and they sat down on the porch to talk before heading off to their respective beds.

"I have an idea," he said. "Tomorrow I'll turn the hogs into the yard; they should make short work of any snakes."

"Sounds reasonable. I'll have to keep Thalia inside. She won't like that much."

"I also need to go into town. I'll try to be back as soon as I can," he said. "Think you can handle her while I'm gone?"

"She's only one small girl. Shouldn't be a problem."

He chuckled. "Yeah, I know. Then how come we're both so tired?"

Allie put aside her mending and gazed down at Thalia, whom she'd kept occupied with a necklace made of buttons.

"Pretty?" the child asked.

"Very pretty."

The little girl pulled herself upright and toddled toward the window. "How?"

"He'll be back soon." Laying the patched shirt to one side, she, too, went to look out the window. A squealing drew her attention to the side yard, where three hogs grunted and churned the ground. One of them tossed a long, slender object into the air. Another grabbed the opposite end in his jaws.

Allie shuddered and turned away. At least Hal's plan was working.

"How! How! Papa! Eee!" Thalia called, patting the window glass.

Allie saw the child was right. Hal, her father, and her oldest brother had ridden into the yard. She poured them some lemonade.

"Howdy, honey," her father said, tossing his hat onto a peg by the door. "There's my little darlin'," he said, lifting his laughing granddaughter into his arms.

"Hal tells us you've been having a problem," Lee said. "I think I know why. When we were digging that well, we found a rattler's den. We thought we had taken care of them, but it seems we missed a few."

"What can you do?" she asked.

"We brought some kerosene. We'll burn the den and shoot the rest."

The men drank the lemonade, then loaded their rifles and carried them out into the yard.

Allie watched from the window and saw a column of smoke rise from an area beyond the barn. Then shots sounded, first a volley, then only a few, until the ranch was again silent. Hal, Lee, and her father returned to the house.

"That should take care of them," Hal said, wiping a hand over his smoke-blackened face.

"Might not hurt to leave the hogs out the rest of the day. I don't think we missed any, but you never can tell."

"Got anything around here to eat?" Lee said, rubbing his middle.

"I think I can find something—after you get cleaned up. While they washed, she sliced some bread she had baked that morning and filled it with thick cuts of roast beef. She refilled their glasses and set the pitcher of lemonade on the table.

"By golly, you're getting to be a pretty fair hand in the kitchen. How 'bout I send Meredith on vacation and you can come and cook for me," Lee said around a mouthful.

"What about Mrs. Cooper?"

"Heck, I guess you haven't heard. She's going East to take care of her sick sister."

"She is?"

Her pa, his own mouth bulging, nodded in affirmation.

"Yeah, and after she leaves, I'm liable to starve to death," her brother said sorrowfully.

"*You* could always learn to cook," she teased. "Or you could have Bo Jack teach Meredith how."

Lee sighed. "My wife just don't have the temperament for cooking. And I break everything I touch. Think I'd better hire somebody else—unless . . ."

Allie shook her head. "Not me. I've got other plans." She glanced at Hal, who was feeding Thalia a piece of buttered bread.

"Well, reckon we'd better get back to town," her pa said, getting to his feet. "Mighty good, Allie. You're gonna make some man a good wife." He winked, hugged the baby, then put on his hat and went out the door. Lee and Hal followed. Thalia toddled close behind.

Thinking about her pa's words, Allie cleaned off the table and put the dishes in the sink. She would make somebody a good wife, if only she could get the knucklehead to see it.

"Awie! K–kee!" Thalia called from the porch.

"Kitty?" C. J. and Lizzie didn't have any cats. She peeked out the doorway, her eyes widening as she spotted the squirming creature held wrong side up in the child's arms. Allie saw only the fluffy black-and-white tail, but that was enough. "Put the kitty down, honey," she said softly, hoping the child would obey.

"No! K–kee!" Thalia said, heading toward the kitchen.

Backing up warily, Allie glanced toward the barnyard where her pa and Lee lifted a hand in farewell. She could expect no help from that direction.

"No, Thalia! The kitty can't come in the house. Put it down. Now!" Allie said frantically.

"No! No! No!" the child screamed, holding the wriggling animal even tighter.

"What's all the racket?" Hal asked, coming up the path from the barn.

"Look!" Allie pointed to the animal the child was squeezing.

"So?"

"She's got a skunk!"

Hal glanced from her to Thalia, then burst out laughing.

"What's so funny?"

"A skunk?" He let out another whoop.

"K–kee!" Thalia said determinedly.

The creature wriggled loose and strode haughtily across the porch.

"It is a cat." Allie eyed Hal, who was wiping his tear-bright eyes with his neckerchief. "Where did it come from?"

"I stole it—from the widow Bibble. I figured she owed me something for making me eat that blamed cake."

"Hal Anderson, you should be ashamed of yourself," she said, chuckling.

"The baby needed a playmate. I figured this one would at least be safe." He squatted beside the little girl. "You like the kitty?"

Thalia nodded, then wrapped her arms around his neck and planted a wet kiss on his cheek. "Purdy k–kee."

"There, see?" he said smugly.

"You win." She knelt beside them and ran her hand along the cat's back. Her eyes widened.

"What's the matter?" Hal asked.

"Did you have to steal one that was pregnant?"

"You mean?"

"Any day now." Noting the disturbed look on his face, she giggled.

He managed a one-sided grin. "What do you suppose C. J. and Lizzie will say?"

"Maybe we can convince them it will keep the baby occupied."

"Yeah. And maybe we can help find homes for the kittens as soon as they are weaned."

Her heart leaping with hope, Allie stared at him, but Hal's attention was occupied by the little girl and the purring cat. Had he even realized what he had said? Before, he had planned to ride out as soon as C. J. and Lizzie returned. Now he mentioned finding homes for the kittens. Could he have changed his mind?

Twenty-Six

THE NEXT FEW DAYS PASSED PEACEFULLY, WITH NO MORE SNAKES sighted, and the easy camaraderie between her and Hal returned. Thalia, enchanted by the cat, had been so angelic Allie wished Hal had thought of catnapping the animal sooner.

The only thing that marred her tranquil existence was the fact that her time with Hal was running out. And even though she had taken special pains with her appearance and had busied herself in the kitchen making all of his favorite dishes, he still was no closer to making a commitment. But neither had he said anything further about either staying or leaving, a fact she should have found comforting. Instead, the uncertainty only added to her agitation.

She took a bite of the roast she had prepared for dinner and glanced at the man who sat at her elbow at the end of the table. The meal had been perfect, she thought with satisfaction, certain that Persy could not have done better. Hal had no problem packing it away. Why couldn't he see that she would make a good wife?

Noticing his coffee cup had reached the half-empty point, she rose and refilled it. "Would you like another biscuit? I left some on the stove so they would stay hot," she said sweetly.

"I think I'll pass. I already ate a panful, and besides, I've been trying to save room for that pie." He nodded toward the crusty deep-dish pastry cooling at the end of the table.

"Well, let's cut you a slice right now. I'm anxious to see if you like it." She prepared a large piece and set it before him. After he'd finished that, she gave him two more portions. "Well, how was it?"

"Delicious." He let out a satisfied sigh. "Pard, you're getting to be a better cook every day."

Pard. She leaned forward and ran a fingertip along the corner of his mouth, removing a piece of crust. "I aim to please," she said softly, lifting a lock of sun-bleached hair away from his face. "Am I succeeding?"

Instead of taking her cue, he eyed her like a mouse about to be eaten by a hungry cat. "All that food made me sleepy. Think I'll call it a night," he said hoarsely. He slid his chair back from the table, then gave Thalia a quick kiss on the cheek. He flashed a sickly grin and bolted through the door as if his shirttail were on fire.

"Coward," she muttered. So frustrated she wanted to scream, she washed the dishes and cleaned up the kitchen, making a good deal of noise in the process. Then, aware that the other end of the kitchen had become unusually quiet, she saw that Thalia had fallen asleep in her high chair. She gently bathed the child's hands and face and packed her off to bed.

Not at all sleepy herself, Allie returned to the kitchen, carried the washbasin out, and dumped it into the yard. The mournful wail of a harmonica drew her attention toward the corral. So he hadn't gone to bed after all. The way he'd claimed exhaustion and raced away from the house, a body'd swear he would have expired any minute from lack of sleep. She hesitated, wanting to join him but knowing if she did he would probably either decide to go to bed or find some other way to avoid her. No, she wouldn't go to the corral; instead she'd make him come to her.

She removed the large washtub from its hook on the porch and carried it to a spot just inside the kitchen entrance. That ought to do it. She propped the back door open with one of C. J.'s boots. Her hands on her hips, she surveyed the room, then stepped to the table and turned the lamp down to a golden glow. No sense being too obvious.

A grin on her face, she filled the tub with the water he'd carried in for her earlier, then added two hot kettlefuls from the stove. She tested the third kettle she'd heated for rinsing and nodded. Just right. She wouldn't even need to cool it with the other bucket she'd drawn from the well.

Humming softly, she removed her clothes and draped them over a chair; then, taking the bar of soap from the cabinet, she dangled her toe in the tub. Perfect. Submerging herself in the warm water, she released a sigh of pleasure and wished she could just lie there until the bath grew cold. But realizing Hal wouldn't stay up all night, she quickly doused her hair, then applied the soap. "Oh," she cried, just loud enough to be heard outside.

She listened, frowning when the sad melody continued. Maybe he hadn't heard. "Oh!" she moaned loudly, hoping that she didn't wake Thalia in the process.

The harmonica cut off in midsong.

She sprang upright and vigorously applied the soap until the rest of her body gleamed with an iridescent sheen. Moments later, she heard his footsteps crunching in the gravel on the path to the house. 'Bout time, she thought. If she really was in trouble, she could die by the time he got there. "Oh," she cried out again.

"Allie, are you all ri—?" he began, coming to a sudden breathless halt in the doorway.

"I've got soap in my eyes," she lied. Her eyes squinted shut, she groaned. "Oh, it burns. Hal, help me rinse it off!" Striking an enticing pose, she extended her hand toward him.

"Uh. Where's the rinse water?" he asked hoarsely.

"On the stove."

A moment later, he dumped the bucket of liquid over her head.

"Jehoshaphat!" she gasped, parting strands of hair to peer through the frigid stream. "I said the one *on* the stove. That bucket just came out of the well!"

"How in hell was I supposed to know?" he said, glaring back at her.

"Could you try it again? This time with the right bucket!" she said, her teeth chattering.

"Not on your life." He banged the bucket down on the floor. "Looks like that one took care of the soap in your eyes. Now you can do your own rinsin'."

His heart pounding so loud he was sure she could hear it, he hurried toward the barn. Soap! Not likely. He had a good idea what she was after, and it sure as hell didn't have anything to do with soap.

That time at the river when he had seen her in the altogether, she'd accused him of peeping and chucked a rock at him. This time she stood there brazen as could be. He almost preferred the rock.

He was getting skittery as a June bug in a hot skillet and she knew it. Every time he sat down to eat, she looked at him like she was starving and he was dessert. The rest of the time he tried to stay away from the house, but somehow his feet managed to get him there anyway.

Tonight at dinner she'd looked so pretty, so soft and sweet. And so damned determined. He knew Allie Daltry well enough to know that once she had her head set on something, there was no way to change her mind.

Even though it would have killed him to have her marry Clay, at least then she'd have been unattainable, out of reach. But now . . .

After checking to make sure she hadn't followed, he entered the barn and slid the bar across the door—not that it would have kept her out if she decided she wanted in.

He closed his eyes in the darkness and leaned back against the weathered boards. He didn't know who he thought he was fooling. The bolt wasn't to keep her out. It was to keep him from doing something stupid, like grabbing her and kissing her silly. His throbbing body told him once he'd gone that far he wouldn't be able to stop.

Crying out like that! She'd planned the whole thing. She knew he'd come running to see if she was hurt. He thought he'd swallow his tongue when he saw her, but she hadn't been a bit ashamed, even though she'd been naked as the day she was born. The memory of her silken curves all wet and slick and smelling of soap made him groan. He cursed, yanked off his hat, and sailed it toward his bed in the loft. His jaw set, he climbed the ladder.

He took up his customary position on a pile of hay; then, unable to help himself, he glanced through the loft opening toward the house.

She was still in the damned tub! The golden glow of the lamp made her appear as if she were on a stage. He watched her raise the washcloth and dribble the water over her body. She extended one long leg and washed it, then the other. And she was singing!

"Greensleeves was my delight," she crooned, holding her head back to allow the water to trickle over her breasts.

He let out a moan. *Probably getting wrinkled as a prune by now. She's only in there 'cause she figures I'm watching.* Which he was. In spite of every intention to look away, his gaze remained riveted on that lamplit doorway.

When his nerves felt like they had been scraped raw and roasted on hot coals, she finally got out of the tub and sensuously dried every inch of her body; then, when he thought his eyeballs would fall out from the strain, she doused the light.

He rolled over on his back and ran a trembling hand over his eyes. He was reaching the end of his tether and she knew it.

Two more days.

Two days of pure hell.

Unless he did something desperate, he'd never survive.

The next morning, bleary-eyed and unshaven, he staggered toward the house. The first thing he saw when he reached the porch was that blamed bathtub, bringing back the memory as though it had just happened. His body immediately responded, his staff becoming achingly hard and hot.

"Good morning, Hal," Allie said, smiling from the kitchen doorway. "My, you must be tired. Why, you don't look like you got a lick of sleep." She held out a cup of coffee, which he grabbed like a drowning man would grab a floating log. "Maybe you should have taken a bath last night, too. I slept like a baby."

"What's for breakfast?" he asked grumpily, taking his place at the table.

"Sourdough pancakes, but they aren't ready yet. I thought maybe we could sit a spell before we ate."

What was she up to now? He eyed her warily. At least she had all her clothes on. "Where's Thalia?" he asked, noticing the empty high chair. He'd feel safer if the baby was in the room.

"She's in the living room, playing with the cat. I already fed her, so she'll be occupied for a while." She placed her elbow on the table, then propped her head on her hand and stared at him.

He shifted uneasily and straightened the collar of his shirt. "Have I got straw in my hair or somethin'?"

"No," she said slowly. "I was just noticing how handsome you are."

He choked on his coffee. "Quit your foolin'. Handsome?" He glared at her. "I didn't even shave. I barely combed my hair."

"I know. You look like you just got out of bed. I guess that's the way I'll be seeing you every morning."

"What do you mean, every morning?"

"Why, after we're married, of course," she said, reaching out to caress his cheek.

He jerked away as if he'd just been bit. "Who said we were getting married?"

Wearing a smile as old as Eve, she slipped from her chair and onto his lap. Her fingers made a tickling trail of fire around his neck, then she pulled his head forward until his whiskered cheek rested against the swell of her breast.

She felt so good, so soft, and smelled deliciously of soap. Helpless to do anything else and knowing he was lost if he hugged her back, he desperately wrapped his fingers around the seat of his chair and held on for dear life.

Her heart beat against his ear, strong and determined. "Well, we don't really *have* to get married." She touched her lips to his perspiring forehead. "At least not yet," she whispered, her breath seductively warm against the side of his neck. She wriggled into a more comfortable position.

He closed his eyes and gritted his teeth so hard his jaw ached. Then, when he was sure he'd reached the breaking point, she sighed, got up, and sashayed across the room.

One second more and it would have been all over. That knowledge made him quiver. Sanity and freedom beckoned just beyond the door, but his legs were too weak to carry him.

She returned and poured him another cup of coffee; then, her bottom swinging, she strolled back to the cast-iron range.

He spilled a good portion of his cup just trying to find his mouth. She intended to marry him. Even though she claimed it wasn't necessary—yet.

Yet?

He downed the rest of the scalding brew in one gulp. The fragrant aroma of pancakes wafted toward him, but he had lost his appetite.

"Now, don't these look good?" The heavy platter of pancakes in her hands, Allie turned toward the table. Hal was gone. He hadn't even stayed for breakfast. But maybe that wasn't all bad, considering how much he loved to eat.

She'd put her cards on the table. Stated her declarations loud and clear. And while he hadn't exactly set the date, he hadn't said he wouldn't marry her, either. He wasn't as insensitive to her presence as he liked to pretend. This morning, even though he'd sat there like a red-faced wooden dummy, his body had given him away. He was weakening, and now it was only a matter of time.

She figured she had him hog-tied right where she wanted him; now all she had to do was slap on the brand. A triumphant grin on her face, she filled her own plate and began to eat.

Twenty-Seven

HAL STARED TOWARD THE HOUSE, MORE CONFUSED THAN EVER. Had she given up? He didn't know.

After this morning when he'd sneaked out without eating, he thought she would have been hanging onto his shirttail all day. Instead she'd ignored him.

After what she put him through at breakfast, he hadn't the stamina to go back for lunch. But now that it was supper time, his hunger wouldn't let him stay away.

He washed up at the horse trough and put on a clean shirt and combed his hair, then headed for the house.

It sure was quiet, he thought, pulling the screen door open. When he went inside, he found the kitchen empty. A single place was set at the table. Then he saw the note propped by the side of his cup. He picked the paper up.

Hal,
    Thalia and I ate already. Your supper is in the warming oven.
                                    Allie

Scowling, he wadded up the note and tossed it into the stove. He opened the oven, removed a bowl of stew, and carried it to the table, then sat down and began to eat. The food was steaming hot and mouthwateringly delicious, but with no one there to share it, he might as well have been eating sawdust.

Where was she? And where was Thalia?

He took a few more mouthfuls, then shoved the dish aside. He sniffed the air. The kitchen didn't smell like stew. It smelled like . . . ? He wasn't sure. Something good, anyhow.

He prowled the room, peering into all the cupboards. Nothing. Had she fixed something special for herself and the baby? If so, surely she would have saved some for him.

Still sniffing, he followed his nose up the stairway, stopping just outside her room. A sliver of lamplight came from beneath the door. He knocked. "Allie? You in there?"

"Yes, I am."

He waited. Why didn't she open the door? He impatiently shuffled his feet. "Can I come in?"

"No. I'm not decent. I'm in my nightclothes. Thalia and I were getting ready to go to bed."

Not decent? Last night, she hadn't worn a stitch and it hadn't bothered her a bit that he had been there. Tonight she had on a nightgown and she wasn't decent.

He sniffed again. "Allie, what's that smell?"

"Must be stew."

"Don't smell like stew." It wasn't stew—not unless she'd started making it with cinnamon. Not having any other alternative, he reluctantly returned to the kitchen. He was still hungry. He sat down and finished the plate of now-cold stew. He was also mad. And lonesome.

The truth was he'd grown accustomed to having decent meals, clean clothes. He'd grown accustomed to Allie and to Thalia. Now that he'd seen what it could be like, he wanted a home, a wife, a family. The truth was he wanted Allie. And he didn't want to wait ten years to have her. He still didn't have any more to offer than he had a week ago, but he had his youth, a strong back, and a willing spirit. He couldn't give her the luxuries the Daltrys could, but together they could have a good, if simple, life.

But it appeared that she had already abandoned the idea. It irritated him that she would give up so easily.

He propped his head on his palm and stared at his empty cup. If Allie had been there, she would have filled it. But she wasn't there; she was hiding in her room.

He shoved back his chair and tramped out of the house, slamming the door behind him. Damn it, she was the one who'd said she wanted to get married. Now that he was willing to let her have her way, she seemed determined to avoid him.

Allie carried Thalia into her own room and told her stories until the child's eyes closed and she drifted into a deep sleep, then she tucked the blanket around the little girl and kissed her good night. As she bent to blow out the lamp, her gaze touched on the cat nestled at the foot of the bed, and she wondered if k–kee's kittens would be born during the night. Smiling, she extinguished the lamp and closed the door.

Back in her own room, Allie brushed her hair until feathery curls hung in a soft cloud around her shoulders, then she pinched her cheeks and bit her lips until they were a deep rosy red. Eyeing herself in the mirror, she untied the sky-blue ribbon that secured the ruffled neckline of the fine white lawn nightgown and adjusted it to reveal a provocative swell of breasts.

It had been hours since Hal had stormed out of the house. Hours that she had used to frost the cake. He'd sure sounded mad when she wouldn't let him in. Served him right for getting so upset over a simple kiss. Knowing her whole future rested on the outcome of this night, her hand trembled as she picked up the cake, then carried it through the house. She stopped at the kitchen table to cut a few large slices, leaving them in place until she reached the barn. She grabbed up a napkin on her way out, then softly closed the kitchen door.

A lovers' moon rose on the horizon, casting a silver hue over the ranchyard. A warm, gentle breeze rustled through the treetops, fluttering her nightgown around her legs and ruffling her hair. The night seemed romantic, magical. She only hoped Hal would succumb to its spell.

What if he was asleep?

Then she'd wake him up.

What if he was still mad?

Then she'd feed him cake. It wasn't as large as the one she'd made for the social—she hadn't had enough ingredients for that—but it was the Daltry cake just the same. Knowing his love for sweets, he couldn't resist the treat, even if he could resist her.

The idea that he might resist her made her legs grow weak. Somehow she'd make him see they belonged together. She had to.

Balancing the small seven-layer cake in one hand, she quietly opened the barn door with the other. She stood there in the filtered moonlight, feeling more uncertain, more vulnerable than she ever had in her life.

"Allie? That you?"

"It's me." She hastily removed one of the slices she'd cut earlier, then placed it on a napkin.

"What are you doing out here?" he asked, looking down over the edge of the loft. "What's that you've got?"

"Cake."

"Cake? At this hour?"

"Don't you want any? I made it especially for you." Carrying the huge slice in one hand, she moved two steps up the ladder. She heard a rustling of cloth, then barefoot and shirtless, he extended a hand and helped her into the loft.

"You shouldn't be out here like this." He motioned to her nightdress.

"Don't you want your cake?" She opened the napkin and held it under his nose.

His nostrils twitched like a hound dog's on a scent, then he took the napkin from her hand and began to eat. "Um, that's good."

The moonlight slanted through the open loft door, capturing Hal in its silvery beams. He sensed her scrutiny and turned toward her. Aching with longing, she stared as if seeing him for the first time. She lifted her hand to caress his cheek, his brow, his nose, then ran her fingertips over his lips. All so familiar, yet with the awakening of love, excitingly new. He smelled of soap, summer-sweet hay, and cake. She leaned forward and touched her tongue to the dab of frosting at the base of his throat, marveling at the heartbeat that hammered so fiercely it threatened to burst through his skin.

Suddenly she was overcome by the need to run her hands over his body, to touch, to learn every part of him, as if only by doing so could she ever truly make him hers. Would he think her too bold, too eager? Her own pulse thundering in her ears, she lay her head against his chest and slid her palms up and down his back, tracing, caressing the muscles that rippled under her fingertips. She felt a tremor go through his body, but he made no move to take her into his arms.

"Hal? What's wrong?"

The cake in his hand forgotten, he sucked in a breath. "Wrong? Everything is too damn right."

"Don't you love me?"

"Of course I love you. I love your spirit, your honesty, your independence. Fact is, I love everything about you—including your stubbornness. But Allie, I'm only human. And right now, you're driving me crazy." He freed himself from her embrace, then running a hand through his tousled hair, he stepped away. "Pard, I think it might be better if you went back to the house."

Pard again. "And what if I don't?" Her mouth curved in a hint of a smile; she ran her hands over her cotton-covered hips and thighs, stretched herself tall, then slowly pulled at the blue satin ribbon. The garment slithered over her shoulders, her hips, and fell to the hay at her feet. She stepped free.

Hal gasped. "Allie, what are you doing?"

"I'm trying to seduce you." She moved toward him, then reached up to curl her fingers in the hair on his chest.

"Sedu—" He slapped her hand away. "Allie Daltry, I ought to paddle your bare backside." Instead, he snatched up the night garment and yanked it down over her head, then, when she was trying to find the armholes, he drew the ribbon up and tied it in a knot.

"Dang it, Hal, I can't breathe."

"I'm doin' enough of that for both of us." Clutching her arm, he marched her to the ladder. "The house. Now!"

Well, he'd made that plain enough. Her eyes filled with tears, she stumbled down the rungs. Keeping a safe distance, Hal followed.

"Here's the rest of your damned cake." She picked it up and shoved it toward him. The moonlight shimmered on the towering layers—all seven of them.

"That looks like—" He stared first at the cake, then at her. "Aw, Allie."

Not wanting his pity, she straightened. "I told you I

only intended to make this cake for the man I aimed to marry, but since you've made it plain you don't feel the same way about me, we'll just say it's my way of saying thank you for helping with the stock, with Thalia, and—" Her voice broke. Not wanting him to see her tears, she whirled.

Before she could escape from the barn he grabbed her into his arms and crushed her against his chest.

"You're squashing the ca—"

His lips silenced the rest of her protest. He kissed her softly, tenderly, then he gazed into her eyes. "I love you."

"No, you don't. You're just saying that because I'm cry—"

"Allie, darlin', you talk too much."

Moonlight slanted through the open barn door, making the expression on his face easy to read. His dark eyes locked on hers, and in them she saw hunger, lust, possession, and . . . Before she had time to decide what else, his lips captured hers and clung with a fierce joy. "Allie," he said softly. The love—no, adoration—on his face flowed over her like a spring shower on a drought-stricken plain, caressing, nuturing tiny seeds of desire until they budded then burst into splendorous bloom. He kissed her mouth, her throat, her neck, taking bites of smashed cake as he went. "I do mean it," he said, nibbling the frosting from her skin. "And I expect you to make this cake every anniversary for the rest of our lives."

"Anniversary?"

"You did say you aimed to marry me."

"But I thought—"

"That's the trouble—you think too much. Just listen." He took the platter with the squashed cake out of her hands and carefully set it on top of a feed bin, then he imprisoned her hands in his. His lips twisted into a gentle smile as he gazed into her eyes. "Atalanta Daltry, I love you to distraction. Will you do me the honor of becoming my wife?"

"Yes," she said quickly, afraid he might change his mind. "Oh, yes." She launched herself into his arms and hugged him tight.

He kissed her hungrily, fiercely, as if he could never get enough. When he finally allowed her to take a breath, she looked at him and smiled. "Aren't you going to eat your cake?"

"I certainly am." He bent his head and nibbled a mouthful from her neck. "Even if you couldn't cook, I'd love you." He claimed her mouth, her chin, then his impatient hands snapped the satin ribbon, allowing his nibbling lips to nuzzle her icing-smeared shoulder. He licked his lips. "Remember, every anniversary."

"I hope you don't expect me to wear it every year, too," she said breathlessly as his head dipped lower.

His mouth and cheek covered with cake crumbs and frosting, he grinned. "Oh, but I do. I want it served exactly as it is tonight. In fact, I plan to do a little decorating on it myself. I'd put a spot of frosting here"—he kissed the tip of her nose—"and here and here." He touched the hollow of her neck and a sensitive spot beneath her ear.

When he continued to touch and kiss each spot he planned to embellish, Allie trembled with delight and wished she'd thought of coating herself with frosting sooner.

Determined not to be left out, she ran a finger down his chest, then popped the frosting-covered member into her mouth and licked it clean. "Not bad. Maybe a little sweet."

" 'Bout the sweetest thing I ever tasted." He bent his head and licked at the cake, his efforts plastering the slick nightgown against her breast. "Delicious." Seemingly intent on removing every trace of the cake, he drew that portion of her lawn nightie into his mouth and captured her puckered nipple between his teeth.

Allie gasped as a shock of exquisite pleasure radiated through her core. "Ohh. If I knew cooking could be this good, I'd have taken it up a long time ago," she cried, tightening her arms around him. His skin was smooth and hard, and cool to the touch, but the passion of his kisses seared her flesh with a fierce heat.

He moved a hand down her shoulder, sliding the damp nightgown down to expose the top of one breast, then the other. "You are so beautiful," he whispered. Almost reverently he freed the pale, swollen globes and cradled them in his palms, then his thumbs circled the pink crests until they drew into hard, demanding little knots. When he drew one into his mouth and began to suckle, Allie quivered with pleasure. By the time he bent to the other, she was giddy with desire.

"Thank God you didn't marry Clay," he murmured. "I don't know what I would have done if you had married another man."

"Don't think about what might have been, just love me. Focus on today."

"Impatient—and bossy," Hal teased. His eyes dark with passion, he leaned back against the ladder. He slid his callused but gentle hands underneath the nightgown and cupped the rounded swell of her hips and lifted her to rest on top of him. Her own body responded by arching against him, her moistness hungering to be filled by his swollen heat.

As his fingers roamed her fevered flesh, her craving grew to a desperate pitch, making her respond to his touch with mindless abandon. She met his passion equally as a woman, with a woman's need to take and submit, to conquer and be conquered. While he kissed and hugged, nuzzled and stroked, until she thought she would lose her mind, she sensed he was holding back and knew that he would not go any further unless she made him. Wanting more, much more than a simple caress, she raised her hands and pushed him away. Her breathing ragged, she stared into his bewildered face. "Hal Anderson, if you don't make love to me here and now, I swear I'm going to die."

"You don't want to wait? Honey, are you sure?"

"I don't want to wait. And I've never been more sure of anything in my life." Her heart brimming with love, she stepped back into his arms. "Please, just love me."

His face serious, he held her for a long moment, then he took her hand and led her up the ladder to the loft. Slowly, lovingly, he removed the cake-smeared nightgown, then his lips on hers, he lowered her to his blankets.

She lay back against the soft hay bedding, waiting for what seemed like an eternity for him to unbutton and slip out of his britches. He turned, his body transformed to marble by the moonlight, reminding her of the statue she'd seen of David. She held up her arms, and finally his naked body covered hers, and he worshipped her face and body with fervent kisses. She welcomed his touch with eagerness, matching him kiss for kiss, touch for touch, savoring the weight of his hard, muscled body, loving the feel of his skin against hers, the tickle of his chest hair against her breasts. Never had she felt so wildly alive, so eager to experience the mysteries that only Hal could teach her. Consumed by her burning need, she entered a mindless void where there were only Hal's lips, Hal's caress, Hal's hard, demanding body.

"I love you, Allie." He cupped her face in his hands and gazed into her eyes, then he slowly parted the area that he had made ready and eased himself inside.

Allie felt a hard, insistent pressure, then her eyes wide with love, she arched toward him. After a moment of sweet pain, her body opened to welcome him. She clutched his slim hips, drawing him further into her tight, hot heat. As their bodies became one, he surged forward, giving her unbelievable pleasure as he filled her to the very core. Then his dark eyes on hers, he began to move, slowly, his body quivering with the tension of trying to make his loving gentle, enjoyable for her. Although inexperienced, her own body answered his surging passion in a dance as old as time. Her hips lifted, pushing against him, giving, receiving, until the pace reached a frantic urgency. The tempo of his thrusts increased, urging her onward and upward until she was aware of nothing but the broad shoulders she clung to, the mouth that caressed and murmured soft words of love.

He carried her toward a blinding brightness, until she was beyond seeing or hearing; then, reaching her zenith, she cried out as her body exploded in brilliant wave after wave of undulating light. Reaching his own peak, Hal arched against her, shuddering as their life forces melded and he made her his own. Spent, his sweat-sheened body collapsed on hers and she heard him heave a contented sigh. Her eyes wide with wonder, she slowly floated back to the top of the world. "Jehoshaphat," she whispered.

Still buried deep inside her, Hal propped himself up on his elbow and gazed into her face, then he reached up and lifted a curl out of her eyes. "I didn't want it to be over so soon; I wanted to make it better for you. But, sweetheart, I just couldn't wait."

She nuzzled his hand and kissed the palm. "I couldn't wait, either, but I'm not sure I could stand any better."

"Did I hurt you? I tried so hard to be gentle." He shifted his weight and withdrew.

Afraid he would leave her, she wrapped her arms around his waist and held on tight. "It didn't hurt at all. In fact, it felt so good, you could do that all day long and all night, too, and I wouldn't mind a bit."

"You liked it?"

"Ain't I supposed to? You don't think I'm a hussy, do you?"

Hal laughed and gathered her into his arms, pulling her over on top of him. "A hussy? Allie, you silly, wonderful, adorable little innocent. I'm glad you liked it. In fact, I think I'm the luckiest man on earth."

"Really? Then could we try it again?" She threaded her fingers through the hair on his chest. "Since I haven't done it before, I'm sure I could use the practice."

Hal let out a whoop, then he rolled her over and pinned her wrists at each side of her head. "As long as you don't practice with anybody but me," he growled. To her delight, his long, hard heat sprang to life and sought entrance to her secret place.

Eager to learn all he had to teach, she welcomed him inside. "Lots and lots of practice."

"Allie Daltry, you'll be the death of me."

But as Hal began the lesson, he couldn't think of a more pleasurable way to die.

Twenty-Eight

"To the bride and groom," Odie said, raising the glass in a toast.

Allie smiled into her husband's green eyes. "I love you," she whispered softly.

"You'd better," he answered. " 'Cause you're stuck with me till death do us part—and then some, if the good Lord is willing."

Through eternity. Even that didn't seem long enough, considering how much she loved him.

After the toast, Odie strode across the room and looped his arm around Hal's shoulders. "Son, I think it's time the men in this family let you in on a few secrets— such as how to handle the opposite sex."

Hal shot her a questioning look and Allie nodded. "Go along, just don't believe a word he says." When Hal and her father were out of earshot, Minerva took Allie's hand and led her toward the couch.

"Well, Atalanta? Have you figured out why I gave you those particular labors?" the old lady asked with a smile.

Allie remembered that day, not so long ago in time, but

eons in experiences, when her grandmother had given her not one but three tasks to complete for her labor.

The cake. The first one, a disaster. The last one . . . She sighed, remembering the night when she and Hal had made love for the first time in the loft of C. J.'s barn.

The dress. She gazed down at the simple but elegant wedding frock she wore, a far cry from the first one she'd attempted. This one, too, she'd made herself, with her mother's and grandmother's help. She intended to pack it away and save it for her daughters.

The week with Thalia. If Allie lived to be one hundred, she'd never forget the incident with the snake. Or, she grinned, the mistaken identity of the black-and-white cat, k–kee. The kittens, all four of them, had found happy homes. One, identical to her mother, had been returned to the widow Bibble. Two had gone to the family, one with Lee and one with Minerva. The remaining little scamp now prowled the barn Hal and her father had built on the section of Daltry land that adjoined the piece Hal's grand-father had left him.

Built on a tree-shaded knoll, their new home was small, only two bedrooms at present, but when they outgrew that, her pa would build them an addition. Her kitchen overlooked the river, and their parlor had a good view of the horses and pastures.

Allie thought about the three labors—all so foreign to the tomboy she'd been at that time. All three tasks calculated to make her come to grips with her feminine side. "Yes. I think I have. You wanted me to realize I was a woman."

"That's right," her grandma said with a nod. "You are a beautiful woman, Atalanta. Never forget it."

"I won't." Allie gazed across the room to the tanned, earnest face of the man who would be forever by her side, her pard, her lover, her husband. She wondered what would have happened to them if it hadn't been for her grandmother's intervention.

Minerva, the goddess of wisdom. How aptly named she was. She smiled into her grandmother's gray eyes. "Thank you," she said quietly, sincerely.

"I seem to remember a time when you thought I was a regular tyrant," Minerva said with a wink. "But maybe this will make up for it."

Minerva got to her feet. "Hal, don't listen to any more of Odie's nonsense; it's liable to get you into trouble. You'll do just fine on your own." She grinned at Allie. "Now if you and that fine new husband will come on up here, I have an announcement to make."

Allie took Hal's hand and together they followed Minerva to the front of the room.

Looking ever so much like her benevolent namesake, Minerva beamed them a broad smile. "Atalanta, you have completed your labor, and even though it hasn't been a year yet, I decided it's time for you to receive your prize." Minerva opened a box and took out two halters. One she handed to Allie, the other to Hal.

"They're beautiful, Grandma," Allie said, admiring the fine leather, the silver embossing.

"I'm not finished," Minerva said sternly. "The other part of the gift is in the corral. Your prize is a pair of Arabians. The stallion will take some handling, but his bloodlines make up for his fractiousness. The mare is gentle and a beauty. The two of them should give you a good start on that horse ranch you're so bent on having."

Hal and Allie stared at each other, then both let out a whoop and hugged Minerva until she begged for air.

Their dream. Now a reality.

Allie and Hal darted to the window for a quick look, then arm in arm they ran out the door.

Dear Reader,

I want to thank you for buying my book and hope *The Tomboy* has given you a few hours of entertainment. I thoroughly enjoyed the time I spent with the wonderful, eccentric Daltry family and hope you feel the same.

I value your opinion and welcome any comments you may have about *The Tomboy* or any of my previous novels. I cherish every letter.

You may write to me c/o Jennifer Lata, Berkley Publishing, 200 Madison Avenue, New York, NY 10016.

If you would like a reply or a flyer of future books, a self-addressed, stamped, legal-size envelope would be appreciated.

Happy Reading,

Mary Lou Rich

If you enjoyed this book, take advantage of this special offer. Subscribe now and...

Get a Historical

No Obligation

If you enjoy reading the very best in historical romantic fiction...romances that set back the hands of time to those bygone days with strong virile heros and passionate heroines ...then you'll want to subscribe to the True Value Historical Romance Home Subscription Service. Now that you have read one of the best historical romances around today, we're sure you'll want more of the same fiery passion, intimate romance and historical settings that set these books apart from all others.

Each month the editors of True Value select the four *very best* novels from America's leading publishers of romantic fiction. We have made arrangements for you to preview them in your home *Free* for 10 days. And with the first four books you receive, we'll send you a FREE book as our introductory gift. No Obligation!

FREE HOME DELIVERY

We will send you the four best and newest historical romances as soon as they are published to preview FREE for 10 days (in many cases you may even get them before they arrive in the book stores). If for any reason you decide not to keep them, just return them and owe nothing. But if you like them as much as we think you will, you'll pay just $4.00 each and save at *least* $.50 each off the cover price. (Your savings are *guaranteed* to be at least $2.00 each month.) There is NO postage and handling—or other hidden charges. There are no minimum number of books to buy and you may cancel at any time.

FREE
Romance
(a $4.50 value)

Send in the Coupon Below

To get your FREE historical romance and start saving, fill out the coupon below and mail it today. As soon as we receive it we'll send you your FREE Book along with your first month's selections.
